The Winning

Adrian Harvey

First published in Great Britain in 2025 by February Books

ISBN 978-1-9191750-0-3

Cover design by Daniel Keeffe

'The criminal regimes were made not by criminals but by enthusiasts convinced they had discovered the only road to paradise. They defended that road so valiantly that they were forced to execute many people.'

The Unbearable Lightness of Being, Milan Kundera

'The capacity for self-surrender, he said, for becoming a tool, for the most unconditional and utter self-abnegation, was but the reverse side of that other power to will and to command. Commanding and obeying formed together one single principle, one indissoluble unity.'

Mario and the Magician, Thomas Mann

Memory

He told me I should keep a diary. On my first morning in the office, as soon as the pleasantries were done, Joszef had let the words slip into the air as if the idea was the most natural thing in the world. But his words had simply floated past me and they became lost amid the thrill of it all. Had the old man already known, even then?

That first morning is stamped into my memory, sharp as the light cutting into the office through the smoke-hazed air: the way it settled on the dark wood of the tight-packed desks; the way it caught Ana's hair. I can still hear the scratching of Georg's pen on a document; smell the tobacco clinging to Joszef's waistcoat. All of it bright as the day itself. My first day in the private office of the mayor.

At the time, it had seemed ridiculous. Why keep a diary? There would be things I would want to remember, of course. This was already the pinnacle of everything I could have dreamt, if only I had known how to dream. Just two years since I had graduated from the University and I was already at the very centre of the world. But there was no need to keep a journal. Being there was enough. The act of writing, I told myself, would merely be a re-imagining, a means to distance myself, to insulate myself from the crackle of it all. A diary would fail to capture the colours, the odours and sensations, the immediacy of events; all would lose their intensity in the process of transcription. I had no need for another unopened notebook. Better simply to be there, to participate rather than to record. Just to be there.

But memory is an unreliable well-spring, even for an eyewitness. The simple rhythm of events, those concrete nuts and bolts of existence, can become muddled. What hope does memory have with all the rest, with the interpretation of their meaning? Given where I am, it seems a reasonable question. I am in the boot of a moving motor car, that is certain. For the first time in my life, I regret my height. The presence of the two men in the front of the car is also certain. The identity of my assassins, the belief that they are in fact assassins, may be conjecture, but it seems well-reasoned conjecture. They took me from the street an hour ago. I had been on my way to the racecourse, to meet a girl I barely know, to ride the whirligig. I saw her across the street, glimpsed her beauty as if for the first time, and then the blackness covered me. The thud and clang of metal. The grumbling of a motor. Some things, then, are certain, or so close to certain as to make no difference. But everything else is opaque. I know that I am confined and bound, being driven through the city streets. Each jolt of the cobbles confirms the material reality of my situation, even if its meaning is not yet clear.

Could I have acted differently? Could this ending have been foreseen? Could it have been avoided? Maybe Joszef had known from the start but, even so, he failed to alter the course of things just as much as I have. Another jolt. I do not know how long it will be before the car stops and the men inside it come for me. My story has run its course in any case. In the telling of it, I hope that some meaning can be found. It is too late for me, but it must mean something. It cannot end – I cannot end – for no purpose at all.

Belonging

As usual, I found Kem down by the river, kicking through the detritus along the muddy bank, seeking out something worth stooping for, something that would bring a smile to his father's face. This was not the river that curled through the centre of the city, the one that, on sunny days, reflected the grand buildings and the villas that existed somewhere beyond our world. This river barely deserved the name. And yet this sprouting thicket, stretched along a thin brown ditch, strangled with filth of every kind, was ours.

Kem's hair hung over his face, a mass of coiled hawser, slick like oil. I called out to him and his black eyes flashed a welcome in response, a hand raised, his sifting forgotten. At the side of the street, where the mud blurred with the asphalt, we clasped each other's hand in emphatic greeting and then, without a word, set out into the neighbourhood, seeking new corners, places undiscovered and magical, that could take us out of the monotony of life for a few hours, until the darkness closed off the sky. It was in hours such as these that I lived out my childhood.

'What's so special about the university anyway?'

Kem spat a gobbet of phlegm at the empty can that he had declared to be our target. Again he found the mark, and the dull thud of contact punctuated my uneasy silence. A pigeon cooed from the beam that had once held up the roof of a paint factory. I had, I realised, been dreading this question and all the antipathy it contained. Rather than answer, I pulled noisily at the back of my throat to construct a projectile of my own. It was pointless; Kem would win the contest as always. But at least the effort allowed me to maintain my silence, to prolong the certainty of our childhood friendship a little longer. I would miss this. It would be gone. It was already gone and had been from the moment that I had decided. Even though everything would stay the same, everything would change. I would still live with my mother in the same little apartment above the dirty courtyard that had been my home for as long as I could remember. Probably longer. Probably even while my father had been alive. But I already understood that life as a student at the university would change things; that my connection to the neighbourhood, to my neighbours, to my friend, would wither. No matter how hard I tried to stay the same, I would change. I looked at Kem, smiled a twisted smile and let fly a viscous ball of mucus in the direction of the paint can.

Neither of us noticed if it hit or missed, because at that moment gunfire crackled in the street below. Some shouts followed, the sound of feet slapping the cobbles, the shouting of men. Kem was rigid, unable to move to the broken window to take a look. I knew it wasn't fear. Kem was fearless. But he knew the stories of the crackdowns before the war, when the police would rattle through the camps, clattering the vans to dislodge their residents, to push them on to another patch of scrubby waste ground where they could settle for a few days before the police returned and the dance began again: heads cracked, teeth dislodged, the bloody display of pointless resistance performed. He knew that, for people like him, it was usually best not to be found near trouble.

Things had changed after the war, when the government decided that the solution to the problem of people like Kem and his family was to build cement houses and hand them over, to anchor a once transient people. Kem's father had been one of those that had helped the project take root.

But the problem had not been solved: the people of the neighbourhood, people living in crumbing tenements, had been angry, envious of the new houses. There had been little enough love before, but then, in the deathly days after the war, hatreds had bubbled blackly beneath the insolence. Traces of that insolence remained, and Kem Haluska faced it every day, even from his own neighbours. Even from my mother.

'It's the anarchists. The police are dispersing a demonstration, I think. Shooting over their heads, by the looks of it. No-one is on the ground, at least. It's OK.' I turned back to look at Kem, who frowned quizzically. *'I didn't know there was going to be a demonstration today. Are you sure they're anarchists? Were they coming from the works?'* Kem usually knew what was going to happen in the neighbourhood long before I did. His family seemed to catch wind of disturbances and trouble before they happened. The anarchists had been throwing bombs, daubing slogans and spitting threats since before the war. But they were no longer the only source of disorder, and the texture of the city's angry dissatisfactions had become richer since the men had come back from the front, since the strikes had started at the steel works.

The plant dominated the neighbourhood in every way imaginable. Its bulk defined the eastern edge of the district like a mountain, and its stacks could be seen from every street corner. The railway lines that brought in the ore and coke and took out their progeny marked the district's northern border. Everyone knew someone who worked there; every shop, café and bar relied on the wages of those that did. And the politics of the works defined the politics of everyone that lived in the neighbourhood; the leaders of the union were the most prominent men, and even the Party officials did nothing without their say so. Before the war there had been no real elections, but since the armistice had brought democracy, the whole neighbourhood voted unanimously for the Party.

'Those anarchists are trouble. They should fall in behind the Party. Without unity, we're all doomed.' Kem looked at me scornfully as I spoke. For Kem and his father, politics was something to be mistrusted, even when it couldn't be avoided. My growing political consciousness was incomprehensible and faintly comical to him. I recited the words I read in the newspapers or heard on the steps outside our apartment, as if their incantation could create understanding, and he would listen with that same scornful smile, hoping simply that the foolishness would soon end.

In the street below, a few shouts flared up. Policemen dragged a couple of anarchists across the cobbles towards a waiting wagon. This was unusual. Normally they would simply chase the demonstrators away, back into the alleys and courtyards, their tails between their legs. Arrests were rare, only for the ringleaders of strikes and the most prominent agitators. I stared more closely at the two men kicking and wrestling between the uniformed bodies. One was wearing the Party badge. They weren't anarchists after all. I twisted to get a clear view of his face and froze at the recognition. It was unmistakeable, a face familiar from a hundred leaflets, from the photographs in the city's newspaper.

'It's Andreas Hofmans! They've got Andreas Hofmans! Andreas! Andreas! We are with you!' I knew as soon as I started shouting into the street that I was making a mistake and yet the clout Kem landed at the back of my head still surprised me, knocking the words from my mouth. Below, a tall police officer scanned the façade of the warehouse building until his eyes found my startled face. He barked an order and three others set off at a pace towards the entrance on the street below. Before Kem could drag me back I caught a glimpse of Andreas Hofmans' smile.

Slipping away was easy enough and before the three pursuers had reached the third floor, Kem and I were two streets away, melting into the gathering dusk. Near the river, we paused, gulped at the thick air and smiled slyly to each other. As we parted, Kem embraced me then punched my arm, without malice.

'You're an idiot, you know that? If they hadn't been such dolts we could have got arrested.' I was laughing by now, but Kem's face hardened. *'That might be funny for someone like you; for me it's deadly serious.'* I straightened my face as best I could, tried to see events with the same gravity. I wanted to tell him that Andreas Hofmans had smiled at me, but it seemed too absurd to say out loud: Andreas was like a father to the whole neighbourhood; he came from here, grew up among us, offered hope that things could be different. But I knew that sounded childish, so I simply apologised for my foolishness and clapped his shoulder. I promised to see him by the river again tomorrow. In a few weeks, I would not be able to make that promise and my final school exams would start. Over the summer, I would spend only a few days ranging over the neighbourhood with him. Most days would be spent working to raise a little money to see me over the first term at university.

Discovery

Only once I had left the familiar streets of my childhood did I begin to understand how little I understood. The safety I had known within the limits of the neighbourhood had not always been apparent: there had been many occasions when violence and threat had come too close. My adventures with Kem often put my body, my life even, at risk. But those threats were understood, familiar. Moreover, no one threatened my understanding of the world. Whatever idiosyncrasies they held, my neighbours essentially had the same view of how the world turned. That certainty disappeared with the beginning of my student days.

The university was woven into a collection of buildings that clung to the north bank to the river. To reach it each morning, I crossed the ancient bridge under the gaze of dour statues, kings and dukes and their generals. Beneath me, cobbles glistened, polished by ten thousand feet, by hooves and wheels, and each day they carried me forward with less resistance. At the bridge's southern end, trams and motor cars tussled on the broad esplanade, but none crossed. Their range was limited to the boulevards of the newer districts; the old city stood resolute against progress. It was a world away from my neighbourhood, from the city I knew. But at least the streets around the university itself were comfortably narrow; the avenues I walked to reach it were wide enough to swallow whole tenements.

On my first morning, I had set off earlier than necessary, eager to be away, to be bound for the future. I crossed the railway track casually, confident that this new world would cause me no difficulty. And yet I was lost almost as soon as the neighbourhood slipped from view. The deeper I plunged into the frenzy of the city, the more it writhed; the streets became wider, but the buildings rose into canyon walls, six then nine floors of polite apartments, dressed with window boxes. Below them, cafés and shops sucked in, then disgorged, their clientele in a steady rotation; the broad pavements teemed with people busy with the beginnings of their day, oblivious to my faltering progress. I heard the squeal of a tram, and scanned the street for its stopping place.

I had taken a tram before, of course. I had visited the city centre and been to the river, had seen the grand buildings along its banks. But it had been as a visitor. The scale and pace had belonged to people who were not me. The knowledge that I did not have to know this, that I had only to understand my own neighbourhood, had always reassured me. I had been a guest on these streets, a stranger, and my ignorance could be excused. But on that first morning, standing at the tram stop with a hundred others, it struck me that these streets were now mine too. My ignorance was shameful.

I squeezed onto a tram eventually and pressed myself into the mass of humanity in all its stale softness; I let myself be decanted a couple of stops early, carried on the wave of office workers pouring from the car. The last few hundred metres were a blur. The shapes and colours of the city's autumn washed into me but did not bring me understanding. I resolved that I should conquer my ignorance: on subsequent mornings, for the whole of my first term, I walked the three miles to the bridge, letting the streets guide me as they would, spending my time extravagantly, exploring the city's districts in turn.

Houses, shops, apartment blocks, cinemas, grand cafés, churches, offices and factories, close cut lawns, parks and gardens, columns and triumphal arches, warehouses and theatres: I would return to streets after the passing of a few days or weeks, and every time I was startled by the discovery of some facet that I had failed to notice at my first encounter. It was as if the fabric of the place was in a state of constant transformation; everything fluid up to the moment that I looked at it, when the scene would solidify momentarily, anxious to be in motion once again. Eventually, I came to know something of some of the parts of the city, but I don't think I ever came to understand the whole. The randomness of the buildings and streets when among them did not seem to correspond to the simplicity of the city's silhouette when I looked at a map. The city was unknowable in its entirety. I would have to satisfy myself with a partial understanding, knowing that I would never be happy with such incompleteness. And yet, the city's very unknowability became intoxicating. I continued to walk to the university each morning, always taking the route offered up to me. Sometimes, giddiness would overtake me, a dizzy fainting pulling me left or right, staggering like a drunkard, uncertain of my legs; I would have to pause, gather up my strength and wait for the nausea to pass.

By the time the first snows swept through the city, when the air pinched the faces steaming in the grey morning light, I had overcome whatever doubts I had carried into my studies. Unlike the city beyond, within the lecture halls and study rooms of the university I was certain that the knowledge I had yet to acquire awaited me. It would not shift and mutate with the seasons. It would be solid and reliable; it could be acquired through regimented exploration. I fell quickly into a routine, absorbed by books and deadlines. While the other students bundled into classes, boisterous and unprepared, I recognised the rare privilege that learning offered. By the third week of term, they no longer asked if I wanted to join them in the nearby cafés and left me to the library, laughing, already seemingly half-inebriated. Most came from wealthy families, from market towns and the smaller cities of the region. None came from neighbourhoods like mine. They could afford to squander the opportunities for learning that I could not, and I hated them for it. Even those few studious fellows, who haunted the libraries as I did, seemed beyond my understanding. Almost none sat among the stacks of economics texts but instead were to be found reading the works of long dead romantic poets or else immersed in the study of anatomy or law. Occasionally I would pass some words with them in the corridors or on the stairs, but their lives had begun in such different circumstances to mine, and were heading towards such unimaginable destinations, that I found I had little to say once the necessary civilities had been exchanged.

I had one regular companion in the economics reading room, however. She would arrive before I did and was there most evenings until after 8 o'clock. While I always sat in the same place, comfortable with the familiarity of the surroundings, she took up a different seat each day, never returning to the same location. It was inevitable then that I should find her one evening sitting at my table. I stalled, hanging in the doorway, unsure of how to proceed. Despite the evenings we had spent together in this room, we had never acknowledged each other's existence, much less spoken. Both would be impossible if I took my usual seat. I tried to calculate how it would appear if, instead, I moved to a different place. My dilemma was resolved by her quizzical look and open palm indicating the seat across from her. I sat down.

'Anton Guebler.' I offered my name with a serious smile, but she did not look up from the pages spread on the table in front of her. Her breathing sped up fractionally and the hand, now resting palm down beside the book, tensed and did not release. I waited for a moment, then took books and pens from my satchel. From my jacket pocket, I retrieved my

glasses: I put them on as calmly as I could, but I managed to trap some hair behind them, covering my eyes. Unseen, I heard her laugh.

The next evening, she was again seated at my table, and the evening after that. On the fourth, in barely a whisper, she told me her name, held my gaze for what felt like several minutes, then pushed a thin pamphlet towards me, glancing left and right so as to be sure that we were not observed. I did not need to look down to know that the pamphlet had been produced by one of the many revolutionary groupings that fed on the atmosphere of economic and political upheaval rumbling beneath the city's streets. Whatever its other merits, the pamphlet was certainly seditious and I took the publication quickly, without question. With what I hoped was discretion, I placed it inside *The Foundations of Economic Theory*, conscious of the incongruity of such radicalism within the torpid orthodoxy of the established text. I smiled across at her, but she was already deep in her book, something by a German writer that did not appear on any of my reading lists.

Klara was not in the library on the Friday evening of that week. Perhaps she was never in the library on Friday evenings. To be honest, Friday evenings were not so unlike any other evening that I would have noticed before. But that would have been the fifth day of our acquaintance and I had wanted to talk to her about the pamphlet. I had so many questions, and I had spent the night and most of the day trying to answer them, so that I would be able to demonstrate the sophistication of my understanding. But she was not there and, since many of my observations remained as questions, I was grateful to have a little more time to resolve them.

I got home a little after ten. The tram had been full to bursting, but with laughter and carousing. A large group of red-faced young men had sung bawdily, passing an unlabelled bottle between them, hoping to impress the young women on board. The women looked down at their hands, rather than at their would-be suitors. I imagined their revulsion at the drunkards and relished our unspoken complicity.

The neighbourhood streets were mercifully calm by comparison. The air still rang with the familiar shouts and laughter, the arguments and the clatter of tenement life, but it felt like the stillness of a monastery after the tram. On the stairway of our tenement, women's voices clanged down from above; I climbed slowly and, as I passed each dwelling, I caught glimpses of family life, picked out in yellow light, frozen in doorframes. I knew through years of practice how to greet my neighbours without intruding, but some unfamiliar undercurrent was present and I could not help but catch their eyes as I passed them in the half-darkness of the stair.

I reached the doorway to the small apartment that I shared with my mother. The light was on, as usual. My mother finished her shift at nine each night and was typically still eating when I found her. I was surprised then to smell no cooking as I shuddered open the front door. No light crept out from the kitchen, nor from my mother's room. It took me a moment to fathom the meaning of this: my mother was not at home.

She had worked at the garment factory for so long that it might as well have been forever. Since before I was born, in any case. She must have hoped that once the children came, she would have been allowed to withdraw from the noise and acrid air, but there had been only me. My father had died during the war and she had never remarried. I had no siblings, no wider family: whatever relatives existed had chosen to leave us to ourselves. While there was a small widow's pension, it was not enough to pay for bread, let alone rent and clothes. When the war ended, she had simply carried on. What choice had there been?

My childhood had formed itself around shift patterns, with much of the care entrusted to the neighbourhood itself. Often, as a small boy, I would eat my supper with Kem's family. I would bathe in the warmth of their home, a warmth that came from the love they had for each other and for me. The thin concrete walls held little heat, but I lingered as long as I could, until the factory hooter sounded and it was time to head up the hill to the tenement building, usually with a piece of sweet pastry in my closed palm, a gift from Kem's mother. From the third landing, I would see the yellow light of the lamp above the door and I would know that my mother would be home, already wrapped in her blanket at the kitchen table, a chunk of bread and sausage on the board in front of her, a bottle of beer beside it. Her absence that Friday evening was like a jolt of electricity.

I looked at the table in the empty kitchen. No crumbs. She had returned after her shift, or how else would the lamp have been lit? And yet she had left before thinking about supper. I looked in the cupboard, but there was bread there, beer too. She had not needed to go out to borrow some food from the neighbours. Anxiety tightened in my chest. The sudden eruption of commotion from the courtyard below distracted me from the mystery.

At first it rose like steam from a cauldron, a hiss of voices roiling up the stairway. The accustomed noises of evening sank beneath it, doused or replaced. I went to the front door and leaned over the balustrade. Beneath me, a crush of bodies was crammed into the tight space of the courtyard. It seemed that most of the tenants of the building had abandoned their suppers and the warmth of their kitchens. Instinctively I scanned the heads below for my mother's familiar scarf.

She was at the centre of the crowd. I could not hear her anger above the fizzing voices of the others, but I could see her jabbing finger punctuating its explosion. Others in the crowd were also animated and appeared equally vocal, even if I could not discern the sound that they made. If outrage has a collective face, I was looking into it; without its content, it was faintly comical. At the sound of footsteps on the stairs, however, I managed to smother my smile before Mrs Toporowitz's boy raced onto the landing.

The Toporowitzes lived upstairs from us and, while far from friends, they had always been kind to us since their arrival a few years after the war had ended. Mr Toporowitz had come to work in the machine plant, where he earned enough to ensure that his wife did not have to work at all, and simply had to care for the children. The eldest of these stood before me now, eyes rolling in his head, his breath still catching as he gulped it down. Eventually, I realised that his inability to speak was caused more by my unexpected presence than by his rapid climb of the stairs. I decided to break the spell.

'Good evening Tomás. What's all the fuss about down there?'

He remained silent for a moment, regarding me with disbelief. It seemed inconceivable to him that anyone who lived in the neighbourhood should be unaware of the cause of the commotion below.

'Anton Guebler, I think you should fetch your mother. Fetch her home before she says much more. The machine works is to close next week. It's just been announced. The whole block is incensed, but your mother is arguing that the garment factory should not come out in solidarity with the machine workers. She says that her hunger will not bring back the jobs. The men will only take that kind of talk for so long.'

I understood of course that he meant his father. The closure of the machine works would end the relative comfort of the Toporowitzes' lives, bringing misery in its stead. My mother was under no immediate threat from this closure, so her lack of concern would appear doubly callous. Of course, she was not even a shop steward at the factory and could have no say, beyond her own vote, over whether the garment workers would come out on strike in support of the men whose jobs were lost. But memories ran deep in the neighbourhood. In the tenement itself, a further six families beyond the Toporowitzes relied on the machine works. My mother's lack of solidarity would be remembered in the lean times to come.

As the boy scuttled up the next flight of steps, I paused to watch the confrontation. The outrage of the crowd was still as vivid but my mother's part seemed transformed. Her jabbing finger was now simply a defensive gesture, an accusation to mask her own shame; her lost words pleading and bitter, rather than heroic. The anger of the others was focused rather than diffuse. I sighed. She understood so little of the world, as it was and as it would become, despite her greater exposure to it. I thought in that moment of Klara, of her pamphlet and her resolution. I promised myself that I would find her somehow, before turning to trudge down the stairway to rescue my mother from the bear pit below.

Praxis

Klara did not appear in the library the following week, nor the week after that. By the second Thursday, I no longer turned in my chair when I heard the sound of a step in the corridor. Little by little, my attention returned to my studies and the equilibrium that had governed my student life seemed to have been restored. I knew this to be so because, that evening, a paragraph over which I had laboured for a week finally released its meaning, unclenching like a fist. I flopped the book closed and slid down the leather of the chair, my hands behind my head. The clock showed a quarter past seven. I felt enough pride in myself to justify leaving the library early.

I reached the bridge in time to hear the clock above the town hall chime the half hour. I skated over the icy cobbles, my feet hungry for the pavement. I wanted to be out of the city before its darkness became threatening. Demonstrations had always been common in my neighbourhood but, since the closure of the machine works, and the announcement of layoffs at three of the city's other factories, discord had spilled over onto the polite boulevards and avenues of the central districts too. Here, anger sat uncomfortably, and the police were more confident in its enthusiastic suppression. Already that week I had seen glimpses of violence in the shadows, and witnessed men go down under the thrashing of slick batons in the gloom of side streets.

I turned up my collar, as much against the leer of police officers as against the cold. I pushed my hands deep into my pockets, burrowing into the soft fibres in search of comfort. Small groups of uniformed men stood at street corners, watching. The glint of black metal occasionally caught in the lamp light, sending a deep chill through me. The effort of keeping my pace perfectly balanced between respectable progress and guilty haste provided me with the necessary distraction, and I focused on my feet and my breathing, timing each to the other.

Buildings slid past, unnoticed. Just after the Electric Cinema, where the street stepped back in deference to the grand villas that lined it, a too-familiar ball of sound rolled through the air: the murmur of feet and voices that signalled a crowd. Something caused me to glance over my shoulder. Behind me, at some distance but not far enough, a black line of police horses stretched across the full width of the street. Their stillness threatened more than the riotous commotion advancing through the darkness.

The head of the march turned the corner. Some of the strikers held lanterns, others simple torches; still others carried sticks, cudgels, ironware: the tools of their interrupted trade. I thought of the glint of black metal, the flash of sharp hooves. My heart thumped, implored me to escape, but there was nowhere to run to. There were no side-streets or alleys anywhere between the ragged mass ahead of me and the stern line behind. I was caught full square in harm's way, like a novice.

Blood thudded behind my ears and I scanned the gateways and walls that protected the genteel gardens of the street's wealthy residents. The gates were shut tight and I did not need to test their handles to know that they were also locked. The whitewashed walls rose two metres above the pavement. I could see no niche into which I might bolt once the shouting began, before the gunfire crackled. There was no decision really; there was no question of which side I should choose. That choice had been made for me in the womb. The only debate had been how far I would be willing to declare that allegiance in the face of a threat to my safety. I walked, as calmly as I could, towards the demonstrators, sweat prickling under my hat.

I heard the beating of hooves before I could make out the flame-licked faces of the men and women filling the street. Terror sank through me, down into my stomach, draining through my knees; I don't remember where the sinking dread crossed with the wave of shame that rose almost simultaneously, but both emotions were in flood as I pressed myself into the recess of a gateway, flattening myself out of harm's way.

The gate swung open. I fell backwards and the garden's darkness swallowed me. Horses and uniforms flew past, orange light gilding leather boots and polished batons. My senses returned only slowly, but I had managed to push the gate closed with my boot before the first of the police officers on foot trotted past. As shouts and cries carried over the wall and wove their way between the wrought iron of the gate, I scudded across the concrete until I sat on the hard, wet soil, my back against the wall. No-one on the street would be able to see me, just as I could see nothing of the turmoil beyond. Even the house was largely invisible, shrouded by trees and shrubbery, lost in its empty blackness. Just a few metres away, the bodies of men and women were being broken and bloodied, but only the noises of this violence reached me in the darkness, like the sounds of an argument carried on the midnight air in summer.

The crash and thud of the body froze me in my place. I could not see it, but it was certainly now on my side of the wall. For a moment, there was no movement and I imagined the body as a corpse, tossed over the wall by the force of a racing horse that had been whipped into frenzy.

My mind darted back and forth: they would come in to collect it, would not want the owners of the villa to find it in the grey light of morning, interrupting the calm of their routine. I searched the blackness for another place to hide, a corner of the garden where I might remain unseen. Her gentle sobbing called me back, subdued my panic only to replace it with another fear. I watched the space where the impact seemed to have occurred, tracing the grainy air for movement.

'Hello?'

I hissed my question into the darkness. The silence smothered all other noise: the clatter and thrash in the street, my stuttering breath, the blood trembling through me. I waited, my breath like lead in my lungs. I could picture her, mouth stopped by terror at the presence of another.

'It's OK. I'm not police. Not the owner of this garden either. I was on the street. Found a place to hide here. Like you.'

Her reply was a muffled animal noise. Another sob, then stillness. I sat in the darkness for a moment, listening to the violence beyond the wall.

'Anton? Is that you?'

I could not imagine how she had recognised me in the gloom, but the voice was undoubtedly Klara's. I could barely make out the simplest impression of her as a solid thing, but even through the tears, the tone was resolutely hers. I heard her scrape across the earth towards me.

'I didn't know you had joined us; sorry, I didn't see you. Earlier, everything was such a whirl. It was hard enough to focus on the tasks at hand, let alone recognise friends. Are you hurt?' Her hand on my sleeve made me flinch and she must have assumed that my arm had been injured, perhaps a baton blow, maybe even a bullet. She apologised and her faith seared into me.

'*No, I'm fine.*' My honesty felt insufficient, since it may have been received as bravery, and I felt compelled to explain further. '*I wasn't with the demonstration, just on the street. I saw what was going on, was walking towards you all, when the horses charged and, I have to admit, I was terrified and found my way in here to hide. It's shameful, I know.*'

Her sigh filled me with a melancholy that clouded every rational thought in my head. The glimmer of light from the street coalesced in her eyes and I could see them looking directly at me, laced with a sad smile.

'*If it is shameful, then I should be ashamed too. I didn't even wait for the first horse before I fled. Others stood their ground, but I flung myself at this wall. Momentum and terror must have carried me over it. I have no idea how. I'm hardly the athletic sort. In any case, I landed badly. Think I've turned my ankle. But it wasn't that that made me cry.*'

At this, she leant close into me and left the soft impression of her lips on my cheek, before withdrawing. I wanted to reach out, pull her back to me, feel her warmth again, her softness, but I had no idea how that could be achieved, so I sat tracing the shivers on my skin.

'*Listen. I think it's over.*' The noise from behind the wall had stilled. No shouts, no voices of any kind, not even footsteps. We both strained into the dark night, listening for any trace of the battle that had raged, but there was none. I crept along the wall, inch by inch, to where the gate's hinges clasped the mortar. Cloaked by iron work, I glimpsed, then scanned, the street. There remained some debris: extinguished torches; discarded make-shift weapons that had once more assumed the forms of the harmless implements of working people; here and there a forlorn hat; even a lone boot, its tongue hanging breathless in the lamp light. I took my father's watch from my coat pocket, felt its solidity in my hand. I squinted at the white face, seeking out the nervous hands. Not yet midnight.

We waited for another two hours before we were willing to chance the street. We passed the time in hushed voices, talking about the factory closures, about our studies and what had brought us to them. She had brightened when I'd told her about my neighbourhood, talked less and listened more. Encouraged by her interest, I told her about my mother's work at the garment factory, but not her views on the strike. And, despite her enquiry, I did not tell her about my father's inglorious death in front of a firing squad, only that he had died during the war. Unsure what more to say about myself, I paused. She must have taken this for emotion, for her hand again rested on my arm and my shame burned beneath its warmth.

Klara was the first person to describe my upbringing as proletarian. It was, in fact, the first time I had heard the word spoken out loud. Until then, those five syllables have remained unsounded in books and the thought that it described the lives of my mother and I, even my tenement neighbours, had never occurred to me. When Klara turned to leave me at the junction that separated my way home from hers, I was unsurprised that she turned towards the modest suburbs of the comfortably off. She had hobbled maybe five steps on her injured ankle before she turned back, offering a fleeting embrace. The flickering kiss to my cheek ended before I fully understood that it had happened.

'Listen, Anton. I won't be around campus for a few days. There's too much going on. I need to make up for disappearing tonight. But we're holding a meeting next week, at the Steel Workers' Mission. Wednesday. You should come. I could introduce you to some people. Please say you will.'

I accepted the invitation with too much enthusiasm, then stuttered into an uneasy silence. She smiled and turned once more, and I watched her limp into the darkened city. The blackness of the night wrapped around me like a blanket, insulating me from the terrors of earlier and the mundanity of what I knew would follow. I wanted the days to collapse into themselves, hastening my arrival at the Steel Workers' Mission. I trudged home, willing time to bend.

Through the weekend's aimless hours, and then in lectures and the library, I was able to function with my usual industry and drive, but my mind remained resolutely elsewhere. I analysed each gesture, murmur and inflection from that night over and over. At times, I became utterly convinced that Klara's only interest in me was political, and then in the next instant the exact same evidence would allow for limitless hope. I realised that, for the first time in my life, I was adrift on an ocean of desire. The unfamiliar terror was delicious; the blandness of everything else drained all colour from the world.

Wednesday arrived and trudged its way through grey light and back again into darkness, its passing measured minutely by the reading room clock. With the ending of the day's last lecture, I regained my purpose and set off, heading out of the university's precincts. As I left the library, I felt a twinge of guilt and of self-doubt. But my heels clicked defiantly on the cobble stones and carried me into the web of narrow streets that snaked beyond the fringes of the city centre. I felt an unexpected lightness to my step, a levity that persisted until I reached my destination.

Outside the Steel Workers' Mission, men stood in small groups, smoking and muttering, occasionally breaking the evening's stillness with rude laughter. Yellow-grey light oozed through the smeared windows and around the half-opened door. I stood in the shadows for a moment, at the brink of the final decision to enter this otherness.

Political rallies and Party members had always surrounded me, but they had always been other: the scenery to my life, not active players within it. The grouping to which Klara belonged had been unknown to me and if its fibres reached into my neighbourhood they had remained submerged. The language of revolution was not uncommon, but it was vague, romantic, spoken of as other poor people spoke of heaven, of salvation. An end point, ill-defined, with no clear map with which to reach it. In Klara's pamphlets, the revolution was a technical process that could be measured and described. Importantly, the way to it was clearly mapped.

I stepped from the shadows, past the men outside, and into the yellow-lit hall. Through the smoke, I could see her hair. I tried to slip through the crowd towards her, but my polite apologies yielded no avenues and I had to prise the bodies apart with the palm of my hand. She was talking with a small group of earnest young men and women. Some I recognised, and I assumed that the rest were students too. They were pulled together into a tight knot, as if huddling for protection from the other men and women filling the chamber. I saw her palm flat against the back of a tall young man.

'Anton! So glad you decided to come! Everyone, this is Anton Guebler. He's a student at the university too.'

The tall young man turned, smooth ripples shifting in his woollen jacket. The glow of the lamp light caught in the down about his ears. His face was serene and he smiled warmly at me. I looked from his face to that of Klara, and saw that her wide eyes were on him, not me. He introduced himself as Gustav, said he was pleased to meet me after all he had heard, but the fact that Klara had spoken of me did not cause me any joy or pride. It was instantly clear that I was simply a curio to her, that I had been described to Gustav as an interesting and possibly amusing discovery, nothing more. I was simply a small, proletarian trophy rather than a friend. Even a friend.

I found a store of stubborn bitterness within me and overcame the urge to turn and run. Even so, I was grateful for the hush and rustle that danced at that moment through the room. Those still standing began to shuffle to the remaining empty seats, and I was carried on this movement away from Klara and her friends. I found myself near the back of the hall. I sought out a place and made my way to the centre of a row of wooden folding chairs. An older couple, hands gnarled and entwined, twisted to allow me to pass. I fell into the first vacant seat.

'Desperate times, comrade. Let's see if this bugger has anything to offer us.'

My neighbour, a man in his late forties, his crushed face marked with a frozen sneer, nodded towards the stage. I followed his sour gaze to where three men sat unsmiling behind a table festooned with banners. It took only a few moments for me to recognise him. I felt my pulse race again. Andreas Hofmans filled the stage, even though he simply sat at one end of the table. His black moustache was immobile and pristine, but his cold blue eyes ranged restlessly across the room, scouring the faces of the audience as it settled into the creaking chairs.

'Show some respect! That,' I pointed at the figure seated on the stage, *'that is Andreas Hofmans. The greatest man in the city. In the country.'* My enthusiasm swamped whatever reticence I might have felt. *'If anyone can lead us through this, it is him. Have faith, comrade. Have some faith!'* My neighbour watched me along the length of his nose and, when I had finished, he vented his lack of faith in a scornful snort. I opened my mouth to challenge him once more, but the room fell into a deep silence. One of the other men on the stage, his broad musculature evident beneath too-crisp, too-clean blue overalls, rose to his feet by

degrees, from seated to crouched, to stooped, to erect. His fists were planted on the table in front of him.

'Comrades, welcome. I must confess that this is perhaps the largest rally we have so far assembled during this latest time of strife, and I think that shows that we have had enough. Our patience with the factory owners, with the authorities that protect them, is running out. So, I'm very pleased that Comrade Hofmans, political secretary to the Party, is here to witness this. Maybe he can take the message back to the Executive Committee, that the time for appeasement is over. But I don't want to put words into the Secretary's mouth. He can speak for himself, and I for one am eager to hear what he has to say.'

The young man sat down and a ripple of applause criss-crossed the room. Andreas Hofmans' moustache twisted into some kind of smile and, as he rose, his eyes remained locked on the young man who had introduced him. I prickled with excitement at the menace they conveyed. At his full height, the political secretary stood at no more than 170cm tall and yet before a word had been uttered, he dominated the whole room. His head turned from the young man seated beside him and panned across the audience beyond the stage. I felt those blue eyes as they passed over me, and I can only believe that each and every man and woman present felt them too, sifting through their consciences, their will. When he began his oration, his voice had none of the reediness of the younger man's and its solidity was such that one might build a city upon it.

Parade

There was something about the light that morning. Spring mornings often shone lemon, and carefree Sundays always quivered with an excitement that was denied to working days. And yet the crystal clarity of the air over the neighbourhood startled me. Even my mother felt it. The unpleasantness of the fracas in the tenement courtyard had long been forgotten, erased by my persuasion and by the chiding of our neighbours, and she too blossomed with the excitement of the day. We stepped out into the street together and greeted strangers like old friends, merging with the growing knot of people moving towards the polling station.

Until the election campaign began, I had barely thought about Andreas Hofmans since that evening at the Steel Workers' Mission. The duty to study hard, and then the need to earn a living, had left no time to think of such things. However, on the morning of the election that would see Andreas Hofmans become the mayor of the city, I understood that, in fact, I had stopped thinking about him in order to forget Klara.

It had taken a few weeks, but I had eventually been able to shut out thoughts of her by burying myself in my lectures and my reading. Study also enabled me to recover some of the pride that the experience had taken from me. For the rest of my time at university, the few acquaintances I had made on campus were shunned, and I was able to strangle any butterflies that rose in my stomach at the sight of a pretty smile in the library. These were not people like me. I resented the ease of their lives, and I anticipated their condescension. I was aware of the reputation I had among my peers, but I also knew that my grades were exemplary. I derived sufficient satisfaction from the knowledge that a humble young man from my neighbourhood could outstrip the golden-haired darlings of the wealthy villas. The produce of luxury and advantage did not ripen so fast, nor so well. Eventually I had a first-class degree, a commendation, and the Pritzler Prize for Political Science, which was presented to me by the mayor at my graduation.

That was the old mayor, of course. His moustache had bristled over thin lips shaped into a smile, as his thick, smooth hands enveloped mine in congratulation. My success was also his prize, a trophy for the whole city as well as the university. Taking my ballot paper on that morning, it was hard to recall how fondly I had thought of him on the day of my graduation. I felt no rancour towards him, simply that he was an irrelevance, something spent and about to be swept away by the future. I made my mark next to Andreas Hoffmans' name, just as everyone else in the neighbourhood would do, with a giddy hopefulness, and with pride. We knew that the new mayor had grown up on the same streets that we had. Instead of a silver spoon, he had come into the world with the taste of steel and coke on his tongue. He was ours and, naturally, we were his in return.

I had taken my mother to see him speak at a rally early in the campaign. Something of the excitement of that evening at the Mission Hall had been reignited and I had cajoled her into accompanying me. Most of the neighbourhood had been there too, crammed into the narrow streets, the windows of the houses trembling with excited anticipation. When it came, the speech had set the whole neighbourhood aflame. The power of Hofmans' oratory washed all trace of cynicism and suspicion away. Almost all trace.

Kem had declined to join us. He had made some cursory excuse, sufficient only to avoid the need to express his cynicism. We had found a way to sustain our withering friendship in evasions of this kind. It was I that had left, that had abandoned my friend, and I had no right to demand that Kem stepped across into this new world. My guilt, my betrayal, meant that whatever confected excuse Kem offered was accepted without argument, if not without resentment. It was still the only friendship I had known. Since graduating, I had been working as a clerk with one of the city's leading accountancy firms. I spent my days at a desk in a grand office, built at the height of the Empire, in a pressed suit and stiff collar. At the same time, Kem's life continued much as it had in our shared youth, ranging over the neighbourhood, helping his father or his father's friends in whatever enterprise they had embarked upon. The other clerks in the office were alien to me, neither like me nor like the wealthy intellectuals that populated the reading rooms of the university; most were older, already grey, drained. I spoke little during the day and had nothing to say to either my mother or to Kem in the evenings and at weekends. I existed between worlds, never fully at home in either, much as I had done while studying.

However, unlike university, the excitement of employment began to wane as soon as I understood the rudimentary nature of my duties and the limitations of my position. I mastered all that needed to be mastered in order to fulfil my role within ten weeks and, soon after, I came to see my position as a bookkeeper as utterly mundane and a waste of my talents. When the election campaign erupted into the slow circling of my days, it revealed another life, another future. Instead of simply reconciling profits and loss, it seemed that something else was possible. I realised, for the first time, that there was work to be done in changing the world, not merely in maintaining it. In the instant that I saw Andreas Hofmans' name on a poster pasted to a grimy wall, the constraints I had put on myself were broken. Perhaps the pamphlets Klara had given me had engrossed me in themselves, and not simply for her sake. I volunteered without hesitation to help with the election campaign, and I spent every evening and weekend carrying paste buckets and trestle tables behind Party officials as they went about the business of overturning the world.

Everyone I met in the neighbourhood greeted me as part of a victorious army, garlanding me with smiles and salutes; a firm, tender slap to my shoulder, an occasional embrace. I had lived in the neighbourhood my entire life, was part of it, and yet I had never before felt this kind of recognition, this kind of love. I was no longer simply one of the eternal cobbles in the familiar streets. I was notable.

As the day of the election approached, the entire neighbourhood was dressed in the colours of the Party, inscribed with the name of its leading son. Even Kem wore a strip of ribbon by then, even if he lacked the enthusiasm of the others, content simply to blend in with his neighbours. It seemed impossible that the election could fail to fall our way, and I waved away the warnings of the Party stalwarts, old hands who reminded me that the neighbourhood was not the city, that votes were needed in neighbourhoods where no-one felt any pride in Andreas Hofmans; among the other industrial districts that had been laid just as low as ours, but also the middle class suburbs, the homes of my fellow clerks. There was no certainty that the future would arrive with this election, they told me. But in the bright clear Sunday air, such a possibility seemed outlandish.

When it came, the victory was overwhelming. Not only had the working-class districts given their emphatic support to Andreas Hofmans, but also the suburbs and even some of wealthier enclaves. Across the city the people voted in sufficient numbers to end the era of the flaccid former mayor. As the banners floated above the crowds filling the streets of the neighbourhood, I felt nothing but hope.

Blissful as it was in that moment, hope soured soon enough. Even before the posters had begun to fade, I felt the dust of my workaday life closing over me. There were no more rallies, no more boxes to be moved, no chairs to be stacked: I was no longer making the future, simply watching, a spectator. My neighbours no longer smiled at me when I returned home from the office. Once again, I was a person of no distinction. Days became weeks, and hours passed like months. Months themselves crawled past unnoticed. My work became even less significant, my colleagues even greyer. I still attended Party meetings, but they offered little respite, filled with procedural motions and interminable committee reports. For a year and a half, I trudged through empty days, ever more envious of Kem's freedom, of the life I had abandoned. It had perhaps lacked meaning and importance, but it had been mine to shape.

In the week before the Christmas after the election, once the partners had finished for the year, only the stacks of unprocessed papers stood between me and the holiday. Some of the other clerks took to shortening their days, either by arriving in the office after ten or leaving before four. As such, there was no one around when a barrel of a man, with thinning grey hair and a grey tweed waistcoat, appeared in the stairwell one evening as I was leaving.

'Anton Guebler? I am very sorry to disturb you — and please, there is no need to be alarmed, nothing is wrong. I wanted to talk to you about an opportunity that has arisen which may be of interest to you.' Joszef pushed his glasses up his monumental nose. *'Will you allow me to buy you a cup of coffee?'*

Initiation

The office did not have windows in any meaningful sense. The four desks were illuminated by thin shafts of light that sliced through three reeded fanlights, set high on the wall opposite the door. The faint illumination they offered was supported by electric light that hummed in sympathy. If it were not for the desk lamps that burned from 8am until 8pm, or whenever the office finally emptied, it would have been impossible to read the documents that arrived in thick bundles from the mayor's private office. Even the once-white ceiling had a sombre tone, so lacquered was it with nicotine. The walls were panelled in unstained oak, interrupted only by a single frame: a map of the city over which we ruled.

If the office was sombre, it seemed to glow in comparison with the corridor beyond. Its darkness seeped under the door. Occasionally a head would appear from the gloom: one of the private secretaries with a file or telegram, or Miss Gelber with coffee. Its brooding presence lurked like the threat of bad weather.

Little had been said since Joszef had made his introductions on my arrival. Neither of the other advisor's had even glanced at me, absorbed in whatever it was that lay on their desks. Eventually, Georg looked up. He pushed the document he had been scrutinising under a manila folder, so that as-yet-untrustworthy eyes could not intrude. From his desk chair, he studied me for some time before he raised an eyebrow, a smile flickering on his face, and he offered the merest nod of greeting. A curl of blond hair had fallen across his forehead, and his slender hand scooped the wayward strand back into place.

'Coffee?'

Without waiting for a reply, he stepped lightly across the room and took up a small brass bell. This he rang with three short cranks of the wrist, the chimes hanging uncertain in the still air. It was clear that he was much younger than Joszef: taller, and with a suggestion of athleticism. He stood with his ear cocked towards the door until the sound of clatter and scraping confirmed that the order had been received. He turned back to the room, satisfied. Only then did he extend a hand in welcome; the brisk and sudden handshake ended before I knew what to do next. Georg let slip something like a laugh. His eyes remained fixed on me, but his question was addressed to Joszef.

'He's not particularly sharp, is he? I hope the Boss knows what he's doing.'

In the office, he was simply the Boss. The private secretaries would most often refer to him as the Mayor, or even His Honour, but such conventions appeared unnecessary here. Or perhaps the forced informality reflected the need for Georg, and Ana too, to signal that they were not cowed by the potency of Andreas Hofmans. This breeziness, I quickly learned, did not represent an absence of deference. From across the room, Ana sighed.

'Don't be an arse, Georg. Do try.' She flashed a smile at me, but did not stand, nor offer her own handshake. 'Welcome Anton. It's a pleasure to have you here. Joszef has had such positive things to say about you.'

I wanted to ask her what it was that Joszef had said about me. It remained a mystery to me how my name had even come up, let alone how I had been selected for the position. At first, I had assumed that perhaps Klara, or even Gustav, had suggested me, but when I mentioned their names at that first conversation over coffee, Joszef's face had registered no recognition. My curiosity was no match, however, for my joy at finding myself working once again with Andreas Hofmans, and I pushed the question away. In truth, some small part of me was afraid to know the answer.

Ana sat at the back of the office, under the fanlights, from where she could survey the whole room, on those rare occasions that she looked up from her desk. To face her, I had to turn fully in my chair, but even so I was always aware of her presence behind me, the scratching of her pen, the pauses that would punctuate her thoughts. She was my superior, the Principal Economic Advisor. She had been a professor of economics at the university in the Capital, completing her doctorate long before I had graduated. I was in awe of her, not least because she did not display the same self-importance that Georg did. Already, on that first day, I saw her as an ally. At least, someone I wanted to be my ally.

We mainly worked in silence, each advisor focused on their own work, but it was not an unfriendly place. Certainly in those first days, I shared more moments of camaraderie with Ana, and even with the supercilious Georg, than I had in the years I spent at the accountancy firm. But there was little to puncture the atmosphere of productive studiousness for much of the time.

There was, however, a telephone on Joszef's desk. It seldom rang, maybe once or twice a week, but it was always answered with reverence. By the end of my first month in the office, I had become used to the drama of the telephone call, but I still paused whatever I had been doing to watch, breathless, as Joszef raised the receiver.

'Yes Andreas, of course.'

Joszef was the only one that used the Boss's name freely. They had a shared history, had been friends before; it was in many ways unremarkable. He had been the trusted confidante of Andreas Hofmans long before he was elected, when they were comrades in the steel workers' union. He had been an agitator in the trenches as a young man, and later a leading figure in the struggles that followed during the years of the Depression. Despite his thinning grey hair and pot belly, despite the tufts of bristle sprouting from his over-large nose, he still dominated any room he was in, except when his old friend was present. Then he would seem to shrink, to become less solid, allowing Andreas Hofmans to fill the space he left behind. He seemed content to play the role of tactician to the Boss's showmanship.

Joszef sighed as he rose to his feet. The creaking of his chair vied for attention but was drowned out by the weariness of that exhalation. *'Right, I'll be back in a while. Don't know how long. He wants to talk through the rent control paper. He has some questions, apparently. Anton, you put that together, didn't you? Be ready; I might have to send someone through to fetch you, if I need some more detail.'*

The darkness of the corridor swallowed him, smothered the sound of his shoes on the floorboards. The office rested in silence for a few moments, and I could hear Ana shift in her chair, percussion to the melody of her breathing. Georg was smiling at me.

'I think some coffee would be in order. Anton?'

Until the day he disappeared, I was never certain whether Georg's suggestion of coffee was an instruction or an invitation. On that morning, as on every other, he waited for my nod, studying my face, looking for a flinch of pride. Finding none, he rang three short trills with the bell then returned to his desk. He leant back in his chair, smiling, his hands woven behind his head, amused by thoughts that remained opaque. Between his fingers, a flick of fair hair pointed towards the grey light crawling through the fanlights from the world beyond the office.

'For pity's sake, Georg! Anton has better things to do than to play games with a farmer's boy.' I looked at her, perplexed. Georg fumed behind his desk.

'My family are not farmers! And even if they were, stop being so bourgeois. Your disdain for working people is so unbecoming.' Georg reclaimed a little of his pride, but his lip still projected his annoyance into the room.

'Ha! You have the nerve to call me bourgeois! Whatever the precise involvement of your father in the production of wheat, it doesn't alter the fact that you are a petty bourgeois dilletante.' Ana's iciness cracked into laughter. *'Did you know, Anton, that you should show some respect for our comrade here? He is the eldest son of one of the wealthiest grain merchants in the south. A touch provincial, of course, but his daddy's money got him into law school and then secured him a place within chambers in the city. That was before he found his conscience, of course, and gave some of his precious time to the steel workers' union and then offered his services to the Party. Unpaid, of course. Truly a hero of the proletariat!'*

'Shall I tell Anton about your own comfortable ascent, then? I think, for a man from his background, the smoothness of your path to greatness will grate at least a little. It's clear that he understands the cause better than either of us. This is not just an intellectual game to him.' He spat the last words, then offered a weak smile to me, one that read as an apology of sorts. I

wanted the tension to break, and so I spluttered out the first thing that came to mind.

'What do you think the Boss wants with Joszef? Do you think that I did something wrong?'

At the end of my first week, I had been given the task of drawing up a proposal for rent controls across the city, to accompany a programme of house building that had been announced shortly before I arrived in City Hall. Joszef had stopped me in the corridor as I was leaving for the weekend and, with his paw resting on my shoulder, he had breathed the barely audible instruction into my ear, carried on brandy fumes and tobacco smoke. The architecture of the idea was straightforward, a simple intervention entirely in line with the mayor's wider platform: there were technical difficulties to resolve of course, but the principles were hardly revolutionary. The clandestine briefing was therefore unnerving. I did not understand why Georg and Ana had been excluded in this way. I consoled myself with the conclusion that Joszef was presenting me with an opportunity of which my comrades would be jealous, not least given that I was still a novice. A gift then, and maybe a test. I had begun work that evening under the kitchen lamp while my mother muttered in her room. If the paper had been a test, perhaps I had already failed. Perhaps Joszef's confidence in me had already landed him in trouble with his old comrade.

'Don't worry Anton, I'm sure the paper is fine. The politics are, uh, a little more difficult of course. But that's for Joszef to square with the Boss. Everyone has their role to play here.'

She was smiling and, for a moment, I forgot about her row with Georg. I smiled back, reassured, until the footsteps in the corridor, unmistakably Joszef's heavy tread, caused me to turn towards the door, expectant, terrified.

Joszef filled the door frame, his stomach pushing rhythmically at the buttons of his waistcoat. The yellow light of the room accented the wisps of grey creeping from his nostrils; the bags hanging beneath his eyes were magnified by his reading glasses. He sighed, looking every day of his age.

'Everything is fine. Nothing to become agitated about. Mayor Hofmans thinks the proposals are solid, so well done, Anton, well done. I'll need you to do some more refinement, of course, before I speak to the councilmen, make sure I have enough to secure sufficient support for an overwhelming endorsement. But for now, everything is fine.'

Later, after the others had left and the corridor was silent, I sat at my desk staring at the paper I had written, no longer pretending to revise it, but simply to admire it. Georg had nodded to me with something I took to be respect as he left; Ana had left her hand on my shoulder as she wished me a good evening. When Joszef had creaked out of his chair, slipping his watch back into its waistcoat nest, his smile had wrapped itself around me and a tingle had spun down my spine. We would talk in the morning about what more needed to be done, but for now he was off to meet with the faction leader in a bar in the city, to sound him out on the plans. There would be jobs, and houses, and a poke in the eye for the rentier class. The faction leader would not need to hear the detail or understand the finer points of the economics. All would be well, and I had played my part. My colleagues no longer had reason to doubt my abilities, nor my commitment. And the world would move forward, nudged on by my hand.

I leaned back in my chair and threw my feet onto the desk, my fingers knitted behind my head. It must have been after ten, but I had no desire to leave, despite the low rumblings of my hunger. My mother would be sewing by the stove, one eye on the clock, but I did not care that she would be worried by my absence. Why should I care? She had no need of my presence. It served no purpose. She would sew until her eyes grew too tired to spot the needle and then she would slip off to bed and into dreams. When I inevitably slipped into the apartment, I would make no noise, would not disturb her, and she would leave for the factory before I emerged from slumber.

Hunger tightened my stomach and I felt for the coins in my trouser pocket. I resolved to leave, to find some bread and soup in one of the cafes that stayed open into the late evening, before heading home. It would be good to wander the streets of the city, to feel its pulse on the air. With a smile I switched off my desk lamp and disappeared into the darkness.

Breaking Earth

A photograph of Andreas Hofmans filled a quarter of the front page. His eyes bore through the lens, through space and time and paper, directly into you. Something like a smile lurked beneath his moustache, but otherwise he appeared solemn, serious; aware of the gravity of events. His left hand clasped the shaft of a spade, his right its handle; its blade cut into the turf under the weight of his foot. By autumn, one hundred new houses for workers' families would have been completed at this site alone; work on 17 other sites would have begun.

Somewhere behind the Boss, obscured and obscure, had been Joszef, ensuring events occurred according to plan. Ana was nowhere to be seen in the photograph, although it was unclear whether that was by choice or omission. My absence was more straightforward. The ceremony had been a prestigious affair and, naturally, I had not been invited to attend. While the others were out in the world, I had remained at the office with Georg, confined by oak panels and resentment. Our only glimpse into events came through this picture and the journalist's account that accompanied it.

'*They hate it. Good.*' Georg jabbed his finger at the paragraph alongside the picture. Under a headline praising the new houses, and the work they would bring, the *People's Observer* had contrasted what they saw as the laudable house building programme with the rent controls introduced, quite deliberately, on the same day. *'There's no enthusiasm there. It's the bare minimum, just what we said, no more.'*

Georg was pacing. He paused at my desk, hanging for an instant before flipping fiercely through the pages of the newspaper, until alighting on the editorial. His finger jabbed at the page once more. The sharp thud of his finger drew a fleeting glance from Ana but no more. Her eyes returned to her desk, leaving me the only audience for Georg's triumphalism.

'See? "Many will have their doubts about both the good sense and the justice of such a policy. Some may say that it is motivated more by class-envy than by prudent public law. We await the implementation with interest." Interest! They expect it to fail. They and their masters will be disappointed!'

He flicked back his head, as if expecting applause. When none came, nor any other reaction, he resumed his pacing. I did not watch him; my eyes had alighted upon a sentence that began *"Anton Guebler, architect of the rent controls…"* by way of introduction to a quotation that used many of the words I had given to the reporter the day before, although here in ink, in this atmosphere, they appeared crude and suspect.

'It's brilliant!' Georg turned sharply on his heel and laughed. *'They are clearly rattled, and their defensiveness creates the space to go further. They will bleat and moan on behalf of the landlords and, when not a single one of them has to forgo a kilogramme of flour, their protestations will be shown up for what they are. And we will push further, knowing their next objections will not be heard.'*

He clapped his hands on my shoulders, his fingers squeezing into the flesh with gentle pressure.

'Anton, my friend, you may not know what you've done, but your rent controls have opened a whole field of possibility. Bravo.'

He withdrew his grip and walked back to his desk, more calmly than his pacing but still with purpose. I could not tell if his chuckle was scornful or congratulatory; if congratulatory, it was unclear whether it was meant for me or for his own cleverness.

'My rent controls? I only worked up some of the detail. The idea, the plan: that belongs to the Boss, surely?'

He shook his head in benign disbelief.

'Details are everything, Anton. Without the details there is no action, and without action there is no progress. Those details, your sums, are the bedrock of what has transpired here. We need a drink. Who wants a drink? I'll buy.'

Before Ana or I could respond, the door swung open. A smile split Joszef's face into a joyous arc. It was clear that the Boss was also happy with how the announcement had been received. Joszef said nothing, but managed to flash a wink towards Ana, ignoring both Georg and me. I felt that I had found myself in the wrong alliance.

By his desk, Joszef took his watch from his waistcoat. It flashed a warm glint across the room and I instinctively felt for my own watch, the last trace of my father, made of baser metal. Joszef glanced at the watch face and clicked it shut. With a sudden but practiced movement, he reached into a desk drawer and pulled out a bottle of brandy, stroking the label with the palm of his hand.

'Georg is right. We should take a moment to congratulate ourselves.'

Before the bottle thudded onto the desk, Georg had fetched glasses from the water stand under the map of the city. He waited for Joszef to uncork the bottle and pour out four measures, then he passed glasses to Ana and to me before taking one for himself. Ana cupped her own glass in both hands, her fingertips closing gently around it, while Joszef spoke of how the work went on, about the tide running fast, and the need for renewed effort and vigilance. The slow burn of the brandy raked my throat and I stifled a cough as we drank a toast. Once all the glasses had been drained, and the bottle returned to its place in the filing cabinet, the office returned to seriousness. I, however, was still mesmerised by my name printed in the newspaper. Later, when the afternoon post arrived, I would quietly ask the porter to buy a second copy of the *Observer* for me.

Over the next days and weeks, we received written representations from some of the largest landowners in the city, eager either to sell some of their holdings for new housing estates, or to complain about the unfairness and unworkability of the rent controls we had introduced. We had decided to implement the controls immediately, so that the landlords would not have time to find loopholes through which they and their money could slip. Another consideration had been to ensure that the tenants felt the benefits as soon as possible: elections to the council were scheduled for the next summer.

In the days that followed, the *Observer* continued to report on the complaints of the landlords, and Georg, Ana and even Joszef laughed at their petulance. I laughed too, but without conviction. I still understood little about the politics of what we were doing and took the criticism at face value. But I laughed along with my comrades until the landlord's complaints gave way to a front-page article reporting on rumours of corruption in the house building programme. The mood darkened instantly.

'No, no, no, no! They can't do this! It's lies. All of it. We never even met Svankmajer. It is a complete fabrication!'

Georg's anger flared with the first paragraph and burned brightly even after he had slammed the newspaper with his open palm, sending his pen skittering from the desk and across the floor, as if terrified by his rage. His occasional explosions of bitterness and cynicism had sometimes appeared as anger, but there had always been control. Now there was none. His eyes glistened slightly and the left nostril quivered. His palm slapped the desk again, before his hand curled into a fist. Had there been a meeting between the Boss and the owner of the city's largest construction company, I would likely not have been aware of it. However, Georg's incandescence reassured me in my conviction that it would be inconceivable for the Boss to have agreed to channel all of the building work for the new houses through Svankmajer's firm in exchange for payments to his personal account. The *Observer*'s lies were naked. Anyone who knew anything about Andreas Hofmans would know that this was impossible. And yet, here it was in print, served up for the city to read over their breakfast.

'It was inevitable. Only a matter of time. I'm surprised, Georg, that you didn't anticipate it. You are usually more astute.'

Ana was calm, almost pleased that her comrade's intellectual pride had been punctured so forcefully. She looked back at the newspaper on her desk and I caught sight of a flicker of her mouth. She seemed amused by her colleague's rage. Georg was about to turn his anger onto Ana, when Joszef returned from his meeting with the Boss. The door slammed behind him.

'Well. He's livid. Wants to know how we let this happen. I want to know how we let this happen. Did Svankmajer talk to them? Angry that he didn't get more of the contracts? Well?'

He glowered at each of us. None of us answered because none of us had an answer. We had no idea who had said what to whom; had no knowledge of any dealings with Svankmajer.

'Nothing? Alright, then what do we know about this, uh, Jakob Eisener?' He had had to pause to read the by-line of the article. 'Surely someone knows something about him. What are his politics? Is he squeaky clean? For God's sake, this is not a game! You are not amateurs. Even if it appears that way right now.'

As he spoke, he scrubbed his glasses on his shirt tail, his pale grey eyes darting in unaccustomed freedom. Georg began to say something, but halted, unwilling to invite Joszef's wrath upon himself. Ana's calm interjection pacified him a little, and the redness of his face faded to a blush.

'He has no known associations. Arrived from the Capital a few months ago. An unremarkable, workaday reporter. No-one knows anything because there is nothing to know. He's just trying to make a name for himself, Joszef. It was inevitable that someone would run with this angle at some point.'

Absently, Joszef nodded slowly and replaced his spectacles, curling the wire arms around his ears. He took his seat heavily, then picked up the receiver of the telephone and dialled. Ten minutes later, there was a knock at the door and a man entered the office.

I had not met Kelemen before and his appearance shocked me. He was stocky and his broad frame made him look shorter than he was. He was maybe in his late 30s, but the grey flecks in his cropped hair and the deep wrinkles that scored his face gave him a timeless quality. He appeared incongruous, ill-defined. But most surprising of all, in the rarefied confines of the Mayor's offices, were his workman's clothes: black trousers, a red crew neck sweater, and heavy boots. He was concrete and ephemeral at the same time; when you looked away from him, he melted into the air, leaving simply an uncertain trace of menace.

While he waited for Joszef to acknowledge him, he nodded to us. A gold tooth flashed from behind his smile. It was not a smile that carried any warmth. I wanted to see the faces of Ana and Georg, to be reassured that they were unmoved, that my anxiety was needless. But Kelemen's smile trapped me, his eyes drilling into me, pinning me into immobility. An eternity passed before Joszef rose from his desk with a sigh.

'Franck, thank you. A word please.'

Both men slipped into the darkness of the corridor; Joszef clicked the door shut behind him and, in the silence, I heard the breathing begin again. I twisted in my seat and cocked my head into the shape of a question. Georg looked away and it was clear that he had no intention of looking up from his papers. A pen balanced across his index finger, pointless.

From behind, Ana's sigh hung like a kite on a slack string. *'He's the Boss's driver. Been with him almost as long as Joszef. Different though. Worked in the steel-mill, but on the shop floor. There's loyalty there, but it's not clear what the basis is. Not entirely. Don't take against his manner. He came from a poor home and his life has been hard.'*

A bitter laugh slipped from Georg' mouth, but his scorn faded rapidly into silence.

'He helps out. With practical things. Removes obstacles. Everyone has their part to play, worker and intellectual.' She smiled at this last word, and I felt a twinge of recognition, of specialness, so I smiled back. I pulled off my glasses and polished them needlessly on my handkerchief while I waited for my words to gather again.

'Give me a cigarette, will you, Ana? I'm out?'

She tossed the packet over to where Georg's waiting hands were cupped. A match flared into life, its flame consuming paper and tobacco, and then there was a flash of white as the packet arced back to Ana. She tapped out a cigarette for herself and looked up at me. Her left hand held out the packet.

I lit my first cigarette under Ana's amused gaze. My cough raised a broader smile, one which was warm enough to melt my embarrassment. The uncurling of her fingers, to nudge the ashtray across her desk and towards me, settled the queasiness I felt as I leaned over to tap the ash into it. The swimming of my head and the blood-tang on my tongue did not yet feel as natural as they would become over the months to follow, but the sense of belonging I felt in that instant carried me through the discomfort. The three of us smoked in silence.

The sound of the door creaking open panicked me, and I stubbed the cigarette prematurely into the ashtray, guilty at my discovery. Joszef's face was like a November sky. He said nothing, simply resumed his seat and rifled through a sheaf of papers, fumbling the edges despite his close attention; Ana and Georg also lost themselves in the detail of their desks. The questions I still wanted to ask formed momentarily, but too late. There was no space for questions anyway, and I tried to give my attention to the document in front of me. The nicotine turned stale on my tongue and time crept by under the unbearable weight of the day.

Dawn

Sometimes, you surface into the city and it is as if you have been buried in the catacombs, as if you have pushed up, through the soil piled above you, into unfamiliar air. There is commotion and conviviality, life in abundance. The isolation of thought gives way and the fecundity of the city crowds in, leaves you aware of your own deathliness. That evening, the messenger of my release was a bar, open late. Music and light flowed from its windows and doorway and figures gathered by the entrance. There was laughter and it sounded like another language, as if the whole street were speaking a language that Berber and I alone could not comprehend. I felt like a stranger in my city, or rather an outcast; perhaps invisible, a ghost.

I had planned to walk directly home. It had been some days since the *Observer* published its lies, but an anxious tension still hung over my colleagues and the brooding fury beyond the darkness of the corridor could still be felt. The day demanded sleep, or at least seclusion and separation. And yet I had found myself in an unknown part of the city, unaware of the route I had taken to arrive there. I must have walked for forty minutes before I surfaced from my thoughts, breathless and bedazzled. And yet there I was, lost among carefree souls, all oblivious to the weight of the world.

I would not know for several days that the journalist Jakob Eisener would decide to return to the Capital, once his injuries had healed sufficiently. But the news, when it came, would feel inevitable. Ana's calmness, the matter-of-fact way that she would suggest that we simply get on with it, would make me believe, or at least hope, that the official report of a violent assault on a city street might be true, that my unease at Kelemen's smile was unfounded. What did it matter, in any case? Eisener would undoubtedly be happier back in the Capital, anyway. While the injuries were reportedly severe, they were not life-threatening. The wounds would heal and the world would keep turning. What were some fractured ribs set against social progress, after all?

The glow of the bar proved irresistible. I found a small table by the counter and sank into a chair. I ordered a beer from the lean waiter and, after a moment of hesitation asked also for a packet of cigarettes. As he pulled at the frayed white collar of his shirt, I asked if there might also be something to eat. He took a notepad from his apron and conscientiously wrote down my order for bread and sausage.

Somewhere, a band played and the frenetic, stumbling rhythm ricocheted around the columns and brickwork such that it took some time to locate its source. A tall man with a trombone towered over his seated fellows like a lighthouse and, were it not for him, I doubt I would ever have determined the origin of the music. I watched the brass of the instrument flash and swoop for a time, before my eyes slipped to take in the faces gathered around the other tables. There were men and women in equal measure, many red-faced, their eyes glassy, mouths open, their shouts lost amid the general cacophony. There was joy here, aimless, forgetful joy, and its presence heightened my own melancholy, my otherness. I felt the distance between myself and the vitality of the room. The mouths and eyes of the young women were a particular fascination. I would watch how one laughed, tilting her head or rolling her shoulders, and trace the shape of her back. When I was spotted, I would tear my eyes away in panic and embarrassment, shifting my attention to another. As the beer flooded my mind, I wondered what it would be like to feel the warmth and softness of their skin, and a different kind of shame crawled over me.

Once the sausage had been consumed and a second beer begun, I ate the slices of pickled cucumber left on my plate and tried to concentrate on the music. It was slower now, mournful and sensuous, quite unlike the folk tunes of the neighbourhood or the clanging strings of university concerts. The trombone spoke of pains and desires that I could not recognise, in a language quite alien to my own. I listened for what felt like an eternity, trying to decipher the meaning of it all, to fathom its depths. Sometimes I sensed that I was close, but then it would slip away once more.

In a lull, while the band took a break, to eat and drink, to marshal their reserves of misery and longing, I heard a voice I recognised, made strange by the laughter that wrapped around it. I scanned the other tables and eventually caught sight of his back. He was seated opposite two young women, closer in age to me than to him. A bottle of brandy, mostly consumed, stood on the table between them and, while the women laughed and gazed intently at him, he wafted a glass airily.

It was undoubtedly Joszef. The voice and that back were unmistakable. Only the setting made them unnatural. Every so often, his head would turn slightly to the left or right and I could see the tufts of grey hair, the glint of his glasses. It was him, without doubt. And yet I could not reconcile this man to the solid, serious person with whom I shared an office. I thought of the photograph in the plain wooden frame standing on his desk: the plump woman under a heavy hat, with two joyless children dressed in jackets and short trousers; they were standing in front of a polite rural house with neat curtains and a wooden roof. This same house appeared in another picture there, this one of an older couple with weary smiles; the man wore a dog collar, the woman an apron.

Joszef's shoulders shook, his back quivered, and I heard his laughter crash above the voices between us. His hand fell onto that of one of the women, consuming it like a wolf. She did not pull her hand away, however, but instead placed her other hand over the top of his, building a tower of entwined fingers. She glanced at her friend with a laugh, while the other turned a lock of blonde hair between her fingers; I watched her mouth, followed her tongue as it slid along her lip.

A greasy white apron fell like a curtain across the scene. The waiter was back, a tray of full glasses swaying on his upturned palm. He nodded to my empty glass, and I fished out some coins to stack on the table next to it; with a single move he placed another beer before me and scooped the money into his apron pocket. In irritation, I watched him move on to other tables, then turned back to see what I had missed.

Joszef had turned to try to catch the attention of the waiter, the brandy gone. But instead his eyes found me. The smile melted in an instant and the blurred exuberance of the room drained into the floorboards. I regretted that I was not, after all, invisible. We held each other's gaze until the blonde-haired woman reached across the table and pulled Joszef's hand towards her, wrenching him back into the lightness of conviviality; the redhead caught the sleeve of the passing waiter and whispered something into his ear that brought a sly smile to his pinched face. By the time the bottle of Sekt had arrived, with fresh glasses and a bowl of cherries, I had moved my chair fractionally, and a pillar interrupted the line of sight between Joszef and myself.

My new position also gave me a clearer view of the band and I spent the time it took to drink three more beers watching the trombone flash and dance extravagantly, while a man with lost eyes flailed at his drums; I could see the back of the man at the piano, but not his face. Every so often I would find my eyes fall upon a pretty girl, but shame and seriousness would drag me back to my consideration of the musicians and their technique.

A little before dawn, Joszef stumbled towards the door and left the bar alone, without a glance in my direction. I looked over to see if the blonde woman was still there, but Joszef's former table was empty, the bottles and glasses cleared, and both his companions gone. The room was much emptier in general. Only a few tables remained, and the music had become almost soporific; a slow dialogue of brass and ivory, the brushes barely rattling the snare drum. The waiter leant over one end of the counter, his attention far away. I raked through my pocket and found I had no more coins.

A pink-grey light was seeping into the streets when I emerged into the air. It was cold despite the season and I fastened my jacket against the chill, turned up my collar and clasped the lapels across my throat. It was too late to bother with walking all the way back home and my intoxication demanded something other than sleep in any case. So I walked the unfamiliar streets and watched the first lights appear in bedroom windows. The shutters clattered on blind shop fronts, scattering birds roosting in the street trees; the squeal of the first tram on a nearby street sliced through the greying air. Eventually I found my way to the embankment from where I could read my location in the river's bridges. It would take at most an hour to walk back to City Hall. I had time yet. I leant over the parapet and watched the grey water rush beneath me, carrying branches and other detritus, washed down from the mountains on melt water. The sun clambered above the roof tops and cast its light onto the river's course, picking out pinkish spots that tumbled into the murk, only to reappear a little further downstream. I fished out the last of the cigarettes and lit it in the flare of a match; stifling a cough with the back of my hand, I looked at the matchbook. On it was written the name of the bar; I resolved to commit this information to memory, to return to see the band once more. Yet I do not now remember the name, only the drawing of a black cat with a red collar and a smile without warmth.

Winter

When it came, the snow fell on the city like a vampire. Only a few weeks before, the streets had been full: workers slowing their arrival at offices and factories so that they could absorb the last of the late-autumn light; couples strolling hand in hand under streetlights; old friends suspended in unexpected encounters. The burr of summer had clung on into those golden days, but now, under the grip of icy grey, the few people visible on the streets hurried to their destination or stood in groups at tram stops, great clouds hanging over them.

Standing on the embankment, I was the only person neither mobile nor impatient. Beneath me, ice floes jostled each other in the turbulent stream, grey hulks in a milky-blue stew. I smoked a cigarette as they passed, vapour merging with fumes into a billowing plume. It struck me that I no longer coughed when I smoked, so inured to it was I by then. My mother had at first chided me when she smelled the sour tang on me but, like the coughing, this too passed.

I sucked hard on the last of the cigarette and tossed the stub into the river. In an instant it was gone, swept away downstream. I pulled my new coat about me, coddling myself in the wool. The coat was a present from my mother, paid for with the pay rise she had received from the factory, and she had presented it to me proudly. It was a fine coat and I came to love it, more so once the snow began.

The clock of St Nicholas chimed the quarter hour. I turned away from the water and began to take cautious steps on the slick pavement, slowly building to a steady rhythm as my feet regained their certainty on the snow. I had a quarter of an hour to cover ground that in other seasons would take just five minutes. But one was not late for a meeting with Karel Svankmajer.

It had been a surprise at first. Only months before, I had dismissed out of hand the very idea that any sort of deal had been done with Svankmajer. I thought back to the debacle over the article in the *Observer*, and the suggestion of impropriety. I had been naïve. It was perfectly possible, necessary even, to deal with men like Svankmajer. At some point, a perfectly proper arrangement had been reached, with the best interests of the city at its core. The scandalous piece in the *Observer* had threatened that; no wonder Joszef had been furious. A tram squealed around the corner and I paused to let it pass, then continued out onto Armistice Square, towards the Svankmajer building. I crossed the street and entered through the overlarge and ostentatious doorway, to which abstract motifs had recently been added in a fashionable decorative style.

'Good morning, Mr, uh, Mr Guebler. Do please take a seat. Ilsa! Some coffee please!'

The young man faced me across a broad teak desk, a distracted expression stubbornly clinging to his face. It was obvious now, but I had expected to meet Svankmajer himself and took the presence of a mere assistant as something of a discourtesy. The fact that even this assistant seemed to regard the meeting as an imposition only heightened the indignation I felt. I stretched my neck in the too-tight collar.

'So. I assume that you would like to talk about progress on the three eastern developments?'

I nodded. The firm had been engaged to build three of the new housing estates, the largest of the whole programme, and Joszef had instructed me both to find out how the construction was proceeding and also to impress upon them that, however well it was going, more was expected. Joszef had gone to great lengths to warn me about Svankmajer, although it had been unnecessary. Everyone in the city knew of Svankmajer. An émigré, he had arrived from Bohemia during the War, a young man with nothing to his name except a determination not to be poor any longer and with few scruples about how he achieved that goal. Never actually criminal, at least as far as the authorities had been able to discover, he had none the less found ways to grow a construction business from the flimsiest of foundations: casual labour, long hours and cut corners. Within a decade, he employed 30 men; somehow he weathered the depths of the Depression and was able to expand rapidly in the ruins, while other businesses were only beginning to fumble their way back into the light. The biggest building firms from the days before the war could not withstand the relentlessness of Svankmajer, and most folded. Hundreds of men had no choice but to go to work for him. They muttered about his origins, his avarice and his ruthlessness, suddenly forgetful of the excesses of their former indigenous bosses.

A young woman entered nervously, the cups jittering on the tray. The young man barely looked in her direction, simply paused his account of progress to allow her to pour coffee. As she left, I mumbled a thank you while he remained silent. The door hushed itself shut behind me.

'The trouble is, as I'm sure you'll appreciate, the wages that the City have insisted upon are, uh, unsustainable. Of course, this was stipulated in the contract, and we will honour that part of the agreement. But we must cover our costs, so have identified some savings. The principal saving will be on bricks. The buildings will be perfectly good, it is just that the walls will be, uh, thinner.'

While he spoke, I had been quietly congratulating the Boss on his vision, for seeing how to ensure that the house building programme had even greater benefits for the city's poor. Higher wages meant that the workers would have more for their families; squeezing such a concession from a man like Svankmajer was no small victory. It was galling that the *Observer* had chosen not to report this masterstroke, when they had been so willing to print lies about corruption and collusion. Svankmajer's guile was all the more shocking because of this and my throat tightened.

'Thinner?'

The young man shrugged with satisfaction, like a chess master playing an unforeseen move. He raised his cup to his lips and took a long shallow sip before responding.

'And the floors, of course. Instead of concrete, we propose to use rammed earth. It is a very traditional method. Many of the workers' houses in the city are built this way. And it is entirely compliant with the terms of the contract.'

From a small plate, which I had not noticed until that moment, he took a biscuit and placed it on his tongue. He chewed it so delicately that I could hear no sound; his lips barely moved but that movement was the only indication that he was eating at all. He watched my rising irritation with amusement, until it erupted in impotent pique.

'This is not acceptable. While it may be consistent with the letter of the agreement – and we will of course consult with our lawyers – it displays a disregard for the greater good. I urge you to reconsider your decisions. The Mayor demands it.'

There was no laughter, but his slanted expression told me that he thought my threats comical; moreover, that he found me entirely comical in myself. He made no attempt to counter, nor to excuse. Instead, he poured the last of the coffee from the pot and waited. It was clear that he expected the next words to be mine, and for them to be more amenable. Enraged, I slapped my palm onto the desk, rattling the cups. He remained unmoved, and all the words that swirled within me, all the righteous anger, evaporated before I could harness them. I realised that I did indeed look ridiculous.

Ilsa knocked tentatively at the door before slipping in.

'Excuse me, sir, but you are expected.'

He looked not at her, but at the clock and with an apologetic dip of the head, he excused himself, satisfied that I had nothing further to say that was of any value.

'Thank you again for your time. Please do make sure to explain the situation to your superiors. It is regrettable of course, but such are the fundamentals of business. I know that, on reflection, you will see things as they are. Now, my apologies. Ilsa will show you to reception.'

I followed a few paces behind as she led me in silence through a series of panelled corridors. At the top of the staircase, I was reunited with my precious coat. It looked shabby in her outstretched hand, and she held it as if it were something repellent. But she had sad eyes, and I did not begrudge her disdain.

I don't remember the walk back to City Hall. I was lost in the anger I felt at his arrogance and at my impotence in the face of it. Despite the freezing temperatures outside, this anger had been stoked into rage by the time I reached the office. Joszef's desk was empty and Georg paid no attention to my arrival. Ana looked up briefly from her notes and regarded me quizzically, but she asked no questions. Humiliated once more, I sat at my desk with a sigh. The papers on it received a cursory glance, a nudge with my fingertips, before I slumped back, making roof timbers of my fingers. The blank wall offered no comfort, so I turned my chair to face Georg's desk and glowered at him instead.

'What? Anton, I'm busy.'

Eventually he had looked up, head tilted slightly, eyebrows raised. The words fell out of me, tumbling like water into a drain after a downpour. I could see Georg's limited interest wash out of him with each sentence. At last, he stopped me with his raised palm.

'Do you think this wasn't anticipated? Do you have such little faith? I personally oversaw the drafting of the contract. It is a snare, into which Svankmajer has stepped just like a rabbit. It was foreseen. At the right moment, the poor workmanship will come to light and the foreigner's duplicity will be there for all to see...'

'And at that point, we will have the opportunity to seize the company for the City. It will be a scandal that even Svankmajer will be unable to gloss over.' Ana's calm, cold voice broke into Georg's oratory. *'Don't be too hard on yourself, Anton. It was important that as few people knew as possible, so that everything could be put in place. We should have explained before you went to meet with them, but your anger and frustration were essential. We need Svankmajer to believe that he still has the upper hand. You played your part well. Very well.'*

She smiled and I felt the rage ebb out of me. I had been left to play the fool in a piece of theatre, but I could see that it could not be otherwise. The game was too important for any consideration to be given to my feelings and, while I still did not fully comprehend its rules, I better understood my role within it with each passing day.

Returns

With spring came the return of daylight in the fanlights above Ana's desk, a welcome intrusion from the world outside. The extent of the shadows on the floor receded a little each day. The pace of work accelerated too, as we readied ourselves for the imminent election. The Boss had two more years before he faced the voters again, and the success of the house building programme, as well as the new clinics, meant that he was already secure when that election came. But to be able to go further, the Party had to secure as many councilmen as possible in May.

It was unfortunate, then, that the scandal around Svankmajer's construction company came to light at the end of April. Public money was being spent under the Mayor's oversight, and yet the houses being built were judged to be substandard. For two days, the *Observer* tried to blame the Boss for granting a weak contract in the first place, and a junior official with the Bricklayers' Union was found to corroborate the concerns about quality. The paper's leader writers even hinted at the earlier allegations of corruption. But such coverage soon died and, as predicted by Ana and Georg, the scandal provided the perfect excuse to seize a part of Svankmajer's empire. By the time that the City took a majority interest in the firm, even the newspaper did not object. The people were delighted of course, and other businesses chose to give no opinion, unwilling to draw attention to their own activities. We were emboldened and Joszef asked us to develop some ideas for how the legislation might be applied to the problem of the rent controls introduced the year before. While Georg worked and reworked the legalities, Ana and I spent two weeks working through the likely economic impacts.

'Well, that was a very successful morning.' A beaming Joszef paused in the doorway to slip off his coat. It was early May and yet the air still bit at your skin when the sun slid behind the cloud plumes that rolled over the city on spring breezes. *'Over 700 people at the rally. Andreas is delighted. I think next week will go very well.'* He had the air of a man who had enjoyed not just a successful day, but also a good lunch.

Cautiously, he took his seat and reached inside the desk draw to retrieve the bottle of brandy. *'So, we have two reasons to celebrate.'* The bottle's dull thud punctuated the sentence, its trace hanging in the silent air of the office. Georg's chair creaked uncomfortably, expectant.

'For God's sake Joszef. You know that I'm not the kind to make a fuss of it.' Ana's brittle exasperation eventually filled the hushed void. He had already crossed to the side table to collect some glasses. They clinked in his hand.

'You are young still enough to mark your birthday, my dear. When you reach my age, that's another thing. But at your age, you should enjoy it.' His face was shaped with kindness, perhaps also a little sadness at his own ageing.

'Alright, Joe. I'll have a drink with you to celebrate your good day, and you can drink to my passing days. I'm always willing to compromise.'

Her smile seemed genuine enough but, while her words spoke of compromise, the hardness of her eyes appeared as a challenge. She regarded Joszef with coolness for a moment, and he watched her with curiosity. There was no obvious affection between them, despite the glad faces and warm wishes. I felt the fibres of my loyalty pulling and rending. I wanted it to stop and looked to Georg in the hope that he might do something, say something to break the tension within me.

'I'll drink to whatever you want, as long as some of your brandy is involved.' Georg stretched out an arm, hand flapping like a fish's mouth; Joszef placed a glass on my desk first, then, once he was satisfied that the Georg had looked sufficiently ridiculous, he handed a glass to him too. We drank down the brandy and offered our good wishes to Ana. A trace of the same rigidity clung to her smile, but she took the bottle from Joszef's desk and refilled the glasses to make her own toast to the success of the Party at the polls. The prospect seemed to fill her with greater pleasure than her own birthday, and her eyes softened as she spoke. Genuine excitement trembled through her as she made a toast to the Boss.

'We're not out of the woods yet.' Joszef could be counted on to smother naïve optimism with the merest shake of the head. *'Anything short of every candidate being returned means that we will have to trim our programme. We're going to need unanimity in the council chamber. Even then, the Party will need to be managed. There will be some opposition on our own side for some of what we want to do.'*

'Every candidate? Is that even possible?' I was struck by the scale of the ambition. The Party would undoubtedly do well in the working-class neighbourhoods, and maybe among the residents of apartments in the city centre. It might even be possible to garner support along the streets of modest middle-class houses in the suburbs. But to win where the rich lived, along the grand boulevards and in the genteel enclaves, among the villas by the river, was surely unthinkable without the personal charisma of the Boss on the ballot.

From the corner of my eye, I saw Ana shift in her chair; her impatient sigh whistled like kettle-steam into the congealing air. Joszef allowed her to take up the reins, turning his attention once more to the glass cradled in his hands.

'That's why today was so important. The rally was not in one of our neighbourhoods, but in Fontainebleau.' She paused, allowing the significance of this fact to percolate through me. The calmness of her voice was unexpected. *'Even so, the Boss drew a huge crowd and got a rapturous response. He is a real asset, as you know. And now our candidates know too. There will be less room for disloyalty within the Party, if we can achieve a clean sweep. Every one of them will know that their victory belongs to the Boss.'* Another pause, but one barely long enough for me to wonder how Ana, who had been sitting in the office with me all day, could possibly know about the size of the crowd or the nature of its response. *'And he will have done a lot to reassure those usually antithetical to the Party itself, don't you think?'*

The question did not need an answer, but even so it felt like another challenge. My loyalty was being tested. Gently, but it was a test nonetheless. I wanted to protest, to exclaim that of course I believed wholly that Andreas Hoffmans could turn a crowd, even one as genteelly hostile as could be found in Fontainebleau. But instead I simply shrugged, nodded, and finished my brandy. I had no choice but to believe.

When the votes were eventually counted the following week, every district in the city returned a councilman loyal to the Boss. I told myself that impossible things were merely obstacles to be overcome, and that doubts were simply the threshold to disloyalty. And I did not allow any room for the questions that I might have asked about how such an unlikely victory had been achieved. I was simply grateful that my faith had been rewarded.

That night, we stayed in the office until almost midnight. The work and the celebrations snaked together into an unfathomable knot, such that I could not tell if the work was a celebration, or the celebrations were work. Much of the evening was spent at Ana's desk, drafting a briefing on our economic plan for the city. Her hands swirled and swooped as she explained for a second, then third, time something that seemed so self-evident to her but that slipped through my fingers as I scribbled to keep up. We shared the cigarettes that lolled out of their packet, lying on the desk, cramming the ashtray as we went. I did not notice when first Joszef, then Georg, made their escapes, and I was grateful to her for staying with me while I typed up the papers from my notes. From the corner of my eye, I watched her smoke in the lamp light, her face intent upon some document that I could not see. The shadows clung to the panelled walls like voyeurs.

Severance

It was almost ten o'clock when I surfaced into the morning after the election results were announced. For a time, I wanted to cling to sleep, but the smell of coffee, the stuttering of crockery in the kitchen, roused me with the promise of breakfast; my stomach reminded me that I hadn't eaten the night before. My feet found the sun-warmed patch of rug beside my bed and my toes sought comfort in its thin pile. Light fell in through the windowpane, forming a familiar rectangle of blue.

'Eggs?' My mother was by the sink, pouring water into a saucepan. She spoke without turning, busy with her task. I watched her back as she worked, the scarf tied tight about her grey hair. I grunted a shapeless reply and took my place at the table, studying the slices of bread on the board, selecting the fattest for my plate.

'Won't be long.' She kissed my head, her hands warm on my shoulders. Without asking, she poured coffee and forked two slices of ham onto the plate next to the bread; tomato and pickled cucumber followed. I had always taken her care for me lightly, never fully grateful, believing that my presence was reward enough. I simply wanted to eat and so I did, without even a word of thanks.

She asked when I had got home, whether I had slept, and about the news from the city. *'They say the new councilmen will pass an ordinance setting the price that the merchants can charge for bread. Is it true?'* She took up a chair opposite me while she waited for me to finish chewing the meat. Her eyes were anxious.

'Is that what they're saying at the factory?' It was certain that rumours like this would circulate. Such possibilities had been poured into the flow of city life by the Party. They had swirled though the thoughts of the poor people throughout the weeks leading up to the election, making their vote more resolute. And yet I wanted to chide her for her lack of imagination, frustrated that the people thought first of their bellies when so much more was possible. I wiped my mouth with the back of my hand and smiled at her.

'Things will definitely change now. We have all of the seats on the council, as well as the mayor's office. The price of bread is the least of it.'

She looked hurt, rather than impressed. *'Since when has the price of bread been of so little concern? For us, it is no small matter.'* Her arms were folded across her chest now, better to protect her pride. My cheeks reddened, stung by the suggestion that my interests, the interests of the Boss, were somehow different from hers, from those of my neighbours. She drank her coffee, eyes turned towards the stove where the eggs rattled in the pan.

'Of course it is important, and it will be addressed, I am sure. I only meant that we have the chance to do so much more. You remember that the price of bread was fixed after the war for a few years? Soon enough, the price went back up and the quality was worse. The merchants will always take the opportunity to make money where they can. Unless everything changes, nothing will.' I heard myself using Ana's words and I was surprised by how comfortably they lived in my mouth. *'Besides, you have enough money now that the wages have gone up at the factory.'*

She was fishing eggs from the pan with a ladle as she had done for as many mornings as I could remember. Even when there had been no meat, there had been eggs.

'There's never enough money, Anton, and even when wages go up the merchants take their chance. That loaf cost 20 pfennigs more than it did just a few weeks ago.' She nodded at the grey-brown hunk on the bread board. *'It will cost another 20 before the end of the month, unless something is done. Can you not see a way to make the councilmen take notice?'*

I wanted to tell her that that, and more besides, would be taken care of, but I had been sworn to secrecy. It was important, Joszef had said, to give the merchants no warnings so that they had no chance to find ways around the constraints that they would face. Instead, I simply told her that I would discuss it with the Boss, to see what could be done. At this she smiled, content both that her loaf would soon be cheaper and that her son had the ear of the mayor. She would no doubt share both thoughts with the other women on the tenement's staircase at the first opportunity.

After breakfast and out in the late morning air, I followed the familiar lanes like an aimless wanderer, lost in the forest. Bricks and asphalt, mud and painted timber jumbled together into streets and houses, or else stacked themselves into tenements and workshops, warehouses and chapels. I did not need to look at them to feel their presence. Unlike the city, the shape of the neighbourhood changed only slowly, organically; I had known it for so long, so intimately, that its glacial rhythms were second nature to me. Despite my ostensible lack of purpose, I knew precisely where I was heading.

I found Kem by the torpid ditch that had once seemed like a river. The frayed cuffs of his jacket sat too high on his forearms and the fabric stretched across his back, forming a ladder of ridges along the curve of his spine. A cigarette smouldered between the fingers of his left hand.

'Hello, my old friend. I thought I'd find you here. Taking in a little air?'

His smile blended with his confusion and surprise, then melted into a frown. He threw the cigarette into the stream absently and nodded my greeting back towards me. It had been weeks since I had seen him, long before the election campaign. He had been pulling a handcart along the street behind the synagogue, his mind lost among the cobbles, this same thin jacket buttoned against the early morning chill. My own coat had felt immoderate, vulgar. My greeting then had gone unremarked and if I had not placed my hand on his shoulder as he passed, our meeting might have gone unacknowledged. I had looked at the bricks stacked in cart as I asked for his news with unnatural enthusiasm. A few brittle moments had passed, and then he had excused himself and resumed dragging his burden uphill.

'What's up?'

The stream bubbled over broken pipes, chuckling greasily, slick in the sunshine. When we were young, Kem and I would wade in, hunting the spiny fish that flitted between the weeds. But now the water was thick and dark and, if any fish remained, they had no need to hide, already obscured by the silty gloom.

I took Kem's question on its own terms, rather than as an empty greeting: Kem did not use empty phrases, speaking only when there was need. I sank to my haunches next to him and stared at the water so that I might see what he saw.

'Work is going well, but the hours are long. I don't begrudge it, but it would be easier for me to take a room in the city, rather than spending hours each day getting from here to there. I've found a comfortable house; clean, good people. I'm moving there, leaving the neighbourhood.'

His laugh surprised me, and I watched his face crease, the wide mouth thick with teeth. I waited for it to subside.

'Anton, my friend, you left here ages ago. This...' With his forefinger, he prodded my arm, *'...this is just a ghost.'*

I felt his fingertip through my shirt sleeve like the judgement of God. I wanted to deny it, to defend myself, but I knew that what he said was, in all important aspects, true. By the time I first stepped into the dark corridor that leads to my little wood-panelled office, I had already left the neighbourhood; perhaps even as soon as that first morning on my way to the university. Certainly, I left something of myself in the lecture halls and library, something that never truly returned with my weary body at the end of each day. I had left. Leaving the tenement was simply the completion of that parting, an overdue reunion of my body and soul in the city.

'Perhaps. Perhaps. My mother will be upset by my departure, all the same. I don't think she sees it quite as you do. Keep an eye on her for me. Please.'

I could already picture her face when I would tell her my news later that afternoon. By nightfall, I would be gone. I would sit on a narrow bed, awkward and hushed, in a strange room, with the sounds of a different woman stuttering up from a different kitchen. Sitting by the filthy stream, contemplating my liberation, I did not imagine that I would weep, alone, consumed by the aloneness, an aloneness that was my only companion that night. There, with Kem, I felt resolute, invulnerable, even at the prospect of my mother's misery. I was greater than the smallness of the neighbourhood I had outgrown.

Kem raised an eyebrow when I offered him a cigarette from my own packet, but he shrugged as he took one, felt its velvet length greedily before coaxing it into life with a cheap match. He held out the flame for me, cupping its glow in his hands; I lit my own cigarette with a little bow towards him, accepting this gift as a friend must. We sat in silence while we smoked, watched the thick water creep towards the city, towards the real river.

'Will you walk with me, before you leave? They are pulling down the warehouses by the steel works. There may be some iron.'

I resisted the temptation to explain the house building programme, the cleverness, the importance of it all and instead I savoured my pride quietly, letting it rest on my tongue unexercised. He was already on his feet by the time I'd nodded my agreement, eager to be moving. At first, I followed behind but soon fell into step beside him. We spoke little as we traced the familiar streets, pausing to laugh at some memory etched into the blackened brick before continuing our meander. We reached the street, where once the warehouses had loomed, sooner than I had thought we would. The neighbourhood was shrinking around me, tightening like a vice. Kem had already taken a perch on one of the steel beams that had been ripped from our childhood refuge. Memories of that day, when the police had arrested Andreas Hofmans and I had called out his name, flooded over me. It had been the first time that I had seen him in the flesh. I measured the time and space that arced between that moment and this, between that Anton and this, and I felt giddy. I rested my hand on what was left of a wall, steadying myself until the spinning stopped.

Kem was looking forlornly into his tobacco pouch, his fingers scratching through the crumbs. I smiled, happy that I could do something for my friend and tossed my packet of cigarettes over to him, barking his name in warning. In a single instant, he looked up and snatched the crisp white carton from the air. I grinned, and he smiled back, but with a trace of sadness. In this small moment, I felt the tectonic plates of my life shift into their new alignment. The terms of our friendship were reset in that sunlit clarity.

'You'll visit though? And not simply out of duty?'

I nodded as he dragged a match into life, letting its flame lick the tip of his cigarette. I would think of his question later, when I was lying in the darkness, unable to find my place in the flat evenness of the unfamiliar mattress. Its softness would feel like betrayal and I would slip at last into an uneasy sleep.

Garcia

Georg nodded his greeting from what had been my desk. The strangeness of the previous night had left its mark on me and it took some moments for the pieces to come together. I absently followed his finger to the small trestle table next to Ana's desk, where the papers I had been working on the week before were stacked. An empty folding chair stood awkwardly to one side.

'Anton, you're over here now. Some rearrangements, to accommodate our new colleague.' Ana looked towards the desk that had previously belonged to Georg. A short leather coat hung from the back of the chair; a silver cigarette case was the only object on the desk itself. I looked back at Ana, then at Georg, but both had returned their attention to their work. I shrugged for my own satisfaction and wandered to my new station. There were advantages to the new arrangement. Since I was now in the corner of the room, I could see everything within the office and no longer had to feel Georg's eyes burning into my back whenever I spoke. Content, I settled into revising the plans for the new health centres that were intended for the city's poorer districts.

I was barely two pages into the report before the corridor creaked, signalling the arrival of first Joszef, then another. From the doorway, framed against the gloom of the corridor, the stranger scanned the room over a pair of wire-framed spectacles that were slung low on his tapered nose. Seeing me, he gave Joszef a quizzical glance.

'This is Anton, the junior economics advisor. I mentioned him earlier, if you recall. Anton, let me introduce you to Mr Garcia. He will be joining our merry band.'

Garcia gave me a nod of acknowledgement before taking the cigarette case from his desk. It opened with a snap. He was older than the three of us, but next to Joszef he appeared lithe and youthful; his hair was dark and lightly oiled. He smoked with an intensity that unnerved me, the fingers of his left hand planted on Joszef's desk; occasionally, he would point with the right, cigarette clipped between index and middle finger, asking for clarification of some point in a murmur that I could not discern. When Joszef looked towards me in response to one of these questions, Garcia's eyes also fell on me, narrowed and searching. I felt the prickle of sweat on my forehead.

'It's a good start. But this process, it must be accelerated. The landlords are not yet lowering rents in accordance with what is demanded. Suggestions?'

I had trouble understanding him entirely, so thick was his accent, but the directness of his question was unmistakeable. It was also unanswerable. No mention had been made of making any amendments to the rent controls in the months since they had been introduced. The policy seemed settled, even though some landlords had simply closed up their empty houses and evicted their former tenants. This had been expected. Indeed, I had produced a report anticipating this effect myself and had believed that the Boss had accepted this as a necessary consequence. I stuttered over some syllables, in the belief that making even meaningless sound was better than silence under Garcia's glare. I could see Ana watching me, her lower lip clamped between her teeth in concern. With something like disgust, Garcia shook his head and he turned to Joszef.

'I would have thought the staff would have more about them than this. I heard good things about what you were doing here. I would not have made myself available otherwise. When Andreas briefed me on this assignment, he led me to believe that this was not simply another reformist experiment, a tepid whittling at the margins.'

Joszef's discomfort at the casual use of the Boss's name flickered across his face. I waited expectantly, knowing that when it came, his rebuke would ensure that Garcia never again questioned the ambition nor the talents of Andreas Hofmans. Joszef had the Boss's ear, not this interloper. But the rebuke never arrived. Joszef's shoulders dropped fractionally, and he simply nodded, his watery eyes drifting into the distance while he gathered his response. He sighed.

'My dear Mr Garcia, you'll have to forgive us. We have only now come through a taxing election campaign. Give us a little time to organise ourselves for the new reality, please. Anton here is an exceptionally gifted economist. Task him with a puzzle and he will find the most elegant of solutions. And, as you shall see, Andreas does not lack the determination you expected. His reputation is well deserved. Georg, perhaps you could ring that bell of yours, have some coffee sent in?'

I had not until that moment seen Joszef appear so defeated, so conciliatory. He had shrunk into his chair and Garcia, standing over him, seemed immense, despite his stature. The sound of Georg's bell set him in motion once again and with two strides he was back at his desk. Seated, he bounced slightly in the chair, getting a measure of its capabilities. Satisfied, he snapped open the silver case on his desk and selected a cigarette.

'Ana, isn't it? How about you? Any thoughts on our problem?'

She took a shallow breath, her tongue poised on her lip. I willed her to say nothing, so that she might not compound my humiliation, but when she spoke, I did not blame her.

'It should be possible to devise a special tax. Levied on empty houses. Set at the right rate, it should be sufficient to, uh, incentivise landlords to continue to rent their properties even within the controls we have established. If some of them still choose not to, the City still gains.'

Garcia clapped his hand onto the desk with a laugh. *'Good. Good, really. It is still technocratic tinkering, but a good start. The kernel of something. I like the punitive element.'* He paused to consider his own words and to suck hard on his cigarette. It struck me that he had yet to offer one to anyone else. *'Surely, however, there is a simpler, more direct way to achieve our goals. Just a small development of your thinking. Instead of a tax, why not simply seize the empty properties and rent them at an even lower rate to the people? A token rent, with the houses allocated to the most deserving.'*

He had laced his fingers across his stomach, his feet now resting on the desk. The soles of his shoes were unmarked, as if brand new; there was no trace of the street to be seen. I wondered what sort of a man this was: a foreigner who seemed untouched by the world, and yet one that could shrink Joszef with the curl of an eyebrow. I remembered what Georg had said about me on my first day, and I hoped that the Boss knew what he was doing. I could not imagine how Joszef was able to tolerate such an intrusion.

'That may well be worth investigating, my friend. Along with Ana's thoughts on raising a tax, of course. But while things may be different in your country, I do wonder if there might be some legal constraints on your proposal. Georg, your opinion?'

Georg looked at Joszef reproachfully. It was clear that he had no desire to be drawn into this trial. In normal circumstances, he needed little encouragement to offer an opinion, to demonstrate his acuity. But the presence of Garcia had changed things. Suddenly, inexplicably, there were costs to holding an opinion, to offering an untested idea.

'Technically, of course, the seizure of private assets by the City would be unlawful, without invoking emergency powers. And there are no clear grounds for invoking such powers. This is not like taking a share in a listed company, like we did with Svankmajer. A contract already existed there and, in any case, we simply took equity in lieu of moneys owed. No, this is quite different, and I can't see a legitimate legal basis for it. That said, no municipality has ever attempted such a thing, so it's not certain what the implications would be. It could certainly be tested, but...'

While he spoke, I watched Joszef. His belly clenched closer and closer as the old man held his breath; his shoulders clamped to his broad neck. Only with the last word, before Georg shrugged his sentence to its incompletion, did Joszef's tension dissipate through his unclenching fists. From the corner of my eye, I could see Ana studying Garcia for a clue to his reaction. The room hung momentarily, and I was uncertain who would speak first, Joszef or Garcia.

'A revolution is not made in accordance with the law. Risks must be taken.'

The coolness of Garcia's tone left no doubt that he regarded the matter as good as closed: there could be no contradiction, it was a simple thing, and only a coward or a fool would object. It was a tone that formerly only Joszef would use. As the two men stared at each other, I thought of the times that I had watched the street dogs in the neighbourhood contest their dominance. I swear I even heard a low growl under Joszef's first syllables.

'Calculated risks, yes. Do you think we have been sitting here meekly, obeying all the rules, since we arrived in City Hall? But look here: rushing into a fight with the Capital, now, before we have established ourselves, risks everything, and for no reason. No. This is folly. I propose that we ask Ana to develop the idea of a tax on empty apartments and houses, how that could be introduced quickly and most effectively. And at the same time, Georg can do a little thinking about the legalities and potential sanctions, and put that in a short paper. As a courtesy. To you. This is not the time to poke a stick into the wasps' nest.'

A brief flicker of relief passed through me as he spoke, a welcome sense that order was returning. For months, there had been only Joszef's will, his indisputable, infallible will. Even when I had disagreed with where it led, I had accepted it and found comfort in that acceptance. I believed Ana, and even Georg, had felt it too, for a time. But it was already apparent that Joszef's authority was draining from him. Perhaps it was this moment that marked the start of his fall and ultimate fate. The words were clear enough. They had been delivered with confidence, the courtesy with a snarl. And yet Ana and Georg, even I, were already watching Garcia by the time his declaration had been completed.

'I disagree. Hesitation is death. We have the momentum now. We strike before they have a chance to regroup, to make arrangements, as they have done with your rent controls. You. What is the worst sting that those wasps could give us?'

Garcia had not taken his eyes from Joszef, but his finger pointed straight at Georg, who shifted uncomfortably in his chair. A bead of perspiration formed on his lip. I felt pity for him for the first time, but also a surge of affection and protectiveness that I had not expected. Usually, my starting point in any discussion was to adopt the opposite stance to that taken by Georg, and to take disproportionate satisfaction when his ideas were overruled by Joszef. But there, skewered by Garcia's finger, caught between Scylla and Charybdis, I willed him to find a way to be right, to settle the argument, end the discord, and save himself.

It was Ana, however, who spoke. Everyone, even Garcia, turned towards her at the sound of her throat clearing. Enjoying the lull she had created, she prolonged the period of dead air, spreading her palms onto the desk in front of her, as if preparing to pounce.

'Forgive me, Georg, you will have a far better grasp of the legal position than I, but just from a lay point of view, whatever sanction the National Government could bring would take time. It is law after all, and the courts move slowly.' She paused to allow her audience to keep up with her line of thought. *'The sanctions could be severe, including the risk of imprisonment, potentially. Georg, you should definitely check on that. At the very least, if the courts ruled against us, we would be required to reverse the policy, to return the property. But that could take months, years even. In the meantime, the people get housing, and the landlords get scared. They will be more likely to rent out their properties, and within the terms of our policy. And, if we eventually have to return the property, the people will know whose side we're on and whose the government. If a few of us have to go to prison for a short time, that seems fair enough.'*

Garcia rose to his feet and, eyes fixed on Ana, began to applaud awkwardly, his hands thudding together in a deliberate rhythm, such that each beat was bracketed by its own silence. A smile broadened across his face and then he was dynamic, turning again to Joszef, leaning forwards, all the while jabbing his finger back in Ana's direction.

'This. This is what we do. Come, we must talk to Andreas, make the case.'

He was already at the door before Joszef could stir himself into motion, much less resistance. He remained inert for a moment, while Garcia glared back at him from the doorway, then slowly, so slowly, he began to pull himself from his chair, unable to do otherwise. His authority had by now ebbed completely and, with it, his will. Over the weeks that followed, he was able to recover some of it, and he fought his corner like the Joszef of old. But it was never the same, up until the end. There was something broken in him, the taint of a wound that would never be healed. Perhaps it was because of this lameness that everyone was so willing to believe the worst about him when the time came.

Garcia, triumphant and energised, turned back from the darkness of the corridor. *'You. Gregor, yes? Do what you need to do to determine the worst legal outcome. Most importantly, set out your thinking on who would go to prison. Today, if possible.'*

I could not see his face, so could only imagine the humiliation that Joszef was enduring. Without a glance to us, he followed Garcia out into the corridor, the door clicking closed behind him. I turned back to my colleagues to say something, but my words died on my lips: Georg was glaring at Ana with undisguised fury; Ana was reading through a paper, impassive and unconcerned.

Eggs

A bright clear sky cut through the net curtains that shielded the dining room from the arrival of Monday morning. From the kitchen, busy movements wrinkled the still air, carrying the scent of brewing coffee like a radio transmission, signalling the beginning of the day. My initial ill-ease had long passed and my lodgings had proven to be comfortable and comforting. My heart had arrived a few days after my body, but it had arrived nonetheless and I felt at home in Mrs Kettmann's care. Home: the shape of the word triggered a snap of guilt, and I promised myself that I would visit my mother at the weekend.

'Some coffee, Mr Guebler? Your eggs will be along in a moment. And I thought you might like to look at the newspaper. It has just been delivered.'

Mrs Kettmann dropped the paper onto the table, next to a plate of bread and ham, and poured coffee into my waiting cup; with an indulgent smile she pushed the sugar bowl towards my hand and turned towards the kitchen. I glanced across the front page while I stirred my coffee. Details of a murder filled the columns: a woman's body had been found in the deserted streets beyond the steel works, abandoned, lacerated. The report alluded strongly to the sexual nature of the assault, providing sufficient titillation without specifically naming the incident as rape. The area was well known for being frequented by the city's prostitutes and their clients, and the report concluded that the police would be focusing their inquiries within the red-light district.

I shook my head, both repelled by the sordid nature of the story and by the fascination of the masses for crime and degradation. But I also gave a small chuckle. In a few days' time, such things would be forgotten, replaced on the front pages by news of the requisitioning of empty houses. There would be shrieks of outrage of course, but also grudging admiration for the Boss's audacity. And, over countless breakfast tables, readers would nod their support and gratitude.

But it would be Garcia's victory. This thought circled me as I walked along the few streets that separated my lodgings from my desk. My partisanship troubled me. I had no side in this fight and I owed Joszef no particular loyalty, despite his part in bringing me into the office of Andreas Hofmans in the first place. Afterall, the Boss had brought Garcia into our circle and I had no right to second-guess his decision, even if the foreigner was not to my taste. In any case, Joszef's petulance at being displaced was a weakness and an indulgence, one that showed only that the resolve within the office needed to be strengthened. No, I had no side in this fight and yet, despite myself, I willed Joszef to overcome his challenger and to re-establish the order of things that had existed before the disruption of Garcia's arrival. I paused at the kerb to allow a bicycle to pass. Perhaps this was my weakness, my indulgence. My hand felt for my pocket watch but left it snug in its place. I had no need for it to know the time, since no matter how early the hour, I was already late.

Since Garcia had appeared, life in the office had become ever more intense. An already demanding schedule had become almost unsupportable with the additional pressures of constructing the plan for seizing empty properties. Once the Boss had agreed to the proposal, Garcia had insisted that it be put into action without delay. The pace became relentless and for those few days we survived only on determination and conviction: from eight in the morning until nine at night, no-one left their desk.

Both Joszef and Garcia were there earlier and stayed later, such that I do not know if either of them left for home at all.

The battle between them, while subterranean, was bitter. On the morning of Garcia's second day, I rejoiced to see that Joszef's familiar spirit had reasserted itself, that he no longer meekly followed where Garcia led him, but I could not help but be impressed by the way in which our new comrade so completely set the terms, such that Joszef could only ever resist. This was Garcia's triumph. The meeting later that morning was technically at Joszef's behest, but since it was to plot the enactment of a policy that was entirely Garcia's, even I could see that the old man was, for now at least, limping around his former domain. I had been surprised when Joszef insisted that I attend the meeting, rather than either Ana or Georg. It would be the first time I had seen the Boss in person since I had begun working for him. That this honour should occur at the most audacious moment in the administration's course, and at the expense of Georg, even of Ana, sweetened the distinction.

That particular morning, I arrived at the office before either of my colleagues. Garcia was also absent, although his hat and coat hung from the stand behind the door. Joszef greeted me with a nod and an indistinct word that might have been *'Morning'*. His cup of coffee was already empty. He felt the side of the pot with a frown.

'I'm afraid you'll need to call for more coffee. This is stone cold.' But before I had a chance to ring the bell, he was up and pacing behind his desk. *'Tell me Anton, what is your opinion of this seizure of property. From a tactical point of view. You can be truthful, there is no need to be otherwise.'* He looked forlornly at Garcia's empty desk, then at the door to the corridor. He did not need to explain himself further and again I had to suppress my longing for the way things had been before. I was grateful that he did not wait for my answer.

'It's a mistake, of course. It'll bring all sorts of attention from the Capital, and eventually mean an almighty climb down. If there are prison sentences, the whole game is up. We'd not survive that. The whole Party could be disbarred from office. The judges would like an excuse to do that.'

There was a creak on the floorboards in the corridor and Joszef halted abruptly, raising his hand to indicate that I too should remain silent. In two strides he'd crossed the floor and opened the door a little. His head disappeared into the darkness. Without clearly understanding why I should, I held my breath and waited, motionless. When Joszef's face reappeared, he shrugged and continued.

'Andreas is, however, adamant.' A twitch of the face. *'So be it. We'll just have to make the best of it. You've read Georg's note on the legal position? I'm sure the clerks will have questions, and will want to make sure that they are not going to be liable, if… when…'*

His pacing stopped and he became lost in his thoughts. As if to no-one, I confirmed that I had absorbed the short document that Georg had pieced together from heavy-bound books and oblique phone calls over the past couple of days. Its meaning was clear: the seizures would be completely counter to the law and, should the matter reach the criminal courts, the Boss and his staff could face up to ten years in prison, as well as being disbarred from public office indefinitely. Most likely, an early reversal of the policy would result simply in a surcharge and a great deal of embarrassment: the main point of contention between Garcia and Joszef was whose embarrassment it would most likely be.

We both heard the voices in the corridor at the same time and Joszef snapped back into his familiar animation. I realised that I had still not removed my coat and moved to stand in the corner, such that I was behind the door when Ana entered.

'Just you, Joszef? Enjoying the peace and quiet?'

I watched her cross the room, her step light and confident. Since Garcia had arrived, she had become emboldened, enjoying the disruption and the opportunities it gave her to establish her own position within the office. Since her intervention on that first morning, Garcia had treated her with greater respect than any of us, deferring to her frequently. Ana was not overawed by the attention. The freedom of movement that the new situation allowed suited her. She had not left her job at the university to run errands for an old trades unionist smelling of moth balls.

Her bag thudded onto her desk, and I pictured the folders of documents inside shifting like a nest of snakes. Turning, she caught sight of me and was momentarily startled, her faced briefly fearful.

'Anton! You gave me a start. I didn't know anyone else was here. Why are you skulking behind the door?' The flicker of fear melted quickly and she smiled indulgently at me, as if I were a child discovered in a game of hide and seek. She nodded towards Garcia's desk absently. *'Where is he?'*

She knew of course. Garcia would be in with the Boss, in a private meeting, but she wanted to remind Joszef that his place had been utterly usurped. It was a cruelty that I could not understand or share, much as I wanted to align myself with her. Joszef looked up and stared at Ana over his spectacles, but there was no defiance, only defeat. Despite his anxious animation of only moments earlier, he seemed utterly exhausted. The bags beneath his eyes were heavier than ever, and the tufts of hair greyer. He appeared melancholic or, worse, comedic. Slowly, his eyes returned to the document on his desk. Ana's mouth twisted into a little smile, and she shot a conspiratorial glance in my direction. I could only look away. Satisfied, she rang the bell for coffee.

Once the coffee had been drunk, and that ordered by Georg too, I felt myself relax for the first time in days, able to focus only on the work in hand. When Joszef snapped open his pocket watch to signal that it was time to go through to the meeting room, I rose from my chair easily and we walked along the dark corridor together as far as the door to the anteroom to the Boss's office. Joszef's knuckles brushed the glossed wooden panel, the knock barely audible but sufficient to elicit a grunt from within. The handle fitted comfortably in Joszef's hand, familiar and loyal.

Behind a desk, Kelemen looked faintly ridiculous, his brutishness at odds with the wall of filing cabinets behind him. I looked about the office, but there were no other secretaries. Only Kelemen controlled access to the Boss.

'Good morning, Franck. Is he ready for us?'

Kelemen looked up at Joszef with a smile. There was some warmth in it, but the glint of his gold tooth still sent a shiver through me.

'Yes, yes, Joszef, my friend, they are waiting for you. And the boy.'

His grin widened and he turned his head to make sure that his mocking of me had found its target. Joszef placed his hand on my arm to pull me gently away, but I looked back over my shoulder as we crossed the room to the inner doors. Kelemen was still watching me, still smiling.

My unease continued once we had entered the inner office. Garcia sat close beside the Boss, their heads bowed together in private conversation. None of the other men at the table were familiar, but they sat impassively, waiting for the Boss to call them into action. I took my place beside Joszef self-consciously, and the details of the seizure plans fled from my mind and were replaced by a nauseous memory of school examinations. I barely followed the preamble and introductions. When Andreas Hofmans began to speak, however, the whirling in my head came to rest.

'Thank you Joszef, my friend. Clear and measured as always. The position is clear. Now, Mr Ehrlich, perhaps you could update us all on progress so far. We'd like to begin the process without further delay. Everything is in order, I trust?'

The sunlight streamed into the room like a flood, flaring into a halo around the Boss's head. The Chief Clerk of the Council squinted into its glare. His assistant pushed a paper towards him, but Ehrlich did not pause to note it.

'Thank you, Your Honour. I have to say, I am a little surprised that you remain intent on pursuing this course of action, given the legal ramifications. I have to confess, I have made no preparations for implementation on that assumption. The proposal is not, after all, in line with the policy of the council.'

The air fell to dust around Ehrlich's words. Beside me, I felt Joszef's body tense and, from the corner of my eye, saw him bite his lip. Across the table, Garcia's eyes narrowed. I heard Ehrlich swallow.

'Not in line with the policy of the council? Mr Ehrlich, do I need to remind you?' He paused, straightened his spine and leant forward, his eyes fixed on Ehrlich, the space between them seemingly vanishing in an instant. *'I am not just some fellow with an opinion, I am the fucking mayor of this city.'*

In the silence that followed, I imagined the Boss reaching out across the table and hurling the ashen Ehrlich through the window. Joszef sought to calm the situation, impressing upon the Chief Clerk that he should begin to work up an implementation plan that could deliver to the original schedule. While the Boss glowered and the colour drained from Ehrlich's face, Garcia caught my eye and flashed a smirk in my direction. The Boss had not needed to complete his thoughts, as the meaning had been clear: the wishes of the mayor and the policy of the council were indivisible; indeed, the mayor was indivisible from the city itself. He was its very manifestation. This was not a debate about policy or protocol but a simple statement of fact, indisputable; a truth that the Chief Clerk of the Council could only resist for so long.

Ehrlich rose, seemingly broken, and indicated to his colleagues that the meeting was closed. None followed him until Garcia wafted his hand in dismissal and confirmed that they were no longer needed. The room cleared, leaving me with only Garcia, Joszef and the Boss. There was a moment of silence, the Boss seemingly fascinated by the tabletop between his hands. Eventually, Joszef sighed and turned to me.

'Thank you, Anton. You can head back now. There are some, uh, other matters that we need to deal with and you don't need to be here for them.' His eyes were soft, pleading, and I stood, bowing slightly to the Boss.

'Anton, is it? Thank you for all you do for me, all you do for the city, in fact. Mr Garcia here tells me that your work has been central to the whole housing policy. I intend to keep a close eye on your progress, son. Thank you again for your service.'

I wanted to run into the street, shouting with joy: Andreas Hofmans knows who I am! But instead, I smiled, mumbled my thanks, and backed away as far as the door to the outer office.

History

Ehrlich's dismissal was sudden but not surprising. He must have accepted its inevitability, if not the manner in which it was delivered. According to Georg, the Chief Clerk had worked through the night to assemble a list of the city's vacant apartments and houses, identifying those that met the criteria for confiscation. He had even drafted the letters of notification and the instructions to the Chief of Police. He had presented the thick folder in a closed meeting with only the Boss, Garcia and Kelemen present; he had been thanked cordially, and only then had he been told that his usefulness to the city was at an end. Kelemen had escorted him directly from the building and out onto the street. Any personal belongings that the Chief Clerk had collected during his 20 years of service had presumably become the property of the City.

How Georg knew this was a mystery and I wondered which of the three people present had been his informant. It surely could not have been Garcia, but the thought that Georg was in close communion with Kelemen unnerved me more. I could picture the leer on the face of the Boss's driver as he walked Ehrlich out into the cold air, and I felt renewed sympathy for the Chief Clerk.

If Ehrlich's departure had been unsurprising, what happened next did manage to shock me: Joszef was reassigned to take on the duties of the Chief Clerk, leaving Garcia to run the political office. Seamlessly, the Spaniard assumed Joszef's place and the waters closed over the head of my mentor in an efficient erasure. My return to my original desk was scant compensation for the loss. The day crawled by, a product of my discomfort and an empty in-tray. It was a Friday and, by 5pm, I was already certain that, unusually, I would not come into the office the following morning.

I slept fitfully that night. Things that had seemed solid had dissolved. Joszef's humiliation haunted me, as did Kelemen's smile; but it was Ana's abandonment of her comrade that bothered me most. I could not escape the thought that I had aligned myself with the wrong ally when I made common cause with her. And yet, despite her cold-blooded reaction to Joszef's reassignment, I knew that she had never shown me anything but her support and affection. Every turn ahead of me appeared to be the wrong one. Despite it all, the Boss had thanked me, in person, and with my name. Even as my world became less certain, I could cling to this.

These thoughts tumbled through my mind during the night and into the greying dawn. My waking and rising was conducted negligently and I have no recollection of anything from that Saturday morning until I found myself at the steps of the city's museum of art. I had not visited before, and do not know what drew me there then. Even as a student, the separateness of my life from the weight and rites of this institution had seemed total, but the geometry of that separation had altered. Before, the contents of the museum had been for others, for the rich and cultured; now they were simply frivolities compared to the significance of my work. To visit was not beyond my station, simply beneath my seriousness. I paused under the arched portico, but decided that I had nothing more useful to be doing and continued into the entrance hall. The uniformed warden who watched me as I did so nodded respectfully and let me pass. My transcendence had occurred unnoticed.

I began at the beginning. Flat images of golden saints stared blankly back at me in the first few galleries, before they were replaced by more life-like figures, anguished men and women frozen in the midst of drama and tragedy, or else naked, fecund women were reposed in all manner of settings, natural and domestic, the wisps of draped gauze barely shielding their modesty. I hurried on, through rooms of staring stern-faced military men and self-satisfied industrialists, their pinch-cheeked wives, their horses, dogs, and children. A swirl of landscapes, peasants, trees and rivers under cloud-stacked skies, seemed to stretch to the horizon, each blurring into the last, and into the next. I watched galleons crash through turbulent oceans, conscious that I had not seen the real sea for myself. Despite this, I felt I could taste salt and the tang of fish hanging in the museum's hushed air.

After the tumult of the seascapes, I found myself in a smaller gallery that, in contrast to the beauty of those preceding it, was instead lined with ugly discordance. None of the canvasses conveyed accurate likenesses of the world and its inhabitants. Instead, twisted faces told of torments of the soul. Broken bodies, barely human, bore unimagined grief; still others held no recognisable figures at all, being simply colour and shape and impermanence. Perhaps it was this angry transience that I found captivating, despite myself. The earlier galleries held pictures celebrating what the world wished to be eternal, be it God, wealth or nature's glory. Here, the world was in flux. Terrifying flux. Unmannered, impolite, and bestial.

One small canvass in particular glowered at me, the heavy, dirty red pulling me into its theatre. It suggested a riot or a carnival or a debauched street scene, I could not tell which. And yet the picture mesmerised me. The grotesque faces of the people, especially the women, leered and snarled, but it was only the sight of the priest standing under a streetlamp towards the edge of the jumble of frenzy, naked but for his

97

dog collar, his member engorged, that forced me to turn away. It was then that I saw the gallery assistant watching me, a half-suppressed smile on her face.

I confronted her amusement with a scowl to cover my shame. Her smile widened, her shoulders slackening. Slowly, almost apologetic, she walked across the polished wooden floor, hands clasped behind her narrow back. I watched her oblique approach, my scowl softening into curiosity.

'It's a powerful picture, isn't it? For something so small.'

A brass name badge was pinned to a short dark green waistcoat, buttoned closely across a tailored white blouse. Judith Stern. The hem of a grey flannel skirt hung somewhere below her knees, completing her uniform.

'I haven't seen anything like it. To be honest, I am surprised that the museum allows such things. Surprised but not shocked.'

She tilted her head to consider my observation, and a strand of thick, dark hair fell onto the whiteness of her sleeve. The cuffs of the blouse were long and close fitting, each with seven cotton-covered buttons; the ends were a little frayed from use and washing. She and I studied the painting for a while in silence.

Soft footsteps indicated that someone else had entered the gallery, and it occurred to me that until that moment there had been no-one else present. I resisted the desire to turn, to see what kind of person would also choose to see these pictures. Instead, I kept my eyes trained upon the wanton carnival playing out on the dusty white wall. A dog skulked at a street corner, mangy and broken, yellow teeth fixed into a lascivious grin. I wondered at the lusts of animals, at what the dog could see that provoked it. In my peripheral vision, Judith's lips twisted, either formulating or containing the expression of a thought. Stillness followed and I became uncomfortable in our motionlessness.

'The painter, he's German?'

I had read the little card pinned to the wall beside the painting, inscribed with the artist's name and other particulars. Judith's nod and hum of affirmation filled the gallery. She shifted her weight, paused in contemplation and then was utterly present again, animated.

'There's another of his, over here.'

Without a glance, she led me towards another wall, to another picture, one from which an older couple, wrapped in bulky overcoats, stared back at me, impassive. Unlike the vicious agony and debauchery of the first painting, there was only a desolate sadness in their faces. Those faces were less life-like, but contained more of life, than the finely rendered portraits in the earlier galleries. Their profound calmness was also quite unlike the torrent of Judith's explanation of the image. She raced through references I barely understood, but her enthusiasm was infectious and I galloped alongside her, trying to capture each word, determined to retain them, understand them. At last she paused, her smile apologetic, embarrassed.

'It's funny. They were painted a decade ago, in another country, and yet these two characters are so like the people in my neighbourhood, it's almost as if I know them. Understand them.'

She looked at me quizzically, prompting me to begin an explanation of where I had come from, and then of where I had ended up. Something about the softness of her green-grey eyes, of her pale cheeks, invited disclosure. I seldom talked about my family, my background, with anyone in the city. At work, conversation only revolved around economics and legal instruments. As I spoke, I realised that my life had become depleted of simple humanity, lost amid abstractions. I had become bloodless, desiccated. People such as this old couple, with their discontents and sadness, were simply units of exchange in the political economy of progress. Something within me railed against the pointlessness of Judith's empathy, its ineffective short-sightedness, but also against the emptiness that surrounded the vestiges of my own sentimentality.

'You work for the mayor? How exciting! That must be fascinating, Anton.'

I realised that I had continued talking, that the playing out of my life story had arrived at its inevitable destination in the here and now. Her observation tightened around me and, instead of the free-flowing discourse of moments before, my description of my work became stilted, formal, tied up in the terms in which it was lived. Pompous.

I paused. I had no desire to broadcast the importance and seriousness of the project, to lecture her. I wanted to return to the ease of our earlier conversation, but I realised that I did not have a language for my work that allowed for that. Defeated, I stuttered into silence.

'I should go, let you get back to work. It's been a pleasure to meet you, Judith. Honestly, a pleasure.'

I wanted to say that it had been a joy, a fleeting yet utter joy, but my stiffness and the weight of social expectation would not allow it. Instead, I held out my hand. She laughed gently as she shook it.

'And you. I very much enjoyed our conversation. Perhaps, if you find your way back to the museum, we might continue it? I am usually working in this gallery, unless I'm sent to the Renaissance room. There are paintings there that I'd like to show you. These pictures,' she made a wide arc with her arm, 'did not appear from nowhere. Art has been describing us for centuries. Everything has roots.'

Her smile suggested conspiracy, her eyes exhilaration. It was as if she were inviting me into a secret world. This impression lingered as I coursed back through the seascapes and portraits and icons and ultimately emerged, my head spinning, into the sunlight beyond the museum's portico, into the pulse of the city. What had seemed until then to have been a straight line had begun to twist into a curve, one that would only steepen as the weeks advanced. The squeal of a tram at the far corner of Constitution Square barely interrupted my thoughts and I wandered into the busy Saturday streets consumed by their implications, unknowingly relieved of my anxiety over Joszef's exile.

Blood Soup

It took fewer than thirty minutes before my thoughts returned to Joszef in an irresistible fashion. Leaving Constitution Square, I decided to walk down towards the river, to enjoy the sunshine in the relative calm of its bank. My route took me through some of the narrow streets that jostle behind the principal boulevards of the city: I had no desire to dodge the people thronging the pavements and the quieter thoroughfares added only a little distance to my journey. Just above the embankment, I emerged into a small square set around the entrance to St Augustin's. A café spilled its tables into the space, although few customers had chosen to take advantage of their hospitality in this neglected corner of the city centre. Joszef was one who had.

He sat alone, a half-filled glass of cognac on the little round table before him. His familiar hat sat next to it, but his overcoat was buttoned about him despite the warmth of the sunshine. His attention was elsewhere, his line of sight pointing towards the gable end of a house on the far side of the square; I could easily slip past unnoticed. I hesitated. I had not seen him since he had been removed from the political office, and I did not know how to strike up a conversation without reference to it. Even not mentioning his exile would be to refer to it.

Yet he was my mentor, and I could not forsake him entirely. It had been Joszef that had brought me into the office, Joszef who had shown faith in me, guided me through the frantic swirl of my first days, before I had any real idea of how my contribution should manifest itself. He had supported me. Now, Joszef was displaced and deserved my acknowledgement, if nothing more. I hung on my heels for some moments, watching him, small, alone, and drinking brandy in the late morning sunshine. There had been rumours, although I did not know where they had begun, about Joszef's drinking. Even some suggestion that it was this that had tipped the balance against him in the eyes of the Boss. The drinking, and his acquaintanceships with women that were not his wife. I recalled that evening in the jazz club on the other side of the city, the young women grinning and spilling across Joszef's table. The rumours did not seem groundless, even if they were unbelievable.

Eventually, I made a decision. I would walk past his table, pause, turn back quizzically and offer some greeting. If he offered me a seat, I would under no circumstances take it, claiming some pressing appointment.

'Joszef? I thought it was you. Such a happy coincidence. I'm just on my way to, to...'

I had not, in fact, managed to confect a specific engagement after all, but fortunately Joszef was quick to come to my aid.

'Anton. A pleasure. I too am on an errand, and passing a little time with my thoughts and, uh, an indulgence.' He nodded towards the brandy glass and shrugged in amused apology. His eyes twinkled over his spectacles, but the bags beneath them appeared even heavier than when I had last seen him. *'Please, join me, if only so I do not feel so much of a reprobate!'*

Against my own injunction, I followed the invitation of his open palm and took up the chair opposite him. From nowhere, a waiter appeared and hovered with questioning eyes, his head cocked in readiness. I indicated towards Joszef's glass; Joszef himself gave a curt shake of the head and the waiter was gone again. I watched my hands coil for some moments as they settled into a comfortable arrangement. Joszef was watching me closely when I looked up.

'It's alright, Anton. No need to feel ill at ease. Things change and we all play our part as best we can. I can do as much as Chief Clerk as I could in the political office. And my new office has a window at least. I can look out onto the river and even see the stacks of the steel works.' He became briefly unfocussed. I imagined him thinking back to the early days with the Boss, during the strikes after the war, when their allegiance was forged. I wondered how the constant sight of those chimneys affected him now. Joszef pushed his nose into the mouth of his glass, inhaled the vapour of the cognac and took a long slow sip. His tongue tip traced his bottom lip as he returned the glass to its rest. *'So, it's not so bad. Better than the dungeon that you toil within.'* He chuckled, his head bobbing on the spread of his torso. He smiled at me with such affection that I too laughed at his description of our office. My office.

When my own brandy arrived, Joszef pulled a leather cigar case from inside his coat and offered one of the fat brown stems to me. In the office, Joszef would smoke cigarettes, like the rest of us, and I wondered at his other life, beyond politics, beyond work. From the photograph on his desk, I knew he had a wife and children; I knew he frequented the city's bars, drank cognac, entertained women; but the cigar hinted at a level of self-indulgence greater than I had imagined possible for someone involved in our project. I declined his offer and watched as he deftly pulled the cigar into life. The smoke curled out from his nostrils like a living, sensuous thing. He tossed his usual packet of cigarettes across to me.

'Cigars are not betrayal, Anton. To a man like Garcia, perhaps. But men like Garcia do not understand that all of their beliefs are an indulgence too,

just as much as my cigar. All ideologies are luxuries to those that do not have enough bread.' He sucked smoke into himself and let it roll through him and out of him. I followed its coils like a cat. *'A revolution undertaken by men who do not understand pleasure, men who hold no human warmth, that my friend, that is a revolution that will end in a cold, dark place. Andreas used to understand that, but he's in a hurry these days. I don't know how it will go.'*

I lit a cigarette from the book of matches Joszef had left lying by the ashtray. I watched its tip glow despite the still bright sunshine, heard the crinkling of the paper consumed by the embers. The brandy fused with the smoke on my tongue, forming a doubly warm core within my mouth that spread through me, out along my arms, down to my legs. I glanced at the matches and the familiar image of a black cat peered up at me.

'I come from the neighbourhood to the east of the steel works. My mother works in a garment factory. There were no puritans where I grew up. Not much money either. All we could rely on was pleasure and human warmth. You can smoke your cigar with ease, Joszef. I make no judgement. I'm sure the Boss doesn't either. Garcia, as you say, might be a different kettle of fish.' I paused, took another sip of brandy, drew in smoke, let them work into my bones. *'Things change, of course, and that is as it should be. But some changes can be regretted. I hope that in time, the Boss decides that your part is best played in our dungeon, after all.'*

I had been too bold. A look of discomfort passed over Joszef's face. I had embarrassed him. He shook his head absently and looked up to the gable end of the building behind me. He had resumed the look of distraction he had had when I had first stumbled upon him. He sucked wetly at the cigar, his lower lip bulging and drooping, heavy. I saw, as if for the first time, the loose folds of skin that hung about this neck, the points of bristle lurking in the razor-rasped creases of his face. Everywhere, the weathering of age and sleeplessness. His energy was spent.

Aimlessly, I took up my glass and focused upon the glinting liquid within it. Perhaps it had been inevitable that the Boss would reassign his friend in such circumstances, allowing him to play his part in a less onerous, but no less important, role. My hand trembled, setting currents of light swirling through the brandy, golden eddies, slow and languorous. My pleasure at the shifting light coaxed a smile out of me and only too late did I realise that, to my companion, I might appear to be mocking his situation. But Joszef was still lost among the thoughts he was chasing over the roofs above. I sipped at the brandy, lit another cigarette and waited.

'So, my friend. I have idled enough of this day away.' He gave a sigh and drained his glass, then pulled his watch from his hidden waistcoat and peered down at the passing time. I felt my hand reach inside folds of fabric, searching out my own pocket watch, and had to stay its movement by force of will. *'I have to go. My wife is making blood soup, and I have to buy a duck. Not many butchers sell them alive, but there is one, down behind the train station. So, that is where I am heading.'* He reached for his hat, cigar clenched between his teeth, but pulled back, a moment of hesitation passing over him. I had expected him to stand and, when he did not, I tried to return as discreetly as possible to my own seat. He fixed me with a serious, questioning gaze.

'Do you know how to make blood soup, Anton? First you have to find a live duck. This butcher, he ties up the beak and wraps the bird with brown paper and string, to make it easier to carry. Believe me, you do not want to wrestle with a terrified duck as you board a tram.

'Once you get the thing home, when you are ready to start the preparations, you tuck the bill down toward the bird's breast, and pluck the feathers off the top of its head. With a very sharp knife, you cut through the top of the head...' To illustrate the point, Joszef mimed the cut with a swift jerk of the thumb, and ash fell from the cigar onto the tablecloth. *'...and as the blood pulses out, you drain it into a bowl with some vinegar. This is important, because otherwise the blood will clot and the soup will be spoiled.*

'With the bird dead, you can unwrapped it from the paper parcel and start to dismember it. The gizzard, liver, heart, neck, and even the feet, make a splendid stock, but you must peel the feet and remove the talons first. For the rest, you cut up the meat into pieces and fry it off in a pan with the fat from the carcass, before adding the stock and the blood mixture. Then you simmer for an hour or so.'

He sat back heavily in his chair, a wistful, hungry expression on his face. He looked again at his watch and, with sudden determination, heaved himself to his feet. Knocking the ash and embers from the end of the cigar, he stowed the remaining half in a pocket and took up his hat, turning its brim slowly in his fingers.

'It's a delicious thing, Anton, especially with my wife's potato dumplings. Divine. You should try it if you get the chance. But the making of it is a messy business. You take a whole, intact bird, and you transform it utterly, into something delicious. It takes work. And there is so much blood. So much blood. Cleaning up afterwards is not always straightforward. You have to use very cold water to wash the things. If you use hot, the blood will coagulate and it will be impossible to shift.'

He turned and took a step, then paused, turned again, and took up my hand to shake it firmly, his urgent eyes fixed on mine. *'But it is a thing of beauty, despite the gore of the process. A whole duck, drained and diced, simmered into something quite, quite extraordinary. It is worth the blood that is spilled.'*

Truth

Garcia was staring at Georg over his glasses, his contempt crackling around their wire frames like static electricity. He was extremely short-sighted and when he glared like this, his unfocused eyes took on an enigmatic quality that only intensified their malice. Thankfully, such confrontations were rare. Garcia did not display emotion often. He was more prone to retreating into abstraction and cold intellectualism. Or to sulking.

After those moody interludes, once Garcia had left the room, either to go into conference with the Boss or to stalk the corridors to regain his composure, Georg would joke bitterly about our senior colleague's Latin blood. In the days when Joszef had shared our office, he would chastise Georg for his lack of professionalism, but the impact of his rebuke was undermined by his own smirk.

Now it was the absent Joszef who was the subject of bitter jokes. Since our brief meeting at the café, the whispers about Joszef's fondness for brandy had intensified, as had those about the liberalness of his relationships with women in late-night bars. These rumours of his bourgeois tastes and habits appeared as if from nowhere. I cannot, even now, recall who first alluded to Joszef's wantonness, but oblique references to it sprouted up like weeds. My own attempts to defend him were faltering and counter-productive since they referred to my two meetings with him in bars. It was a miracle that I did not inadvertently mention the cigar.

111

By the Wednesday of the previous week, the first mention was made of supposed familial connections between Joszef and some of the largest landlords in the city.

'I do not care for your obstructions, Georg. We are in the business of making difficult things happen. I asked for a watertight legal justification for the policy of requisitioning empty houses. I did not ask you to give me reasons for its impossibility.'

Garcia's efforts to control his accent in delivering this rebuke meant that each word was clipped and strained. He sucked furiously on his cigarette as soon as the last syllable had been left on the dead air and resumed his glowering.

'I cannot make true something that is not.

Georg's weariness bled into his stubborn refusal to accede to Garcia's instructions. It was becoming clear that he was increasingly disconnected from the new direction that had been set in train since the Spaniard's arrival.

'That is to misunderstand fundamentally the nature of truth. Truth can be made through the mobilisation of power. We do not need to be right, only to win. And all I ask is that you provide an apparatus through which we can win, should there come a challenge to the policy.' Garcia had relaxed markedly, satisfied by the unyielding logic of his argument. Something like a smile pinched his lips. *'I can find another lawyer if the task is beyond you.'*

In appealing to his vanity, he had ensured that Georg's obstinacy would be unlocked. Often Garcia was oblivious to the need to persuade and it was not clear whether he had simply stumbled upon the key or had done so knowingly. The two men regarded each other for a few moments, but it was Georg who looked away first, returning his attention to the papers on his desk with a sigh. Ana crossed the room to offer one of her cigarettes to the defeated combatant.

'Of course he's up to the task.' She cupped her hands around a lit match and, while Georg set the cigarette alight, she looked down at him with a warm smile, an act of silent consolation.

'Anyway, isn't it time we went through to see the Boss?' She looked over to Garcia with cool confidence, lighting a cigarette for herself before extinguishing the match with two steady shakes of her hand. Garcia looked at his wristwatch and sighed. As they left the room, I looked over to Georg, who listened for the click of the latch and the diminishing sound of their footsteps in the corridor.

'Bastard. And she's no better. Patronising bitch.' He sucked at the cigarette, then turned its tip towards him to watch its cooling glow as he exhaled. *'Drunkard or not, I would rather have Joszef back. I don't care who he sleeps with, at least he understood the seriousness of the situation. The Government are not going to let this pass unremarked.'*

'She's only trying to help. I don't think she meant to patronise you.' I stopped myself before I could agree with his assessment of Garcia. Whatever I thought about him, I knew that it was safest to keep those opinions closely guarded, especially if Georg was right. I also knew that there was no legal defence for the seizure of private property that was in train across the city. In some ways, Garcia's argument was sound: it depended on the persuasive power of the Boss. I believed, whatever reservations I had, that Andreas Hofmans knew what he was doing. My own hesitation, and that of Georg, was nothing more than timidity. We lacked the necessary resolve.

'Do you have a cigarette, Anton? I've run out, and I don't have time to pop out to buy some more. Not if I'm going to work out something resembling a viable approach by the time they get back from their conference. Sorry to ask.'

I rummaged through my jacket pockets until I found my pack and tossed it over to Georg's desk. He received it with a smile, before fruitlessly patting all of his pockets. *'Matches? Sorry, Anton. I am at sixes and sevens today.'* Georg never offered apologies, and his discomfort at the dressing down was evident. My fingers found a book of matches in my jacket pocket and I carried it over to his desk.

'Shall we get some coffee? It's after 11. I'll ring for Miss Gelber, shall I?' Without waiting for his response, I strode over to the side table. I heard the match flare behind me, then gave the bell three short rings. *'I didn't have you marked down as a night owl, Anton. You are a dark horse.'* Georg's observation confused me and I turned towards him with a frown. He was holding up the book of matches. I could see the black cat printed on its cover. *'It's a jazz bar, isn't it? Down in the old town. I've never been, but I've heard it's quite something. Attracts a certain, uh, clientele. Are you a regular?'*

I did not have a chance to respond, because Ana and Garcia chose that moment to shamble in through the door, heads close in muttered conversation. They stood at the threshold, as if unable to decide what they should do next.

'Please tell me he's decided to call off the seizures.'

It was Ana this time that glared at Georg. Her shake of the head was not in response to the surly question but to warn him that this was not the time. The brittle silence clung for an eternity. The thudding at my temples seemed to fill the room. Eventually, Garcia fumbled some words out of himself, each stumbling like a new-born lamb, unused to the light.

'Uh, there has been… There is some distressing news. I was, we were, informed by the mayor, just now. It is, uh… Our meeting has been postponed, delayed. Andreas felt that you should know as soon as possible. Before rumours have… a chance to spread. Ana, perhaps you could, uh, since you knew him better than I? Perhaps?'

Garcia leant back against the doorframe, allowing Ana to take centre stage. The hesitancy of his voice was not reflected in his movements, in the easy way with which he reclined, like an unemployed man at a street corner, his right hand tucked into his trouser pocket, a cigarette smoking in his left. Ana cast him a reproachful glance but took up the story, nonetheless, getting straight to the point: Joszef was dead.

He had been missing for two days. The Boss had instructed the police to comb the city for his old friend. Joszef had last been seen in a bar late at night, in the company of a woman known to be a prostitute and, while his disappearance might simply have been drunken revelry gone too far, a matter of sleeping off a hangover or extended debauchery, the Boss had had a nagging worry that something more serious had befallen his friend. Questions had been asked at home, as delicately as possible, but Joszef's wife had known nothing of her husband's whereabouts and had been grateful for the Boss's concern and support.

The body had been found on waste ground beyond the steel works. His throat had been cut, and his shoes and wallet were missing. The third finger of his left hand had been severed, presumably in order to claim his stubborn wedding ring. Ana broke down as she related the depth of the Boss's distress, not only at the fact of his friend's death, but also at the manner of it. At first, he had refused to believe that Joszef had fallen so far, but the evidence presented by the Chief of Police was compelling. The truth, as presented, overwhelmed the bonds of loyalty and the Boss could not deny the facts.

Ana kept talking, never allowing either Georg or I to interject, and so we simply sat and listened, the horror of events layering over us like soil. When she had finished, Georg sat frozen, pale and horrified. I watched Ana's hands, knotted and trembling, and tried to blot out the insistent images of Joszef's lifeless, bloodless face, the ragged opening of his throat.

That Joszef should have lost his way so absolutely, so quickly, was almost unbelievable. And yet the facts seemed incontrovertible. What's more, I had seen him with those women with my own eyes; I had found him alone, drinking before midday: he had been absent, disillusioned and faithless. Perhaps the Boss had had good reason to reassign him to a less central role in the administration after all. A crime of sordid passion had occurred, a pointless, dirty tragedy. I tasted salt-water and rubbed at my eyes, hoping to cover my weakness.

'It is terrible to think that something like this could happen to a comrade, especially one as highly valued as Joszef.' Garcia was upright again, filling the silence that had overtaken us. 'I did not know him as well as you did, of course. But even so, it is hard to believe. Rest assured, the mayor will make sure that the culprit is brought to justice and that, despite everything, Joszef will be remembered, honourably.' He paused again, looking from me to Georg and back again. 'If you feel the need, you should of course take the afternoon to yourself.'

Neither of us moved. Ana made her way across the office, towards her desk. Life was to continue regardless, it seemed. She paused to look at the book of matches on Georg's desk. 'Cute cat.' She nodded at the matches, smiled, and gave Georg a slow and thoughtful glance.

'*Where's that coffee?*' I stood and walked to the door, leant out into the darkness of the corridor and shouted my request out into the void. No answer came, but I returned to my desk without a doubt that coffee would arrive. I returned to my place, but could feel Garcia's eyes on me, felt certain that he would be smiling his disconcerting smile. It sickened me, but when I shut out the thought of his smile, it was replaced by the image of the gaping smile of Joszef's riven throat. I blinked the image out of me and noticed that Ana was still watching Georg.

Intoxication

The last of the day's light disappeared from the fanlights above Ana's desk and only yellow lamplight illuminated the near silence of the office. The scratching of Georg's pen ruffled the stillness, weaving through the ticking of the clock, but otherwise the leaden air, heavy with cigarette smoke and unease, closed around us, still as a tomb. Before, when Joszef had sat at the desk beside the door, the last hours of the day had been a time for chatter and good-natured argument. Georg would preen and provoke, confident in his cleverness, goading Ana into weary, sardonic response, until Joszef had intervened, calming the manufactured confrontation. But now there was no conversation beyond that which was necessary to the work at hand. The presence of Garcia smothered any levity.

This awkwardness remained even when Garcia was absent, as he often was. He was in meetings with the Boss daily, sometimes more frequently. On other days, he would request that Ana accompanied him and they would disappear, silently, into the darkness beyond the door frame. A week after the news of Joszef's death had been revealed, Kelemen appeared in the doorway one afternoon. He did not need to say anything for Garcia to follow him wordlessly into the corridor, leaving the three of us to the silence and our work.

Georg had completed his advice on the seizure of empty properties days before, but he had now been tasked with developing an analysis of the potential for extending the approach. The reasons for this were never fully explained. At the same time, I had been set to work looking at the scope for accelerating investment in the mayor's social programmes. Garcia had not shared with me which programmes were to be financed and Ana, who had been present at the meeting where this had been discussed, told me nothing further. Things were clearly accelerating but neither Georg nor I had any clue as to the destination.

The click of Georg's pen lid fractured the slow progression of the afternoon. I looked over to the clock. Five thirty precisely. Georg pulled a cigarette from his packet and a match flared into life, casting a ghoulish, shimmering shade onto the panels behind. Exhaling, he stretched his arms wide as if awakening after a long sleep.

'Want one? I owe you, I think.' He smiled over at me, packet in hand, ready to toss it in my direction. I nodded gratefully; the packet landed next to the desk lamp and skidded across, coming to rest at my fingertips.

'Well, I'm calling it a day. It is Friday after all. Not much more I can do until Garcia lets me know what's what, in there.' Georg nodded towards the door. After a moment of hesitation, he was on his feet. *'Think I'll head off...'* He retrieved his overcoat from the hat stand in the corner, but did not put it on. Instead, he simply picked at specks I could not see.

'You might as well. He won't be back. I think the Boss has taken him to a dinner with the Observer's *publisher.'* Ana smiled, pleased that Georg had waited for her permission. She shot me a little glance, lips pursed, then returned to her paperwork with an audible sigh. Georg shrugged his arms into its sleeves and began to button his coat. At the last one, he paused, looked up, confusion and mistrust on his face. *'How did you know? About the dinner, I mean.'*

Ana put down the sheaf of papers and looked up at him. '*Garcia mentioned it, in the meeting yesterday. We've had a lot of negative coverage about the empty homes initiative, and we've got nowhere with the editorial people. The Boss thinks we might get a fairer hearing from the proprietor. Might be able to come to an understanding about things. For the future.*'

She flashed the briefest of smiles by way of reassurance. Georg bit his lip, trapping whatever thought had passed through his mind before it could get free and cause trouble. This kind of circumspection was a recent development. Before, Georg had never hesitated in speaking his mind, even after Garcia had arrived. However, since Joszef's death, he had become more sullen and less willing to share either his cleverness or his frustrations. With a careful nod of the head, he fastened the last button of his coat and turned to leave. At the door, he paused, turned and seemed about to say something to me, but again stopped the words in his mouth. Instead, he gave me a sad smile, a shallow nod and then he was gone.

Ana did not raise her eyes when he left, so did not notice this faint farewell. We sat in silence for maybe half an hour, she working on some problem among the sheaf of papers stacked across her desk. Time slipped by to the sound of Ana's breathing and I became lost within its rhythm, within the calm control it created, such that the creaking of her chair startled me.

'*Well. Late enough, I think. What about you?*' She was already on her feet. but she did not move towards the door. Instead, she was at the filing cabinet. She pulled open the second draw and shuffled the files forward, her forearm disappearing behind them, searching. '*Ta dah!*' She held the bottle of brandy like a trophy.

He had left it, hidden. A relic of his time with us. Almost full. Perhaps Joszef had forgotten it. Perhaps this was proof positive that he had become a drunk, that the rumours were true.

'Seems fitting to drink a toast to him with his own cognac, no?' Ana was smiling, hopeful. *'I mean, assuming that you've finished your work for the day? I know how diligent you are, Anton. Your commitment is exemplary.'* She placed two glasses on Georg's desk, next to the bottle. *'You're not just here for the ride, are you? To make yourself feel, I don't know, important. Or to ease your conscience. Whatever, it's certainly not a game to you, is it?'*

She looked at the floor for moment, lost somewhere within herself. Maybe it was a game to her, an intellectual conundrum to be solved through the application of a fierce intelligence. She had no prior connection to the Party, after all. Presumably, she had been appointed for her academic credentials, which were daunting. She had never really spoken about it, but I knew that she had been the youngest-ever professor of political economy, and the first woman to have attained the title.

'Is that what it is to you, then? A game?' The rawness of the last week cracked at the back of my throat. I did not even regret my boldness. If this were a game, then the stakes were very high for some of us.

Ana took a large white handkerchief from her trouser pocket and used it to wipe out the glasses, folding it neatly before returning it. *'No, of course not. Not really. I am committed, of course I am. But I suppose it's different for me. Not that my family were wealthy, like Georg's. My father is no grain baron, that is for sure! But going to university was no great challenge for me. Both my brothers had gone before me, and my father before them. I didn't need to overcome much to get here, just to work.'* She paused to pour two large measures of brandy, then looked up suddenly, her eyes narrowed.

'Do you mind me speaking this way? We don't really talk... not anymore, not since...'

I wanted her to continue, to accuse Garcia, but she stumbled into awkwardness and silence. The clunk of the glasses on my desk reverberated and the slow liquid oozed gold into the lamplight. A brief pang of memory flickered, of watching the sunlight catch Joszef's brandy outside St Augustin's. Ana pulled up Georg's chair beside my desk.

'A toast. To Joszef, the old fool.' Our glasses clinked and I felt the warmth of the brandy. It tasted sweeter this time. *'He had his doubts, you know. About the empty homes initiative. Felt it was a misstep. A strategic and tactical error. Too soon, apparently. Too risky. He might have had a point. What do you think?'* It struck me that, perhaps, Joszef had had the same conversation with Ana as he had had with me, that he had shared the same confidences, and this too was something Ana and I had in common. She swallowed her drink in one go and poured out a new measure, then filled my glass. I gulped half of it down to catch up.

'You're very quiet. Do you not believe me? That I'm not just playing?' I realised that I had said nothing, since I had asked my question. Perhaps I had even been pouting. *'Sorry. It's just been a long week. I still feel dreadful about what happened. To Joszef, I mean. Whatever trouble he had got himself into, he didn't deserve that. No-one deserves to be left like that, in a place like that.'* I drank down the rest of my glass and she poured out another measure. *'Yes, you were close to him, weren't you? He brought you in, after all. Do you also think things have gone too far? Are moving too fast?'* She waited while I gathered my thoughts: I felt the need for my next sentence to be well-judged, to be assembled with serious words.

'From the point of view of political strategy at least, I can see why the policy would have troubled him. It invites confrontation when none is needed.

Whether it is, of itself, the right thing to do, I do not know.' Ana leant in, animated and alert, almost eager for me to continue. Her eagerness inundated the space between us, and I felt my breathing stutter. Sensing my discomfort, she withdrew a little.

'Yes, politically risky. Perhaps, objectively suspect. Who knows where the logic leads? But…' She looked down for a moment to where her hands clenched into balls at either side of her glass, and only at their release did she continue. *'How do you interpret this turn, this change in course, Anton? Garcia is a difficult character, I know, and he has championed the new direction, so I can understand why it might be… how our feelings about the messenger and the message could be conflated. How the policy might be damned by our distaste for the person. It's understandable, even if it is a mistake.'* She watched me for a minute, then topped up my brandy. I could not recall having drunk more of it, but the glass was almost empty.

'Now, the grounds for personal resentment were strongest for Joszef.' She was nodding slowly, her eyes unfocused momentarily. *'I don't know if it was simply that his nose was put out of joint, that he was humiliated because his position was undermined. That would be understandable. But in any case, he certainly objected strongly to the new direction. His displacement damaged him, that's how I choose to explain what happened to him. I don't believe he was always a dilettante, not matter what anyone says. Circumstances drove him. We are all subject to circumstances. Don't you think, Anton?'*

She was now looking directly at me. I tried to piece together the elements of what she had said, feeling the weight of her gaze. I no longer knew what I should think about any of it. I looked at my glass: half empty, again. She was waiting for an answer to her question and I had no idea what the right answer was.

'Of course, we're all shaped by the events around us.' Despite myself I finished the brandy that was left in my glass. 'And I agree, of course, that it is important to separate out our feelings from policy. Joszef had his reasons for disliking Garcia. Good reasons, reasons that anyone could understand. Good god, his entire life's work was taken from him! But, and I think this is the point... The point is that his perfectly reasonable dislike of that, that... but that should not have coloured his judgement of the policy. If it did, I mean.' My glass was full again. I patted my cheek and the flesh felt numb to the touch. 'I mean, I don't know if that was what lay behind his doubts, his concerns about the policy. Maybe the two things, the concern about the policy and the mistrust of Garcia, maybe both of them existed independently, I don't know. Maybe they were both legitimate. Maybe?' I wanted so much to be able to ask him. I wanted so much for him to be here, explaining the right course of action, about everything.

'Do you trust him? Garcia, I mean?' She was frowning now. Shadows cloaked her eyes, and I needed to see her eyes. Outside, in the corridor, there were footsteps. I wondered if it could be him, drawn by the mention of his name, and I turned apprehensively towards the door. But the footsteps passed and the silence beyond reasserted itself. The tension in my shoulders cracked, but the familiar austerity of the office, its sickly yellow light and dismal shadows, left me a little nauseous. I planted my hands flat on the desk to steady myself, even though I was safely seated.

'Anton? Are you alright?' I anchored myself to her voice and pulled myself back to the question she had asked before.

'Yes, yes, I'm fine. Fine. You were asking about Garcia. I think it's just sometimes it feels like he has... his own agenda, that something else is going on. I'm not always sure he's working to the same ends that we are, that he is aligned to the Boss in the way that we are. I mean, let's think about the empty homes initiative.' I was vaguely aware that my language was changing, and with it the shape of the things it described. New labels changing the content of familiar things. I paused, felt my face set into a questioning frown, before letting go of the thought and continuing. *'Perhaps that was Garcia's idea, perhaps he planted the idea with the Boss and, when Joszef objected, perhaps it was Garcia that persuaded the Boss to reassign Joszef, to get him out of the way.'*

'Perhaps. Go on.' It seemed important to explain things to her, to tell her what she needed to hear. What she wanted to hear. It seemed important to reassure her in her own suspicions.

'Just… Joszef, he might have been right, that's all. About the policy and about Garcia. Maybe we shouldn't trust him either, you and me. Or maybe not. Maybe Joszef was wrong. Maybe it was just sour grapes, I don't know. Not anymore.' She leant back in her chair, and the shadows hanging over her eyes vanished. They were as they often were, pale green and razor sharp. She studied me, as she contemplated her next sentence, pausing her deliberation to swallow what was left in her glass. I watched the brandy pulse down her throat.

'One thing is for certain. Georg doesn't trust him.' She was watching me again, as if testing my acuity.

'I think that is an understatement. Statement.' I heard the slurring of my voice as I shaped the last word and wrestled with my mouth, seeking to re-establish control over it. *'It's clear he has no time for the seiz… the empty homes initiative. He's been battling it from the beginning. If he could, I think he would have sunk it already.'* I wondered if Ana had had this conversation with Georg already, if she had sounded him out first.

'Has he said anything to you directly about it? I mean, I can see it for myself. But he has been working more closely on it than either of us. I just

wondered if he might have said something more specific. About his qualms.
He wouldn't tell me. I don't think he likes me very much. You can see that,
can't you?' She needed my help. There was something she could not do
alone. Ana always seemed so self-sufficient, so utterly capable, and yet
here she was asking for my help.

'No, nothing.' I reached for my glass, but withdrew my hand, surprised to
see that it was empty. *'I don't think he likes me much either.'* Ana laughed
at this and she raised her hand apologetically, her slender fingers covering
her mouth, her close-clipped nails resting at the tip of her nose. *'If you*
like, I could try to speak to him, see what is going on behind that knitted
brow?' She laughed again, eyes sparkling. *'Well then, it's settled, I'll let you*
know. If anything is going on, with Garcia I mean. We three should stick
together.' I offered a broad smile of reassurance, and she nodded back at
me, cementing our alliance.

Ana looked over at the clock and her smile disappeared. The cigarette
that she had only just lit was stubbed forcefully into the ashtray.

'Hell, I'm late. I'm supposed to be meeting someone. Can I leave you to tidy
the place up a little?' She was already on her feet, indicating the glasses
and Georg's chair. Without waiting for my response, she claimed her bag
and coat and stuffed her cigarettes into a pocket. At the door she paused.
'It was really nice to talk to you, after such a horrible week. Really. It means
a lot.' She raised her palm in farewell and then was gone.

The room felt unbearably empty then. The thought that Ana had
somewhere else to be, someone else to see, was inexplicably hard to bear,
in a way that it had not been on every other evening when she had
rushed off. Previously, it had seldom occurred to me to reflect on the fact
that, unlike the others, even Georg, I had nowhere else to go, no-one to
watch a clock, wondering where I was. The aloneness of the empty office

dowsed in heavy yellow light closed in around me. I poured out the last of the brandy and raised my glass in a final silent salute to Joszef.

Rebellion

Garcia's desk was empty, but his coat hung from the hat stand as it usually did by this time on a Wednesday morning. In many ways, everything was as to be expected. And yet it was not. The tension that fizzed on the air brought the blood surging to my cheeks. I had forgotten something, missed something, left something incomplete: anxiety spiralled through me. As I sank into my chair, I looked from Ana to Georg, but neither was willing to offer me any clue as to my omission.

The day before, all had seemed normal. Normal for the days since Joszef's murder, at least. Since the Friday evening, when Ana and I had shared confidences and Joszef's cognac, nothing more had been said. I had slipped back onto the treadmill, working up hypothetical mechanisms for raising additional funding for the Boss's programmes. Most were entirely fanciful: technically possible, but utterly unacceptable in the real world. Garcia of course had reacted with encouragement, urging me to explore the limits of ideas that were already beyond the boundaries of what was achievable. I had done as I had been asked; the iciness of the morning remained mysterious.

Georg swore quietly to himself, and I could almost hear the clenching of his fingers on his pen. Behind me, Ana's chair creaked. I turned my head. Her eyes were softer, and she gave an apologetic smile that melted my desire to demand an explanation, but only intensified the sense that I was, in some way, in trouble. The question behind my searching, plaintive eyes went unanswered. And then the door swung open.

'You. Anton, is it? You're wanted.'

Kelemen's presence was as unnerving as ever. Only Joszef had been relaxed in his company. The long years of their shared history had eroded the jaggedness of his manner for both Joszef and the Boss. They had made an odd trio, but I could see why the arrangement suited Andreas Hofmans. Just as Joszef had lent the Boss intellectual direction, his close association with Kelemen demonstrated that he was still one of the people. Credibility, and threat. That threat seemed to fall especially heavily on me as, stunned, I stared back at him, unsure what any of this meant. Kelemen waited.

'You'd better go, Anton. The Boss wants you to minute the meeting.' The tone of Ana's voiced calmed me a little, but her words only opened more questions. Sensing my confusion, she continued, *'The Government has sent a representative. Last minute, no notice. They're not happy. Not happy at all. I think they've come to tell us that the empty homes initiative has to stop.'* Mute, I gathered a notebook and my pen, and followed Kelemen out into the dark corridor, as if headed for the gallows.

We reached the light of the anteroom. As we entered, a tall man, stick thin, sprang to his feet. Like Kelemen, he wore boots, a sweater and coarse trousers, which in his case were bunched around his strangled hips and hung halfway up his calves. Pale, hairless skin flashed between boot top and trouser cuff. He regarded me with cold scorn, but when Kelemen took a couple of steps towards him, he seemed to flinch.

'So, Tomasz, is everything in order?'

The tall man nodded emphatically, and Kelemen signalled that he should leave now with a flick of his head. As he passed me, Tomasz glanced at me with yellowed eyes, and my already cold blood ran colder still.

'In there.'

I complied with Kelemen's instruction automatically and passed through the door into the mayor's office. Andreas Hofmans looked up from his papers, his pen hovering over an unfinished line. I stuttered a vague apology, struggling to explain the interruption of my presence, when I did not understand it myself. Garcia looked at me with confusion and disdain.

'Him? Really? Given the importance of the matter, I thought someone more senior might… Really?' Garcia raised his hand in submission. *'If you're sure, then so be it.'*

The Boss smiled and indicated that I should sit in the empty chair beside Garcia. Again, I complied. Unsure what else to do, I arranged my notebook and pen in a neat alignment, then laced my fingers and rested my wrists on the table edge and waited, as if in prayer. Only once I had settled did Garcia give me my instructions. I was to say nothing, simply to keep a superficial record of the conference. There was no need for detailed notes. Either things would go well, or they would go badly. The precise route to either outcome was unimportant, except to those in the room. He did not say as much, but it was clear that my presence in the room was part of a piece of theatre, a pretence of seriousness, or perhaps of strength. When Gottlieb von Boehmen entered the room with his two aides, I realised that I was simply there to even up the numbers.

He walked calmly and with purpose. Nothing about his manner suggested that he sought to project dominance on the room; he simply assumed that he had it. When he held out his hand to the Boss, the fabric of his grey woollen jacket rearranged itself with supple elegance. When he offered his hand to me, I shook it hesitantly, convinced that he had mistaken me for someone important. I looked to Garcia for reassurance, but he stared intently at our guest, absorbing every detail of his movement and expression.

Once we had taken our seats and pleasantries had been exchanged, the business began. I took up my pen, ready to begin, but the room appeared to pause, time suspended, and I absorbed the pointless details of where we were: the fragrant notes of von Boehmen's hair oil, the lustre of the pale green silk curtains festooned about the tall windows giving out onto the balcony, the snap of the wind in the flag that hung above it; the extravagance of the yellow flowers gathered in the vase standing on the console, their pompoms reflected back onto themselves in the gilt-framed mirror; the curl of a scarlet S stitched into the pocket square of the unnamed aide sitting across from me. Everything hung steady, breathless, and the world surged into me, alighting all of my senses. When the spell cracked, it was at the sound of von Boehmen's fingers drumming onto the table.

'I will come directly to the point, Mayor Hofmans. I am here at the instruction of both the President and the Prime Minister. There is considerable unease in the Capital, across all parties, caused by recent developments here. Developments that emerge directly from the policy that you are pursuing.' He paused, ran a hand through his ash blonde hair. He must have been in his late forties, but he showed no sign of greying and his skin carried no wrinkles to speak of, as if his office and standing had defied time, preserving him in a state of vigour beyond his prime. *'You are requested, by the Government and by the institutions of state, to end the confiscation of properties and to return those already seized to their rightful owners.'*

At the word '*requested*', Garcia had looked up sharply from his own notes. I dutifully recorded the representative's words precisely, sensing their significance, then waited for the Boss to respond, expecting something like the evisceration of poor Ehrlich that had occurred the last time I had been in this room, when this policy had first been discussed formally. But when the response came, it lacked the impatience; it lacked the self-confidence. Instead, the Boss cautiously and politely tested the extent to which this really was a request.

'*Of course it is a request.*' Von Boehmen smiled, pushed his fingertips together. '*For now, at least.*' The two men stared at each other for a moment, while von Boehmen's aides caught up in their own note taking. The scratching of their pens was unbearable. Once they had ceased their scribbling, the emissary began to speak once more, softening his expression and opening his palms wide towards the mayor.

'*My dear Hofmans, the Government has no desire to instruct you in how to conduct the administration of this city. Indeed, I have heard the Prime Minister speak positively in private about the health and employment programmes you have initiated, even if they are not consistent with the governing Party's own policy.*' A flicker of some distant thought rippled his left cheek. '*Even other aspects of your housing policy meet with some approval too. These are dangerous times, after all. But we cannot, will not, allow such an affront to the fundamental principles of our constitution. We will take all appropriate action necessary to protect the legal security of property rights within the state.*'

The tone had hardened again and Garcia inhaled deeply but, from the corner of my eye, I was surprised to see mischief rather than weariness on his face. I watched him slide a slim folder across to the Boss, who flipped it open, studied the document within it for too little time, and then slid it across to von Boehmen who did not even bother with the pretence of reading its contents. The folder found its way to the aide sitting at von Boehmen's right hand side.

'This would all be simpler, of course, if you would simply commit to rescinding the policy of confiscation. There are many other priorities, I am sure, that deserve your attention.' The urbane affability evaporated, leaving only officious detachment. *'We have the order prepared and are assured that the High Court will expedite its ruling. Of course, we expect that ruling to fall in our favour. We will then take steps, under judicial aegis.'*

The aide leant towards von Boehmen and whispered into his ear with such discretion that I could hear not one syllable of the message. All the while, von Boehmen stared coolly at the Boss, the murmur of a smile playing at his lips.

'Having studied your legal justification, our position remains the same. This,' von Boehmen placed the spider of his hand on the folder, *'amounts to no more than wishful thinking and slogans.'*

He unleashed the smile that he had worked so hard to suppress, allowing it to become something close to laughter. The last possible impediment to victory for the Government had been found wanting. Beside me, Garcia scribbled an angry note and I did not need to read it to know that it meant further pain for Georg.

'I am sorry that you feel that our legal advice is insubstantial. But let me assure you that there is no policy of 'confiscation' or 'seizure'. Our empty homes initiative simply makes available unoccupied properties for rent. The landlords are compensated. They receive a proportion of the rent that we collect on their behalf. A level of rent that is commensurate with what we deem to be fair and just, within the limits of what is appropriate within the city.' The Boss was neither apologetic nor confrontational in his

delivery. Instead, he spoke as if simply clearing up a misunderstanding. Before von Boehmen had the opportunity to reply, however, a quizzical look passed over Hofmans' face and he strained as if to hear something beyond the windows. With an apology, he stood and crossed the floor so that he could see out over the square that lay to the front of City Hall. He then pulled on the bell cable beside the fireplace.

In a heartbeat, the door to the anteroom swung open and Kelemen entered. I was startled. I had never seen him in a suit before, even an ill-fitting one such as this. Too long, the trousers bunched around his ankles, largely obscuring the familiar work boots that he still wore. The bristles of his close-cropped hair had been combed and their waywardness partially tamed by the application of oil. He stood with his hands held behind his back while the Boss asked about the commotion outside.

'It is a demonstration, sir. Against the landlords. There are hundreds of them, thousands, all converging on the Square, calling for further action to make property owners open their shut-up houses and apartments to rent by the people. There is great anger, your Honour.' It was impossible to suppose that I was the only one to recognise that Kelemen was reciting a script, and badly at that. Yet when the Boss hurried over to the window in a state of apparent anxiety, the three guests followed, driven by genuine concern. Kelemen scuttled after them, opening the French doors to the balcony, so that both the mayor and his guests could witness the crowds below.

The rush and surge outside was carried in through the open windows, causing the hairs on my neck to prickle. I began to move, but Garcia placed his hand on my arm, instructing me to keep my place at the table, to leave the display to its protagonist and its intended viewers. A slim smile creased the corner of his mouth, and he watched his hands spread across the gloss of the mahogany, his head shaking slightly, as if in disbelief. I heard him mumble to himself: *'Bravo, Andreas, bravo.'*

Although I did not see the demonstrators, the pace and volume of the muttering between von Boehmen and his aides suggested that the sight was impressive. Eventually, they retook their seats across from the mayor. Kelemen stood just behind them, out of sight but present nonetheless.

'As you see, my dear Gottlieb, these are indeed dangerous times. The people urge us to go further than we have, such is their need for decent homes.' The flash of Kelemen's gold tooth glinted behind the troubled face of the Government representative. *'The settlement we have arrived at with the landlords is a compromise. Politics is, of course, a balancing of interests. Our empty homes initiative enables us to meet the legitimate needs of the people without succumbing to their, uh, excesses. We are merely requiring that landlords, where they have no tenants for their property, acquire them, and benefit from the rental income they generate. Where they are unable to do so, we take responsibility for arranging tenancies on their behalf.'*

Von Boehmen shifted uneasily in his chair. He leaned over to the aide closest to him and they exchanged whispers, their comfortable murmur interrupted by the sound of Kelemen's knuckles cracking behind his back. The doors to the balcony had been left open and the sound of the crowd beyond tightened around the meeting. Slowly, I could make out the name of the Boss rising from the white noise. Clearly, discernibly, I could trace its contours: not his title, nor even his family name, but 'Andreas', as if he was their friend, their brother. As if he was the crowd itself. Soon the whole Square was filled with its repetition.

At the other side of the table, the three Government men concluded their conclave hesitantly. Von Boehmen appeared to seek the approval of his aide before turning back to the mayor. His mouth opened to speak but before words emerged, a frown fell like a dark cloud and he shook his head, changing course.

'Can we shut the doors, please? It's a little difficult to concentrate with all this noise.' Hofmans merely shrugged in response, apologetic but unconcerned. He made no signal to Kelemen, to Garcia or to me that we should comply with the representative's wishes.

'Very well.' A heavy sigh preceded von Boehmen's terse concession. *'Can you guarantee that landlords will be properly compensated and that only empty properties will be commandeered, temporarily, that no actual transfer of title will take place? Because we've had reports…'*

'My dear fellow, reports from disgruntled men are worth nothing.' It was Hofmans' turn to condescend, the balance having shifted with the chanting of his name. *'Of course there is no legal transfer of title. How can there be? The laws you have made in the Capital do not allow it. And, of course, the landlords will be compensated, as they deserve.'*

The delegates looked from one to the other, then back across the table, their eyes haunted. One of the aides began to shuffle papers back into a folder, but otherwise there was no physical indication of movement, of advance or retreat. Von Boehmen glowered at the mayor, impotent contempt bulging at his temples. The pen felt fat between my fingers, engorged, superfluous, and I placed it carefully on my notebook. No further notes would be needed, whatever the envoy said next.

'The laws on property rights are clear, Mr Hofmans. I confess, I do not approve of your methods, but in the circumstances, and with these assurances about legal title and fair compensation, I am prepared to recommend to the Prime Minister that no action be taken against the City at this time.' He sighed. It was clear that he was a man unused to making concessions

and that the experience pained him. Some of his years had caught up with him and he no longer appeared to be protected from their advance. Yet I felt no pity for him, only a surge of elation at his failure. When he stood to offer his hand to the Boss, it was done meekly. One of his aides whispered something into his ear. *'Yes, of course. Is there some way that we could leave the building that would avoid the, uh, commotion outside?'* He nodded towards the open window.

'Of course, my dear fellow. Mr Kelemen, could you escort our guests to one of the side entrances, and send word to their driver, so that they might be conducted in safety?' Kelemen grinned his obedience, turned and waited by the opened door into the anteroom while the Government delegation gathered their things hurriedly. With the Boss's name still ringing on the air, I watched them disappear. Once we were alone, the Boss clasped Garcia's shoulder and let out a whoop of laughter. He then turned to me with a benevolent smile.

'So, Anton,' he began and my brain pulsed again with the knowledge that Andreas Hofmans knew my name and used it with easy familiarity, *'it has been decided: now that the empty homes initiative has been vindicated,'* he threw a glance towards Garcia, *'we move on. The work you have been doing on municipalising the regional bank and the city gas company takes priority.'* I was a little stunned. I had not realised that the economic modelling Garcia had tasked me with was the foundation of such a move and I was awed by the audacity of the proposal now that it had been made explicit. A rush of excitement coursed through me, the thrill of being at last central to the work of the mayor. *'Can you prepare a thorough proposition for me by the end of the week?'* I did not flinch. I had no need of sleep, such was my exhilaration, and I was content to work constantly until the document was complete and ready for the Boss to review over the weekend. I nodded emphatically, unable to speak.

At that, Garcia grunted that I should return to the office while he discussed other matters with the mayor. Once the door had thudded shut behind me, I heard their muffled conversation and yet more laughter. I paused and smiled. Kelemen's sweater and work trousers were hanging from the back of his chair. Von Boehmen must have seen them as he passed through before skulking out of City Hall. He must have realised that he had been the victim of an elaborate trap, one that he had been unable to evade. I took in the surroundings of the empty anteroom, breathed in its air; air purified by its proximity to power. In Kelemen's absence, it felt as though I belonged here. Even the darkness of the corridor felt supportive, no longer ominous. By the time I reached the office, an uncontainable grin had split my face and Georg and Ana watched me enter with what I imagined to be admiration and awe. I told them all that had passed, breathless with self-regard, and unrolled myself into my desk chair as if it were a throne. We had won, and the frantic days of work that were to follow could wait a little while at least.

Warmth

The still, cool air of the art museum wrapped itself around me. After my first visit, the idea of its tranquillity had become a refuge, a place to which my mind wandered when the office became overwhelming, as it had during that week. My moment of triumph quickly dissolved into days and nights of toil, and by the time the week ended, I was eager to seek out my sanctuary.

As I entered the museum's vaulted hall, I paused, looked up to where the columns branched out into the ribs of the cavern above, and felt calmness spread through me. Despite the others present, the hall seemed to belong only to me. In the gallery of seascapes, I lingered longer than I had on my first visit. Vessels snagged gently at anchor, the slow tide straining against the hawsers, or else they roiled on tumultuous waves, battling insurmountable force; canvass snapped taut in frozen gales. One enormous painting depicted a sea battle, billows of smoke rising from unseen gun ports. A shattered mast, caught in the instant of its laceration, hung above the deck to which it must surely be dashed at any moment. Banners curled above ornate sterns whose gilding and glazing seemed incongruous amid the violence of the conflict.

I looked for the sailors, men powerless against the forces unleashed upon them. Just as the elements overwhelmed storm-tossed ships, so mere men were overwhelmed by the violence of metal and rage. Within the narrative of the painting, they were incidental, their actions futile, and their histories irrelevant. They were part of the battle, but could not change its direction, could not change their fate.

By instinct I arrived in the gallery with the picture of the riot. The gallery where I had met Judith. She was not there, and I felt an unexpected disappointment at her absence. I resumed my study of the little canvass of the debauched, angry people on the street, but slowly my disappointment became insistent and I looked around me with stubborn impotence, as if willing her to appear. She did not and I lost interest in the pictures on the walls, began again to walk through the galleries, making a pretence of looking at the paintings they contained.

I found a bench in a room adorned with scenes of Gallic gaiety. I did not need to read the cards pinned alongside the canvasses to know that the promenading ladies, clutching parasols to cover their laughter, were French in origin. Their conviviality reminded me of my own aloneness, and I watched dejectedly their animated conversations, their bathing parties and their dancing. That I could not swim or dance, even if I were invited to join them, only underlined my solitude. I thought of Kem. I had not seen him for several months, had not even visited my mother since I had left the apartment, save for one fleeting visit, to bring her a chicken, some flowers and a box of truffled chocolates that had cost the best part of a week's salary. I had stayed only to drink a coffee and to share the scantest of news before hurrying back to the city and my lodgings. There had been no time to take a stroll around the neighbourhood, and Kem had not been conveniently present on the street leading down from the tram stop.

'So you've decided to give the Impressionists some attention?'

Her voice cut through the low hum of mumbled appreciation rising from the other visitors: this gallery was certainly more popular than the one in which I had first met her. She was standing beside my bench and from this vantage I could see that the grey flannel of her skirt ended mid-calf, above thick black stockings and sturdy black shoes. A bunch of keys hung from her hip, and the combined effect made her look like a gaoler, except for her smile. It was a smile as warm as any I had seen in weeks, warmer than any given me by my colleagues, even after the victory over von Boehmen.

'Is that what they are? And what impression are they supposed to make?' I wanted, it seemed, to give her a reason to stay, to explain her world, to share it with me, even if only this fragment of it. When she laughed, her hand came up to cover her mouth, her fingers forming a gate across her chin, her middle finger resting on the tip of her nose. It was not a laugh of derision, but of appreciation. She had liked my joke.

'Movement. The feeling of being among those people, the sense of their gaiety, more than a frozen representation of truth.' She was still smiling, uncertain if her explanation was necessary, if my joke had contained a serious question. And yet she continued, relaxing into the comfort of conveying her understanding to another. To me. *'There's something physical about them, something material, whereas the Expressionists, in the other room, are seeking to convey the inner life, rather than the material, outer world.'*

I wanted to ask about the movement on that street, the violence of the riot, the swirl and anger, but hesitated. I did not want to appear ignorant, or antagonistic, so instead I tried to change the flow of the conversation. *'This must be the most perfect work for you. The love you have for these paintings. Each day must feel like a privilege. Has it always been your passion? Art, I mean.'*

She tilted her head and studied me through narrowed eyes for a moment, before here face opened up.

'I suppose so. My parents have no time for it. They are practical people. But my mother was a teacher before they were married and, when I started to show interest, she did not discourage it. My father wanted me helping in the shop when not at school, but she would allow me to slip out, to come here. I spent my free time looking at these paintings. Just like you.' She smiled, and I felt the reach of communion across the years. She had sat on this bench, or one just like it, as I did now. She wanted, I thought, to share something with me, to find a bridge between our lives. And yet, while she had been studying art history at the university, I had been locked away in the library with books rather than pictures, oblivious to her presence. I felt a pang of regret that, despite occupying the same space at the same time, our paths had not crossed until now. I picked through my memories to try to locate an encounter, a trace of recognition of her face.

We talked for perhaps ten minutes, during which time she traced her path from student to curator, described her parents' home, where she still lived, and listed the pictures that moved her most. She became nervous, embarrassed even, when she talked about the sketches she made of city streets, and about her unrealised wish to make art herself. We moved on from the gallery of the Impressionists and meandered through other rooms. She pointed out canvases as we walked, her explanations of their meaning or quality momentarily punctuating our conversation, parentheses in the flow of family and dreams, until we found ourselves in the entry hall of the museum. I had by then told her a little about my own life, about my mother, about my lodgings, a little more about where I worked, if not what I did. She had asked if I too loved my job and I had answered emphatically, without reflection, with the private doubt catching me only when, with a smile, she confessed that she had little interest in politics herself.

'The machinery of it seems so...' Her mouth hung frozen around the vowel while she searched for the next words. *'...brutal, I suppose. Politics without regard for people, their wants as well as their needs, is a frightening thing, I think... You have to be allowed to dance, or else what is the point?'*

I recoiled a little, resentful at the apparent attack and conscious of my own limitations at the same time. She responded with a touch to my arm. I reassured myself that, as she had said, she paid little regard to such things and probably did not understand the matter fully. She smiled, satisfied that I had taken no offence. Then she gave her apologies, explaining that she had to return to her work, but said that she hoped that we could continue our conversation at another time. As I watched her walk back into the gallery, the warmth of her hand, warmth that lingered on my skin even after she had withdrawn it, brought a smile to my own face and I stood for a time staring into the space she had left behind.

At something of a loss, I paused once more, out on Constitution Square. The sounds of trams and motors, of clashing voices, spiralled upwards like warring butterflies, high over the gable ends of the grand buildings that surrounded me. Bright sunshine shed its warmth, suffusing me, echoing that of Judith's handprint. Most of Saturday remained to me, although I had little to fill it. I thought of Kem. There was time. I could catch a tram and be in the neighbourhood in less than an hour. I could find him and we could spend the afternoon by the stream, smoking cigarettes and talking about the past and about the future. That I no longer knew the shape of his present struck me as out of place. I did not know how he earned a living. I did not know if he had met a girl, if his parents were well, if he still lived in their modest concrete house. Those houses had been built to provide a permanent home for Kem's kin, to show them that their previously iterant lives were not all that they might aspire to. I had been very small when they had been constructed, and barely remembered the spaces that had existed before their creation. Kem remembered, I knew, or had heard enough from his family to feel as if he remembered. Sometimes he had talked about life before, often with a longing, with regret, but to me his settling in the concrete house was only a blessing. I would not have known him otherwise.

I thought again about taking one of the trams that squealed their way around the Square, then decided that the distance was too great. Instead, I turned and began to walk back into the city centre, towards a café at which a modestly priced meal could be secured. I resolved to buy a newspaper to read with my lunch.

Trust

I learned from the newspaper that accompanied my lunch on that Saturday that both the regional bank and the city's gas company had been taken into municipal ownership. My irritation that Garcia had not thought to tell me himself, given that I had undertaken most of the preparatory work for the move, was tempered by my amazement that the editor of the *Observer* had chosen to be so measured in his reaction.

There was no forthright condemnation. The complaints of the former directors of the businesses were acknowledged, but were reported simply as one minor opinion, the sour grapes of clearly biased parties. Those complaints were dwarfed by the effusive reporting of the Boss's predictions for cheaper lighting and the celebration of the end of profiteering. Despite my proximity to the matter, I read the front page as an outsider, amused by its toothlessness and sycophancy. I wondered at the tone and content of the conversation that had accompanied the dinner that Garcia and the Boss had had with the paper's proprietor weeks before.

The rest of the weekend, however, gave me time to dwell upon Garcia's failure to inform me of the announcement in advance, and my dissatisfaction gradually fermented into a caustic stew of resentment. I arrived at the office on Monday morning in a state of agitation. I paused in the darkness of the corridor, suddenly unsure of how I might react to Garcia's presence. I gripped the door handle to anchor myself before I entered

'Bloody hell, Anton. Did you know?' Georg's eyes darted about, hunting something. *'I mean, bloody hell. Bloody hell! This is so...'* He trailed off, aware once more of Ana's presence. I was relieved to see that Garcia's desk was empty. *'No, Georg, I was as surprised as you. More so, I suspect. I only finished that paper on Friday. It has all moved so...'* Ana was watching me as I slipped out of my coat, her eyes curious but without concern. She did not seem at all surprised.

The detail of the takeovers meant that a great deal of work had been done beyond my own efforts, work of which I had been quite unaware. It was clear that Ana had kept from me her own contribution, and much else besides. What I had assumed to be our alliance was no such thing; at least Georg and Garcia made no pretence. I was sullen in her company for several days, maintaining a resentful silence in the office. I was running out of people to trust. Were it not for my faith in the Boss, I might have become disheartened entirely.

'Have I done something to offend you, Anton?'

It was the end of the week following the announcement of the seizure of the bank and the gas company. I had been hunched over my desk, scratching numbers and words into my notebook, oblivious to Georg's departure, his slipping out to find lunch away from the stale atmosphere of the office. Garcia was in conference with the Boss once again. There had only been the sound of my scribbling and our breathing, the unignorable presence of Ana behind me pressing like water against a dam.

I did not respond for a moment. I was grateful to her for breaching the silence between us, and I welcomed the personal nature of the question. But I did not want to give an honest answer, without weighing the implications and so I did not reply at first. Only when my ongoing silence became more damaging to whatever trust remained between us than anything I could say did I put down my pen and turn to face her.

'Not offend, no. I... I'm a little put out that, after all the work I did, I only found out about the bank by reading the news in the paper. I suppose it hurt my pride. But I've been grumpy with everyone, not just you. I mean, I've barely looked at Garcia.'

She laughed through her nose and her pursed lips twisted into a smile. *'I know. And I'm sorry. I should have told you, given you some advanced warning. Your work was invaluable. I wouldn't have been able to sort out the details without it.'* She paused, as if weighing whether to divulge a secret, then proceeded. *'Garcia. He said I was to tell no-one, specifically mentioning you and Georg, and I...'*

My interruption surprised me even more than it did Ana.

'You mean Georg wasn't involved? Who did the legal preparation? You're more than capable of figuring out the economics, much more so than I, but you don't have the background in law.'

The question seemed to unsettle her for a moment but she recovered herself quickly, taking a cigarette from the packet on her desk and lighting it with precision. She offered one to me before answering, watched my hands fumble with it, smiling as it took me three strikes before I could coax the match into life.

'*There was no need. The precedent had been set. With the landlords.*' She qualified her assertion, as if suddenly unsure that I fully understood the implications of the meeting with von Boehmen. I felt patronised but nodded my understanding, unwilling to challenge her logic and thereby appear even more naïve. '*I am sorry. But you know what he's like.*'

I wasn't sure if she meant the Boss or Garcia, but again I simply nodded. I sucked at the cigarette and a fragment of tobacco became dislodged. Its bitterness filled my mouth, but I did not seek to extract it.

'*Of course. But I still don't understand why you were allowed in on the secret, when Georg and I were excluded.*' Before, with Joszef, the three of us had been treated as equals, even me, and we had treated each other as such, to Georg's irritation. But since Garcia had taken Joszef's place, Ana had increasingly been involved in a way that neither Georg nor I were. Ana was undoubtedly the better qualified, of course. But if it were named, if her pre-eminence had been made explicit, things would have been clearer, less cloak and dagger. She simply shrugged, as if helpless, unwilling to acknowledge the gulf between us.

'*I tell you what, Anton. I know that you can be trusted. Next time, I'll make sure to let you know what is happening, whatever he says. As long as you promise to keep it to yourself.*' She glanced meaningfully towards Georg's desk and waited for me to agree to the terms.

'*Have you spoken to him, by the way? To Georg? How is he?*' Deftly, she turned my resentment into guilt. No opportunity to sound him out had arisen since the evening when we had finished the last of Joszef's brandy. The pressures of work and my own sullenness had precluded it. '*No. But I will. I would imagine he feels similarly shut out of things, especially given that he was not even asked to provide legal advice.*'

She smiled, content with my assurance, and stood up. She reached an arm up towards the light, her fingers splaying like foliage rippling on an imagined breeze. Her head stretched first to the left, then the right, the release in her shoulders spreading through her. She did not resume her seat. Instead, she circled the desk, leant against it, her legs straightening towards me, feet crossed. The once-creases of her trousers led a fuzzy line from her shoes to her knees then dissolved entirely. One of her hands rested on the edge of the desk, white against the dark wood and the olive green of her cuffs. The other held her half-burned cigarette. Thus reclined, she seemed even taller.

'Anton, this is more significant that one man's pride.' Her eyes were fixed on me, alert to any self-regard that might creep into my expression. *'This, our work, is more important. Georg should understand that. That he may not is one of the reasons why he's not entirely trusted.'*

She brought the cigarette to her lips, drew slowly and evenly on its smoke. The crackling of the paper punctuated the momentary silence.

'That's not fair, Ana. He is undoubtedly proud, but he is committed to the project, at least as much as you or...' Her stare fell more heavily on me, despite the blue haze. *'I understand, Anton, and it is important that we trust one another. I know you both, so it's easier for me, but for Garcia, well, you're an unknown quantity. Georg, you. You were both recruited by Joszef and he's, uh... His reputation has suffered because of... things.'*

I kept my face passive, relaxed, containing the question wrestling for answers just below the surface: if not through Joszef, then how did she come to be here? Ana was seldom imprecise, and her self-omission felt pointed, almost like a threat. *'Anyway, that's not something you need to worry about. I will always vouch for you.'* Her smile alone would once have broken the tension in my shoulders, but even the touch of her cool hand on my wrist could not release me. I looked down toward the floor, so that she would have to guess at my discomfort.

The hand lingered for longer than it might, but eventually it was withdrawn at the sound of footsteps beyond the door. By the time Georg had bustled into the office, Ana was pacing back towards her desk, her cigarette forming curlicues around her effortlessly constructed complaints about the onerous tasks assigned her by Garcia. She even turned towards the door, with a look of consternation that only dissipated once she had determined that it was her colleague rather than the senior advisor that had entered. The ease with which she slipped into this confection was disconcerting.

'What's he done now?' There was a weary bitterness to Georg's question that almost masked his satisfaction that Garcia irritated others too. *'Not saying?'* He did not expect an answer and so he did not wait for one. Instead, he busied himself in the mundanity of hanging a coat and thudding into a chair; a shake of the head and a hand sweeping through his hair, leaving cropped tufts to make haphazard patterns, pointing to every corner of the room. *'Suit yourself.'* Once seated, his shoulders closed about him. He seemed diminished.

Ana must have been able to recognise the resentment as clearly as I could. It was not only Garcia that made Georg's time in the office uncomfortable. He had always been terse and stiff, but since Garcia's arrival, his arrogant self-satisfaction had twisted into animosity, animosity and… I could only describe it as fear, even though Georg had previously seemed so incapable of any such feeling. Only with me did he maintain his former cocksureness, and then only when we were alone in the office. He did not regard me as a threat, either to his intellect or his position, so he could be freer with me. But his superiority, and my resentment of it, had prevented me from concocting the conversation that Ana so wanted me to have with him. Rather than a lack of opportunity, I had avoided it for fear of feeling belittled by Georg.

21. Caffeine

Neither Ana nor Garcia were there when, a couple of weeks later, I slipped into the office a little later than usual on a drab Tuesday morning. I had slept badly; anxious dreams had pushed me towards wakefulness throughout the night and I had decided to spend a little longer over breakfast, for once accepting Mrs Kettmann's offer of a second pot to coffee. She had accompanied it with a fat slice of cake and some conversation about the weather and the price of eggs. I had resented neither.

The cake still sat heavily in my stomach when I arrived. The atmosphere was heavier still. Georg glowered at me as I entered, and I felt his eyes follow me to my desk. I settled uneasily into my chair, rifled through yesterday's documents searching for a point from which to resume my work. In busyness, I could pretend not to hear his sighing and muttering.

'Intolerable. Utterly intolerable!' I was unable to prevent myself from turning in my seat to face him, my curiosity provoked more by the helplessness in his voice than the defiance of his words. *'Have you seen this? Have you?'* He glared at me while a paper trembled from his outstretched arm. I struggled to focus on the shifting text, hoping that Georg would relieve me of the task by simply telling me what he felt I should know. He did not.

'I haven't, I'm afraid. Should I?' His exasperation exploded into a growling sigh and he slapped the document onto the desk. *'You can't simply keep turning a blind eye, time and again, refusing to see what's going on. For god's sake, Anton!'*

He was on his feet, pacing, fists clenched. I kept as still as I could, fearful that any movement would provoke him to violence.

'I know it's no secret that I had my doubts about the seizure of the gas company and especially the bank. Wrong targets, too soon. That's just tactics. But if you're going to do it, take that risk, then those enterprises should at least work more favourably for the people. The City shouldn't be profiteering like this!'

It made no sense. I wanted to challenge him, tell him that he must have misunderstood. It was impossible that the Boss would allow the City to profiteer. To suggest otherwise was just disloyalty. All of these words blurred through my head, and only my fear of his anger kept my mouth clamped shut. Instead, I rose to read the document on his desk.

It took me some time to assemble the memo's meaning and only at the third reading did its stark reality coalesce. According to the schedule of charges set out, interest rates and gas prices had been set higher than they had been when the enterprises were in private hands. I turned the page, seeking the rationale that would explain this apparent absurdity. There had to be a sound reason for the price rises: the memo came directly from the Office of the Mayor and it was signed by Andreas Hofmans himself.

'But, I... this doesn't make any sense. Georg, what does this mean? There must be an explanation. It's not possible.' My hands flapped open on the desk, palms upwards. Try as I might, I could not reconcile the two

truths that wrestled inside me. There must be something, some way to understand the numbers on the memo that was consistent with what I knew to be the justness of our project. Only Garcia's infidelity could explain the inconsistency. I looked pleadingly at Georg, but he simply stared at me.

'We should go out. We can't talk here. I know a place.'

We walked out of City Hall as discreetly as we could and headed off in silence, me trailing a little behind him, struggling to keep pace with his step. The city streets were busy but no more than usual, the bustle of lives played out under a damp dog sky. The shroud of drizzle that had settled on the streets some hours before dawn clung on, seeping into everything, frosting the sleeves of my coat.

I had not been to the café before, had not even known it existed, despite its proximity to the office. Georg had turned abruptly into a side street I had never noticed and led me through a low doorway into the yellow light of the room filled with people smoking and drinking coffee. At the counter, two men drank brandy wordlessly and I wondered if they were together or simply two strangers who both happened to need a drink this early in the day. I thought, despite myself, of Joszef.

A small table was free and Georg took a seat, shrugging off his coat so that it hung wantonly over the bent wood of the chair's back. Even before I had taken my place across from him, he had signalled to the waiter, raising two fingers to indicate his order. He was known here.

The cups arrived, clinking in their saucers against the tabletop. Georg exhaled. He cast a glance around the room, studying each of the faces within it. Only when he was satisfied that no-one was present who should not be, did he look at me. The mutter and clatter of the café swallowed

157

his question at first, but it finally reassembled itself and I sipped at the coffee while I considered my response. What did I think was going on? There was no simple answer to it. Since Joszef had gone, since Garcia had arrived, much had continued as before. And yet something had changed. Garcia. It had to be him. All else remained the same. My mouth opened to the first syllable of his name but I remembered that this conversation, now that it had finally arrived, was intended to sound out Georg, rather than to reveal my own unease.

'I don't know. Things have changed, since… But you, you have seemed more distant recently. Exasperated even.' The boldness of my observation scared me, and I hurried on in order that he would not have time to take offence. *'By which I mean that some developments, in terms of policy or of procedure, sit ill with you. Which is it? The policy? Or the way that things are done?'*

This framing pleased me. It was a professional question, asked by a professional. It could only be answered in those terms. I waited while Georg removed a fleck of tobacco from his tongue with the nail of his little finger, and waited again as he swallowed his remaining coffee.

'Can I trust you, Anton?' He drew steadily on his cigarette, but kept his eyes fixed on mine. He did not, however, wait for my response: the question was more a signal that what was to follow should not be shared. It seemed that he did trust me after all.

'To answer your question directly, I would say that it is impossible to separate the two. The change in the policy has created a change in the way things are done, and that change has shifted the policy. Round and round it goes, a spiral sinking into a deeper and deeper well. A cesspit. We are not yet there, Anton. But when we are all up to our necks in shit, remember that I saw this coming.'

The waiter was at my shoulder, two cups of fresh coffee pinched in the fingers of his left hand. The trace scent of cooking fat clung to the long apron tied about him. His presence startled me: I had not noticed Georg signalling this new order. He waited for Georg to pause before placing the cups before us and clearing away the cold, empty crockery.

'But...' My objection stuttered to a halt before it had begun and I took one of my cigarettes between my fingers. I watched it tremble as I lit it, unsure if the cause was anger or fear. He was looking at me with the hint of a smile; a slightly twisted smile. The thought occurred to me that his extravagant predictions were more a provocation than an honest reflection of his views. He was playing with me. A test, maybe.

'Let me ask you a question, Anton. Do you think that this would have occurred if Joszef were still advising the Boss? Would the City have seized the gas company, simply to put up prices?' His eyes were aflame, harsh; his fingers drummed on the tabletop.

'So you think that Garcia has come in and poisoned the thinking of the Boss?' I was grateful that Georg had confirmed my desperate hypothesis. Smoke from my cigarette curled above the table, hung there in blue-grey shreds.

His head was shaking, minutely, and he sighed, rubbed his hand across his chin, across his mouth. *'Do you think the change came about because Joszef left? Have you not considered, even for a moment, that Joszef had to be got rid of to allow the change to happen?'* The idea that the old man had been moved from the political office as a way to side-line him had, in fact, occurred to me, but only in terms of my low opinion of Garcia and his ambition. I had supposed that the then new political aide might well have advised the Boss to reassign Joszef so that his own position would be improved. That still seemed plausible, whereas Georg's idea struck me as far-fetched: as Chief Clerk to the Council, the old man would still have an influence, could still guide his friend and comrade against any wrong turn that the newcomer sought to take.

He was watching me, waiting for an answer. I had assumed that his questions had been rhetorical, that he would expand on his conspiracy in due course, but now it was clear that he expected a response. I knew that in giving one, I should offer little, simply invite him to share more of his own views. But his thesis troubled me, and darker implications lurked in the shadows of my mind.

'Is that what you think? That Garcia ousted Joszef so that he could push the Boss in a new policy direction? It's possible, I suppose, but it seems implausible. It assumes that the Boss lacks strength and, indeed, that he had too little loyalty to his old friend. He and Joszef had been close for so many years. Why would he abandon him so easily?' The burr of the café seemed to have stilled. I looked around me, expecting the attentive gaze of others, certain that everyone in the café had heard the thought before I had. I turned back to Georg, who was patiently waiting for the penny to drop. I refused to let it.

'Look, Anton...' He sighed, changed tack, exasperated by me. *'Have you considered why and how Garcia was appointed in the first place? Just think about that, and things start to fall into place.'* He smiled, the exasperation replaced by patience. *'Anyhow, I'm still the same as I was, warts and all. It's not me that has changed, I promise you. I'll stick around and do my job for as long as I think I can make a difference.'* He drew heavily on the remains of his cigarette, then crushed the stub into the crowded ashtray. He looked up with a frown. *'Look, I know I can be a little sour sometimes, and that it might seem that I don't think much of you. I apologise for that. I've always respected you, you know? You and your work. I think we're here for the same reasons. And you can trust me. Just be careful of the others. Joszef was a little*

too sure of his own invulnerability, in the end.' He stopped abruptly and drained the last of his coffee. *'We should head back, before we're missed.'*

It was unmistakably a smile. Not a sneer or a smirk, but an expression of open camaraderie. The coat slipped onto his shoulders, and his hat was retrieved from alongside the empty coffee cups. Contemptuously, some unwelcome flecks of ash were brushed aside from it and Georg's face resumed its more familiar composition. But it had definitely been a smile, however briefly held. I tagged along in his wake as we walked wordlessly back to the office, much as I had done on the way to the café some thirty minutes earlier. Yet something was altered, for good or ill.

It took just ten minutes to reach the office. Ana looked up quizzically as we entered, the arch of her eyebrow an eloquent substitute for any spoken enquiry. The clock showed that it was a quarter to ten. We had arrived late and together, damp from the outside air. We had failed to discuss how these circumstances might be explained, and this oversight struck me as catastrophically short-sighted. I told myself that there was no conspiracy, at least not one that could be clearly articulated, and yet I was profoundly grateful that Garcia was not at his desk as well.

Ana did not drop her gaze, which shifted only from Georg to me and back again in steady waves. She pursed her lips into a stifled smile. *'Is there anything I should know, boys?'* She was looking at Georg when she said this, studying his face for the flicker of a reaction. Georg turned to hang his hat and replied over his shoulder. *'Yes, Ana. It's raining.'* He shrugged off his coat and shook it gently, releasing a mist from its weave. Only then did he face her, mild exasperation his only visible emotion. With a sigh he continued. *'I hung around at home longer than usual, hoping it would relent, but no such luck. I suppose Anton felt similarly, but I haven't asked. Maybe he had a late night, I don't know. We've not exactly been chatty since we bumped into each other under the portico.'*

161

He was seated already, right leg crossed over his left knee. He inspected the condition of his shoe leather, the creases and droplets marking its surface seemingly of greater concern than Ana's curiosity. Bored, she turned to me, eyes wide, expectant; their invitation was irresistible.

'Actually, I just slept badly. Barely a wink. Even so, I couldn't get out of bed and, when I did, I took comfort too easily in my landlady's coffee and a large slice of fruit cake, and then some more coffee before, finally, walking in late just now.' Ana considered my explanation. Lacking Georg's ease with lying, I was pleased that I had been able, broadly speaking, to tell the truth, albeit with some omissions. Were we alone, there would have been no need for subterfuge. In fact, the truth would have put me in a better light, confirming that I had finally drawn Georg into my confidence. But things were as they were, and I was eager to reinforce my chosen account of the day's events and move the conversation onto other matters. *'I'm just glad that Garcia isn't here to see it. Where is he?'*

She rolled her eyes in exaggerated irritation. *'Who knows? Off hatching stratagems, no doubt. Did you hear anything, Georg? Did he mention his plans to you?'* Georg's laugh was as bitter as it was short, and he did not trouble himself to look up.

Decree

Garcia was already at his desk. Something about his smile, rare as it was, reminded me of something; something unsettling. Before the weekend, tension had rippled through the dead air of the office. There had been a meeting with the Boss and, when he had returned with Ana, he had scowled into the middle distance, leaving Georg and I to wonder what had been said. Later, when we were alone, Ana had confided that problems dogged the plans to make more affordable housing available to the city's workers. Several landlords had appealed against the confiscation of their property, taking their case to the courts, an institution over which we still had no control nor even influence. Due process was slowing our progress.

At the same time, the arrangement with Svankmajer had yet to produce many new homes. Money was not being turned into bricks and slates and Ana hinted that corruption was suspected somewhere in the company. Until this could be proven, we could do little despite our partial ownership of the firm. It appeared that we had been too triumphal, too soon. I should, Ana said, begin to think of alternative measures. The next election was still some time off, but without real progress being made, there were concerns that we would not be able to fulfil our promises to the city. The people would withdraw their trust.

I flipped through the scant notes I had made the previous week. Sketches, fragments of ideas, nothing more. My suggestion that we should simply take full control of the enterprise, as we had with the gas company, was immediately discounted by Garcia. With evident irritation, he had told me that that was not an acceptable solution in this case, and that I should work harder. Yet I had made no advances over the weekend, despite devoting my mind only to this. I unscrewed the cap from my pen, but its nib only hovered over the page, unwilling to do its work.

Ana's coat hung from the hat stand and her satchel sat obediently beside her desk. She was in the building, then, but elsewhere. My mind drifted to this puzzle, displacing the more pressing one before me. If she were with the Boss, then surely Garcia would also be in the conference. He did not relinquish his privileged access lightly. Instead of a smile, he would be wearing a look of thunder. Some other meeting then. With Svankmajer perhaps.

The door swung open and Georg bustled into the room. The heaviness of the previous week seemed to have lifted from him, too. I felt very alone.

'*Good morning, Anton.*' He paused to nod amiably to me. '*Garcia.*' He winked at me and I struggled to contain my surprise.

'*Late, I see.*' Despite the rebuke, Garcia's smile remained. '*Never mind. There's news. But it will have to wait until Ana returns. Anton, you should ring for some coffee.*' With that, he returned to his thoughts and the amusement they caused him. I raised my eyebrows fleetingly and walked over to the bell. No sooner I had rung it than Ana walked in.

'*Oh, hello Anton! I hope that means that coffee is on its way?*' She seemed energetic, and her smile was less measured than it often was. I asked if it had been a good meeting, since she seemed so cheery. Her answer was non-committal, as if surprised to be asked. In any case she was unwilling to say too much and turned to Garcia. '*Is it done?*' Garcia nodded, his own smile spreading ever more broadly. Ana released a small sigh and clenched her lips, taut across her teeth. '*So.*' There was nothing more.

Both Georg and I straightened in our chairs with unease, priming ourselves to react once we had a clue as to what had been done and what was about to happen. What had already happened, most probably, and without our knowledge. I looked from Ana to Garcia, but neither saw me; Georg simply glowered at his balled fists, his earlier levity crushed. Eventually, Garcia spoke, but he provided no information that was useful, only deepening the mystery.

'*So, Kelemen will be through presently with the documentation. A formality. The notices have already been dispatched. I trust Andreas will be pleased?*'

When the door inched open, all of us snapped towards it in anticipation, but it was the slight form of Miss Gelber with the coffee, rather than the bulk of the Boss's driver. She seemed startled by the attention and quickly left the tray, hurrying back into the darkness of the corridor, meticulously avoiding the eyes that followed her. Ana poured a cup for herself and took it to her desk, where she lit a cigarette. She did not offer one to me. I followed her gaze up into the shadows of the far corner of the room, hoping vainly for some illumination.

I heard the rattle of a cup in its saucer, the splosh of coffee carelessly poured, the soft pad of Georg's shoes, the pivot and the turn. He was pacing, furious. '*Enough of the melodrama, Garcia. What have you done? It really is utterly infuriating how you behave sometimes. And the rest of it.*'

There was no anger in Garcia's reaction, just more of that unnerving smile. He had no intention of revealing his hand before Kelemen arrived with the mysterious documentation. When the knock at the door came, Garcia's eyes did not leave Georg as he shouted for the visitor to enter.

Kelemen carried himself with an awkward dignity. In his hand were several copies of the freshly printed decree. It was the first decree issued by the City in its 600 years as a municipality, and I pondered on that small, historical detail as I skimmed over its content.

Flight

I did not sleep at all that night. Thoughts crashed through my mind like elephants in the jungle, tipping over any tranquillity that I might have been able to construct. The grey light, when it came, was a relief. I no longer needed to fight the urge to wakefulness. Instead, I could simply wait, calculating the duration of the remaining time before I could rise. The receding darkness left fewer corners in which my distress could muster.

When Kelemen had brought through the decree, it had been an oddity. A thing of potential disturbance, but nonetheless a curiosity. It had only been at my second reading of the short text that the reality of it formed fully in my consciousness. The City had ordered the confiscation of the houses of the Roma people. People like Kem and his family. My best friend, his mother and father, all of their friends and relatives, were to be evicted from their homes and returned to their travelling ways. This was to happen by the end of the following week, but public notices were not to be posted until the measures had commenced, so as not to alarm the families or provoke an unreasonable response from the Boss's opponents.

The tactical rationale was solid, but it was only Andreas Hofmans' signature at the bottom of the document that allowed me struggle to find the virtue in the decree itself. When the houses had been built just after the war, the Roma had been reluctant to take them on, preferring to maintain their traditional way of life. They had had to be cajoled and persuaded through the doors to the little block-built concrete houses and it was easy to see how, after less than one generation of half-hearted occupation, it could be assumed that they would be relatively easy to displace. The grown-ups probably still yearned for the open road in any case. With some effort, the decree could be seen as a liberation more than a confiscation.

Of course, the decree would be well-received by most of the city's inhabitants. The Roma were still viewed with suspicion and, twenty years on, some still rankled at the unfairness of their being given these modest dwellings. The confiscations, even were they to lead to forced evictions, would be popular. Perhaps more so. The decree would free up affordable housing for the people that needed it, but it would also signal a reckoning, some redress for faded resentments. The logic of it all was compelling, both practically and politically, but still the thought of Kem being evicted filled me with horror. I had felt nauseous throughout the remainder of the day and, going to bed without eating, I had wrestled with my conscience all through the night.

My turbulent conscience was, I knew, an indulgence. It was a luxury, and one that stood in the way of social progress. And yet, in the endless darkness of the night, it would not be tamed. My unease at the implications of the decree was joined by my guilt at my treatment of my friend since leaving the neighbourhood. Throughout the dark hours, the weight of this forgotten abandonment piled onto the newer abandonment, and bit into me deeply.

I set off from my lodgings before Mrs Kettmann had set the breakfast table, still unsure what I should do. I was propelled by the emptiness of the streets towards City Hall, dreading my arrival more than at any point during the months of my assignment. Not even Joszef's death had caused me such anguish and doubt. So I strode on, because there was nothing else for me to do.

The women from the northern districts were still sweeping the dust and dirt of the previous day from the gutters as I walked along the boulevard. Their faces bore the hardships of their lives in deep lines and bitter eyes, and they watched my progress with disdain. As always, I nodded a greeting to each, without expecting a response. They owed me nothing, least of all any portion of their scarce good cheer.

The blurred disk of the sun was only clearing the cupola of the cathedral by the time I crossed the old bridge and turned to continue along the embankment. Usually, I barely noticed my surroundings on this portion of the route. My head typically would by now be lost in the tasks of the day. Calculations and possibilities would spiral upwards in a stuttering dance above me, and I would lose myself within them. That day, however, the empty street and the grey flow of the river became endlessly fascinating. I found my pace slackening. I dawdled. Down in the water, detritus from all that the river had so far seen on its way down from the mountains jostled in the swollen current. It must have rained heavily somewhere upstream, for the river raged and foamed. I felt its anger and stared into its face. A child's lost doll, face down, raced by beneath me.

I had come to a complete halt by now. The air's chillness reached me and I shivered. A spasm of hunger joined it. The cathedral bell struck seven times. All the things of the material world announced themselves simultaneously and I felt a little as if I had only just now awoken, that I had been sleepwalking and my dream state had led me here, to the river's brink. I stared down into the slick greyness. Should I fall, my helpless body would be carried speedily away and all trace of me would vanish in minutes, like the doll. But while I was sure that its loss was still felt by the child that had once cherished it, I struggled to think of who would miss me. I tried to force out thoughts of Kem, to replace them with those of my mother, but that served only to remind me of my neglect of her too.

The clock chimed the quarter hour, and the world sharpened once again. I shook the melancholy from my head and censured my self-pity. There was work to be done and doubt could play no part in it. The Boss would not have put his name to a decree that harmed the people. I was simply too stupid to see it yet, but the plan was surely correct. It could not be otherwise, if Andreas Hofmans had put his name to it. Any alternative understanding would shake the foundations of the world beneath me. I unfastened my coat, goading the morning's cold, and walked briskly towards City Hall. I had nowhere else to go.

The stewards had not yet opened the heavy doors beneath the grand portico and I slipped in through the night entrance. No-one walked in the corridors, and no footsteps rang in the stairwells: I reached the office unseen. I hung my lonely coat from its usual hook and crossed to my desk. The inside air already made everything more solid. Understandable. I had been swamped by introspection; with the flick of a switch on my desk lamp, I chased off the last of it. I filled my chest and allowed a little smile to glimmer.

I flipped through some notes on my desk, but they had little consequence and held little interest. The accounts of Svankmajer's firm, delivered to my desk by Kelemen two days earlier without a word as to their provenance, swam before me. Garcia had instructed me to go through the figures to identify any anomalies that might indicate the presence of corruption within the firm. I had bristled at being treated like a simple bookkeeper and had secretly resolved to delay the work for as long as possible. The reason for the delays in building the promised new houses seemed obvious. Svankmajer had the City's funds now and he would undertake the contracted work at his leisure. Our stake meant nothing. Georg had raised his concerns with the laxness of the contract at the time, but he had been ignored. Garcia had been slapdash.

I looked at the door. It was silent, motionless, asleep. Cautiously, I padded over to it, rested my ear against it and, once confident that no-one was moving in the corridor either, I made my way to Garcia's desk. Rather than even pretend to slip through the columns of profit and loss at my own desk, I had decided that another, closer reading of the decree would help to put to death any lingering doubts I had about the redistribution of the Roma housing. The short text lay face up on Garcia's desk, where it had been left the previous evening. I stood close enough to read it, but with sufficient distance to claim otherwise should I be discovered.

There was an envelope on the desk, propped against the lamp. Its whiteness was dazzling, its edges crisp. It was utterly mesmerising, all the more so because Garcia's name was written onto it in Georg's copperplate script. The loop beneath the G was unmistakable. I took a step closer to the desk, drawn like a moth. By tilting my head to one side, I could see that the flap had not been sealed, had not even been tucked in. The triangle of paper hung perpendicular, careless, unconcerned by who should read the contents. A look back to the door, back to the loose flap. I held my breath.

The note slipped easily from the envelope and sprang open at its crease. I studied the page's edge, the margins, and the shape of the paragraph upon it. Only once all this was familiar to me did I begin to read. Despite the ever-present fear that the door would swing open, I read calmly, meticulously, ensuring that each word, each phrase, was thoroughly processed before moving on to the next. In this way I learned, through his four elegant sentences, that Georg had resigned his position and left the city.

My hands trembled as I returned the note to the envelope, careful to place it just as it had been left, in case this was some elaborate test of loyalty being played out by Garcia. And yet, as I returned to my own desk and took up my seat, I could only think of what it meant. It could not be a simple coincidence that Georg had chosen to flee – for fleeing was what this appeared to be – on the day that the decree had been concluded. Georg's doubts about some of the changes that had occurred since Garcia's arrival were no secret of course, but the full extent of his apparent fear when he had spoken about Joszef's sense of security struck me as I considered the actions of my colleague. My former colleague.

Sitting at my desk that morning, my knee moving like a piston on an express train, I felt fear for the first time. I tried to quell my anxiety by staring at the columns of Svankmajer's accounts, then gave up and crossed to where the coffee bell stood on the little table. As I rang it, too many times, I studied Georg's desk. Everything was as it usually was, all perfectly normal. There were no clues. Georg had vanished without trace.

Betrayal

Garcia raged when he found the letter. For two hours, he unleashed the wrath that Georg's faithlessness and cowardice had provoked. Sometimes his anger would abate a little and he would assert that we were better off without him, but this dismissal of our former colleague did not convince even Garcia and soon he was raining vitriol upon Georg's name once more.

I shrank into myself, unwilling to do anything that might provoke further rage or, worse, draw it onto myself. I cast the occasional glance at Ana for reassurance and solace, but otherwise I remained immobile and silent. Eventually, the storm subsided and, after another hour, Garcia calmed a little. Ana judged that it was safe to talk at last and the speculation began. Unforgivable it may have been, calamitous as it may prove to become, but Ana wanted to understand the reasons for Georg's departure.

'The decree of course. It can be nothing else. But what about it? He was never a sentimental person.' The question hung on the air and Ana became lost in her thoughts. She seemed to fade briefly, to become simultaneously substantial and ethereal. Watching her, I tried to follow where her question led, but quickly lost the trail. This meant that I did not see the tightening of Garcia's expression. His outburst came without warning.

'*Because he's a coward! Always was. No stomach for the fight. This...*' He waved his hands about the room, maybe indicating the office, maybe the world, '*....this was never serious to him. He was a dilettante, just like Joszef. His body will also end up in some alley somewhere, his throat slit. It will be no more than he deserves!*' The hands, suddenly lifeless, slapped to the desk in front of him, sending an empty cup to the floor. The sound of its shattering punctuated his verdict. I thought I had understood something of Garcia, but this flailing, animalistic urge to bloody revenge surprised me.

'*You. You were close to him. What do you know? I know that you are also unhappy with the mayor's decree.*' Garcia was looking directly at me, his eyes as cold as his tone. My mouth hung open, dry, empty. It was not clear whether he expected me to reply, or if this statement was simply another verdict. Dumbstruck, my mouth continued to hang open, until Ana's voice cut through the roiling silence.

'*That's unfair, Roberto. None of this is easy, for any of us.*' Her tone was level, calm, like a school teacher gently reprimanding a volatile child. '*And you know that Anton is the childhood friend of one of them. This measure will have special difficulties for him.*' I twisted uneasily in my chair, conscious that my friendship with Kem may already have become a weakness. '*As for Georg, I don't think he was especially close with any of us. Unless, of course, he did share some confidences with you? Anton?*'

Her emollient smile did not soothe me. She had used his first name, with such ease, with such familiarity. Roberto. It hadn't occurred to me that Garcia might have a name other than Garcia. And yet Ana knew it and felt comfortable enough to use it without a thought. I felt the searchlight find me in the darkness, picking out my solitary form. Despite the smile, Ana's quiet question was simply a softer extension of

Garcia's interrogation, and it left no scope for denial. I bowed my head as if at the confessional.

'He invited me to coffee. Once. It was the only time we talked socially and, even then, it was about work. He wanted to know if I shared his concerns with the direction of some of the policy. Some of the practice too. I didn't challenge him, just let him talk and we left it there. He was vague, otherwise I would have said something at the time. Ana was here when we got back from the café.' I looked pointedly at her, to underline that this was her cue to corroborate my story.

'Oh, that was where you'd been? You did look uneasy with him. I thought it was just because you were embarrassed. Because of what I said.' She blushed, almost at will, then looked to Garcia. *'Believe me, I saw them. There was nothing conspiratorial about them, and I was watching for any signs.'*

Garcia watched her for a moment, scrutinising her testimony. A small smile broke on his face and his eyes widened a fraction.

'He should have said something sooner.' He was stern, although traces of his smile clung to his face, but I felt like a child under the weight of his rebuke. *'We might then have been able to isolate the problem, deal with it. Instead, we have a loose cannon at large. Who knows where that might lead?'*

We found out two days later. At around half past ten in morning, the newspapers arrived from the Capital. As always, they sat unread for a time on the table where coffee was served and it wasn't until that had arrived that events crashed into the office. Garcia had gone to fetch a cup, and scanned the front pages, one by one, until the third paper caused him to freeze. He stared in horror as he read the leading story.

He took his coffee and the paper back to his desk. He drank in silence while the colour drained out of him and onto the page. An anger was rising in him that, while quieter than that provoked by Georg's note, was deeper and more genuinely frightening. I watched him read, conscious that Ana too had stopped her work to do the same. Both of us waited, apprehensive yet curious.

'The rat! He has betrayed us, the worm! There!' He was stabbing the page with his index finger, as if by that action alone we would be able to divine the contents of the article. Or maybe he was speaking only to himself, livid and beside himself with rage. *'Puta!'* Something cut through the anger then, and he froze again, this time in terror. Without another word he rose and made for the door. He was practically running by the time his hand touched the handle and I could hear the rapid thud of his feet as he disappeared into the corridor. Whatever the paper revealed on its front page needed to be couched gently if it were not to unleash an even more dangerous rage.

Ana exhaled her relief. For a while, she sat staring at the newspaper that still lay across the room on Garcia's desk. I stared just as intently at her. Eventually she stood, smoothed the creases across the front of her trousers and lit a cigarette. *'Coffee?'* She didn't wait for my grunted answer before setting off across the office, pausing beside Garcia's desk. She glanced down with as little interest as she could bear, then froze.

'Oh my god. They've got the story on the redistribution of the Roma houses.' She looked at me, ashen. *'It's brutal. Damning.'* She flipped the page and drew in a mouthful of smoke. She read on for a few moments more and jolted to a halt, a motor car slamming into a wall: the smoke lay unmolested in her chest until instinct expelled it with a cough. She looked at me again, aghast, her mouth ajar.

'Anton, he describes him as 'dangerous', a 'tyrant in the making'. How could he?' She wanted me to share her horror at whatever was written in the paper, but since I could not fathom who was describing who in those terms, it was not easy to feel the outrage evident first in Garcia and now in Ana. In the end, I could only offer my upturned palms in query.

'Georg. He's quoted. Must have given them the entire story. Now I understand the look on Garcia's face.' She drew again on the cigarette. Smoke rolled from her nostrils as she shook her head. *'This is bad. Very bad.'*

The course of Georg's flight became clear. Incensed by the decree, he must have set off on the late train to the Capital, either seeing an opportunity to take his revenge or to seek safety. Maybe both. Arriving late in the night, he had first to find a place to stay, maybe with a relative or an old university friend. Then, in the morning he had made his way, fully cognisant of the implications, to the offices of the newspaper and shared confidential material with the enemies of the administration. With the enemies of the Boss. And then he had gone home, or to a café, and got on with the business of remaking his life, without regard to the impact of his words and deeds. Whatever fear he had had for his safety before was now more than justified.

Two days earlier, I had found Garcia's verdict of betrayal overblown and unwarranted. Georg was no dilettante and no snake, I had decided. He had taken the work seriously, and had not been playing a game. The decree had simply been the final straw, another policy with which he disagreed, concocted without his knowledge and then sprung upon him. Georg had been fearful before; whatever the grounds for that fear, the decree could only have compounded it. His flight, in its own terms, made perfect sense and it seemed entirely plausible that it had been executed in good faith and for honourable reasons. But running to the paper, decrying the administration, struck me as abhorrent. Only one small piece of the puzzled refused to fit.

'Wait. Who does he describe as a tyrant?' When Ana had read out the quotations, I had assumed that they referred to Garcia, so closely did the terms match my own estimation of the man. But as the words filtered through the chalk of my mind, it seemed impossible. No-one would know or care about a faceless apparatchik in a provincial municipality. The paper would not have reported the abuse, no matter how well warranted, as it was of no interest to its readers in the Capital. Only the Boss himself would have sufficient renown there to be cited in a story about the city. My blood began to chill.

The door was flung wide and a fuming Garcia stalked through its frame. He glowered first at me, then at Ana, who still stood over his desk, cigarette smouldering in a cocked hand. Behind him, just visible, the bulk of Kelemen lurked in the doorway, waiting for something to break. Ana held his gaze, as if daring him to rebuke her, so he turned back towards me.

'Well, your friend has caused all of hell to open. Andreas is understandably disappointed. Disappointed. He can't understand how this was allowed to happen, and nor can I. Once we've cleaned up the mess, there will have to be a reckoning.' He was across the room now, fists drilling into my desk as he loomed over me. I watched his knuckles whitening, felt his hot breath on my head. *'But for now, ideas.'* Without asking, he reached for my cigarettes and took one; he patted his pockets and finding no matches, snapped his fingers in front of my face until I offered my own, which he snatched without a word.

'Roberto, it isn't the boy's fault. You are not thinking straight.' The name again. The shock of it almost smothered the shame I felt at her reducing

to a mere child. I looked at her, stony-faced, and for the first time she saw that her soft smile and gentle eyes were not enough to lighten my heart. The tiniest twist of her mouth pinned the unexpected reaction as something to attend to later. She turned back to face Garcia. *'What does he say? I bet he's incandescent.'*

Garcia idly struck my matches, watching them flare, sputter and die, before discarding the smoking stalks in the ashtray. *'You can imagine. But it's worse. They're sending that bloody envoy back.'*

'Von Boehmen? That's not so bad. We danced rings around him last time.' She took the matches from his hand and he complied meekly. She took one to light a new cigarette, then threw the box back to me, with a wink. Garcia stiffened, became terse.

'It's not play time anymore. Von Boehmen is to be accompanied by a detachment of the Federal Guard.'

Soldiers. The Government was sending its soldiers to the city. That hadn't happened even during the strikes. The local militias had been enough to put down the unrest then. A detachment of guards. Only about 50 men, but that would be enough, should von Boehmen's orders be to remove the Boss from his office. I joined the others in silent smoking.

Ana watched me with a look of concern, her eyes haunted. The weight of the situation bore down on me, as it did on the others, but I also felt the burden of suspicion. I was already seen as unreliable, a potential associate of the treacherous Georg. My association with the Roma made me even more suspect in Garcia's eyes, no matter what reassurances Ana made on my behalf. The thought of Kem shook loose an idea from the swirl within my head, an idea that might allow my weakness to become a strength. One that might allow me to regain the trust of my colleagues, and of the Boss.

'When is he due to arrive?'

Garcia looked at me with curiosity as much as irritation. *'Friday. Why?'*

'I have an idea. Can you spare me for the rest of the day?'

Redemption

The day was brighter than I had expected. The drab interior of the office had hidden the gaiety of the city beyond. With an even stride, I walked through streets filled with people without cares, their levity only increasing the gravity I felt. I sought solace in the feeling of being useful and, through usefulness, of being of value. As a boy, when I ran errands for my mother, the feeling of being useful gave me a degree of importance that otherwise eluded me. Back then, usefulness had seemed like the highest ambition it was possible to hold; as I slipped through the sunlit streets that afternoon, I was carried by the importance of my mission. Before long I left the city centre and headed into my neighbourhood for the first time in months.

The people of the neighbourhood had long since started their days elsewhere: in factories, in shops and in offices. The familiarity of the streets was strained by their relative emptiness, as well as by the time that had elapsed since I had last visited. At each corner, the view appeared as a well-thumbed photograph, more memory than living thing. I had been away too long. The walls of the houses rebuked me for my faithlessness. At the crossroads, I thought for a moment about taking a detour up to the tenement, to pay my respects to my mother, before I remembered that she would be at work, busy at the factory. I was grateful that my errand did not have to be delayed. I turned down the shallow hill towards Kem's house.

The door trembled at my knock. Three short raps. Brisk. Business-like. In other times, I would never have knocked at this door. Most often, I would simply have waited in the street until Kem appeared, as if summoned by my mere presence. If he didn't appear, I enjoyed the unspoken freedom of the kitchen door and would wander inside unbidden, to take a seat by the table, completely at home. While I waited for him to emerge, Kem's mother would shout upstairs and fetch me a glass of water from the pump over the sink.

For a time, the house was silent. While I waited for signs of activity, I straightened my tie. My fingers became caught between the world in which a tie was normal and the world where it was an absurdity. I felt a flicker of disorientation, no longer certain which world, which me, was the real one. I span slowly in this fog until the thump of feet on floorboards reminded me of myself and I dragged my thoughts back to the task ahead of me, into the clarity of the present. By the time Bireli Haluska swung open the door, I was crystalline.

He was a stocky man, topped by a thicket of dark hair. Flecks of dirty grey peppered the temples and his close-cropped beard, and I felt the pull of memory and the passing of time. His sharp, clever eyes peered out at me, unsure at first of who had disturbed his lunch. Only slowly did my features assemble themselves into something recognisable to him.

'Anton? Anton, my lad…' He paused and looked at me again, perplexed. His confusion had turned to joy and back to confusion in an instant. *'What..? Why so formal, Anton? Such a fine suit.'* He reached out a hand to feel the quality of the cloth at my coat collar, but pulled it back, unsure if such familiarity was still appropriate. *'My apologies.'*

I wanted to tell him that he had no need to apologise, but the stiffness of my shirt restrained me and the necktie trapped the warmth and ease of my words in my throat. It was more than the clothes, of course. He too was dressed in a white shirt and tie, as he always was. His dark green waistcoat was buttoned closely, the familiar watch chain looping across it, linking the present and the past. I had never seen him take the timepiece out of its pocket. No-one had. There was even some doubt that he owned a pocket watch at all, if you listened to the malicious rumours. I thought of the times that I had watched Joszef take his own timepiece from his waistcoat pocket to check the passing of time and wondered why I had not recognised my friend's father in him until now.

Bireli Haluska had no menace about him, despite his solidity. He was one of the most respected men of the community, *de facto* leader to the city's Roma. His authority came from his good heart, his honesty and his ability to make peace between feuding parties. He had taken to me, his son's friend but also an outsider, with the optimism of one who believes in the possibility of change: a hopefulness that the divisions between our respective communities might come to an end. And he had been one of the first to argue that the Roma should see the new Government houses positively, even though he too felt the loss they entailed. It was this willingness to overcome rancour, to see the positive in change, that had brought me to his door. I remembered the reason for my visit.

'Mr Haluska...' His eyes immediately clouded at the offence of my formality. '... Bireli.' I raised a little smile of reassurance. '*I'm afraid I'm here on business. I apologise for disturbing your lunch.*' The words felt fragile in my mouth, and their snap and shatter set off a tiny spasm in my shoulders. I did not understand why this was proving so hard. I chose a less direct route to my goal. '*Is Kem here or is he out about his business? I had hoped to find him at table with you and Mrs Haluska.*' I smiled what I hoped would appear to be a relaxed and affectionate smile.

'Oh, he's about somewhere. I can't keep track of him these days. Mind you I never could, with the two of you flitting all over the place as you pleased.' I smiled at the recollection of a time when, unaware of the ticking of clocks, we had ranged through the neighbourhood free of the gravity that sucked at my feet these days. With a silent sigh, I forced my childhood back down and reminded myself of the reason for the house call. I felt my smile smear at the corners. *Come in, Anton. There is coffee in the pot.*

The kitchen echoed with the sounds of clanking pans and half-heard murmurs, blurring the years. The sense of being two things at once returned. Kem's mother fussed by the stove, while his father took up a chair across the table from me, fingers laced in front of him. I wanted to linger in my contentment but his expectancy pulled me back to my task.

He listened politely while I spoke. Throughout, his face betrayed neither anger nor anxiety. He simply heard me out, as if the merest inflection of an eyebrow would distract me, would cause me to falter. When I had finished speaking, he sat silently for a little while. His wife had left the kitchen at some point and there was no sound other than the crackle of his beard, which he rubbed thoughtfully with his right hand; his left drew calculations, the thick fingers sketching mysterious patterns on the tabletop. Slowly, he began to nod, pushing spent air through flared nostrils

And you, Anton. What do you think?

The gaze of Bireli Haluska shone like the sun, leaving no shadows in which to hide. Under its glare I found that I wanted to tell him that I simply didn't know. Moral certainty collapsed under the weight of his good intentions. He wished me no harm, did not seek to catch me out or ensnare me. He did not seek to test me. He simply wanted an opinion. My opinion. One that he valued.

184

'I think your intervention would be very helpful, Bireli. It would stop the Government's emissary in his tracks, turn the troops on their tail, have them hurrying back to their barracks in the Capital. You know what soldiers mean for people like you. Like me.'

I paused, raising my coffee cup to my lips to drown the nausea rising in my throat. I had lied before of course, but this was not so much a lie. I might be speaking the truth, for all I knew then. It might help. The course of action I had proposed might very well be the best course of action available. I might have proposed it in good faith. No, it wasn't what was being said that was a lie, but the person that was saying it. My conscious calibration of the words, my callous exploitation of his friendship, sickened me, all the more because I knew that he trusted me and would not weigh my words as he would those of a door-to-door salesman.

And then there was the actual lie, the last and riskiest part of my manipulation. The myth that people like Bireli Haluska and I might be the same. Even before, as the son of a factory worker, living in a rotten tenement in the same neighbourhood as he and his friends, I had been aware of the difference between us. Neighbours did not look down on me simply because of who I was. To claim affinity now, when I lived within sight of the grand boulevards in the city centre, when I worked at a desk, in a tie, in the office of the most important man in the city, was galling. And yet, I compounded the insult by reaching my hand across to his in communion.

'I'm a simple man, Anton. I am not made for audiences with government emissaries.' His eyes softened, became plaintive. *'And I would need to talk to some of the men first. If I knew I had their support, things would be easier.'*

His bashfulness and probity should not have surprised me. He would of course want to refer to the community before he spoke on their behalf, especially on something of such importance. With his words, he would be evicting his neighbours. To do so without their consent would be unimaginable. And yet it was what I needed him to do. It was what I demanded.

'Bireli, of course. I understand. But there is simply no time. The emissary is on his way. I need your word now that you will speak in favour of the policy. You know the minds of your neighbours. You know that they have never really settled in these homes. You yourself had to persuade them that they should accept their confinement. Now at last you have the chance to release them.' My stomach tightened. I sensed that my rhetoric had exceeded its limits. I was no speech maker and in any case the kitchen of my childhood friend was no place for speeches.

Kem's mother swept into the room, uninterested in our conversation, anxious only to ensure that our cups were full and no mess was being made. Bireli Haluska watched her, and I was grateful that for a brief time his eyes were elsewhere. I felt my shoulders slacken a little and the chair creaked with the slackening. Behind me, Vadima Haluska moved silently but I could trace her busy progress in Bireli's eyes and I wondered what messages the two of them where exchanging.

When she had gone, he spent several minutes studying his hands. I too looked at them, hoping that the ridges and tufts would provide me with some omen as to my success. I discerned nothing and returned my attention to the familiar face. The past seemed very distant now, the future also. There was only this endless present, hanging silently at the centre of a concrete box.

'Are you sure, Anton, that this is for the best?' He looked tired, the whole weight of his life suddenly upon his shoulders. *'If you say it is, then I will believe you. I know you mean us, me, no harm, but if there is any trace of doubt within you, you must tell me.'*

The open warmth came easily to my face, and the ease shocked me. I did not even blink. *'I have no doubts, Bireli. Andreas Hofmans is a good man, you know that. He comes from this very neighbourhood. You've known him for years. He is trying to do what is best for the city and all of its people. He would not propose such measures if he did not know that they were for the best.'* As I spoke, the conviction grew within me that this was in fact the truth. I could not believe that Andreas Hofmans, even with Garcia whispering in his ear, could be in error. The conviction spread into a reassuring smile, of a kind that made it inconceivable that Bireli Haluska could retain any doubts of his own.

Once he had agreed and made his promise to present himself at City Hall on Friday morning, I stood, looking about me for my coat. He too rose from his chair but with a look of confusion. *'Won't you wait for Kem? He should be back in a while, and I know he'd like to see you.'* The idea had already passed through me, but the thought of meeting my old friend filled me with dread. I would not be able to carry the mask in his company for long; under his brown-eyed gaze I feared that whatever conviction I had summoned up would crumble and I would have to construct another edifice of sincerity. I simply could not. I had already twisted through his father's affection for me, and that was enough for one day.

'No, I really ought to get back to the city. I have already been away from my desk too long.' I pulled a sleeve over my left arm. *'Actually, Bireli, it might be best if you didn't mention this matter to anyone before Friday, including Kem. Just in case.'* I did not want to elaborate on what the

case might be. I wanted, above all, to protect him from any complicity should his neighbours, should his son, not see the benefits of the decree's enactment. But Bireli's anxious expression compelled me to continue. '*In case nothing comes of it. Either way.*'

Guilt

I was pleased that I did not see Bireli Haluska on that Friday morning. In fact, to ensure that there was no possibility of a chance encounter with him, I hid – there is no better word for it – in the office alone all day. While this meant that I had to go without lunch, I was pleased not to have to shake his hand or look into his eyes. When Ana and Garcia eventually returned to the office, they were in high spirits. Von Boehmen and his detachment of Federal Guards were already heading back towards the Capital.

'Your Roma played his part admirably.' There was an edge of condescension to Garcia's voice, but this was swallowed by his own self-satisfaction. *'Whatever objections that stuffed shirt had to our plans collapsed in the face of the whole-hearted consent of the very people affected. To watch his pomposity deflate again was delicious.'* He laughed and I felt a twist of regret not to have witnessed the victory for myself.

'Anton, Mr Haluska was dignified and compelling. It was a pleasure to meet him. He asked after you, by the way. He had hoped to see you, I think.' Her eyes scanned my face for a moment, searching for some trace of an explanation for my elusiveness during the day, but soon her interest moved onto other things. *'How on earth did you convince him to make such a declaration?'*

'I just explained the facts of what we are trying to do. The Boss comes from the same neighbourhood as Bireli and I. We know whose side we are on.' I shot a pointed glance at Garcia, but he paid no attention to me. Apparently satisfied with his work for the day, he had begun to push a stack of papers into his briefcase. The corners of the documents snagged at the opening, trying to resist their insertion. Oblivious, Garcia pushed harder until the twisted and creased pages collapsed into the bag.

'Well, I have an appointment.' He snapped the case shut, paused, and looked up. *'Oh, and Ana, before I go, do remember to task someone with finalising the sites for the camps. Maybe not Anton. He might be too close to the issue.'*

With that, he collected his coat and slipped out into the gloom of the corridor. Once his footsteps had faded into silence, I breathed a heavy sigh of relief, my eyes still locked onto the door. The sound of her laughter behind me was unnerving. I turned in my chair to face her.

'So, it went well then? The meeting?' She nodded a modest smile and grunted her confirmation. *'Good. Glad I could be of use. Bireli is a good man; bringing him in was a good idea, no?'* I paused to take a cigarette from my carton; a moment of hesitation and then I was on my feet, offering one to Ana. She took it with a nod and allowed me to light it for her. Leaning on her desk, I let a slow stream of smoke loose into the greying light before continuing. *'That said, I'm surprised it went off so easily. What did he mean, by the way? About sites for camps?'*

Ana looked at me once more with searching eyes. The tip of her tongue traced her bottom lip while she considered how or whether to answer my question. The cigarette smouldered between the fingers of her left hand, resting on the desktop. With a small gulp, the decision was made and she began.

'You were right to be sceptical. There was a hitch. After your friend had left, von Boehmen set out his conditions. That's what took the time this afternoon. We had to hammer out a lot of details.' She seemed uncertain, as if she expected that what she was about to say would land badly with me; as if she cared that it might. *'You know that those houses were built because the Government didn't approve of nomadic citizens wandering about, avoiding taxes, avoiding schools? They thought it inconsistent with the modern state we're supposed to be. Well. They still feel the same way.'*

I wrestled with her words alone for a few moments before I managed to wring out their meaning: von Boehmen had agreed to allow the City to redistribute the houses currently occupied by the Roma, but still expected the families to be settled. The perfect logic of the situation crystallised into awful clarity.

'Camps?' Her eyes dropped away from mine and she seemed to contemplate her cigarette for an eternity. The crooked stack of grey ash now made up a full third of its total length and it hung there, precarious, until gravity did its work and the tipping point was reached: the ash collapsed onto the desktop and turned to dust. Still Ana did not move, did not seem to breathe.

'It's alright, I'm not angry. I understand. I think.' But camps? Bireli and Vadima Haluska, Kem too, were to be rewarded for their trust in me with a patch of ground somewhere outside the city. Canvas to protect them from the winter's cold. Despite my denial, eddies of anger spun through me. I did not understand. This was not what I had promised Bireli, in so far as I had promised him anything. Incipient tears burned behind my eyes.

'Ana?' She still would not look at me. The lamplight spilled from her desk but never quite displaced the darkness of the floor. It must have been

191

evening by then and I had barely noticed the passing of time. It seemed an eternity since either of us had spoken. *'Ana, please. Tell me what sort of camps von Boehmen has in mind.'* I only wanted her to confirm my worst fears, fears that had already numbed me.

'Shall we get some of Joszef's brandy?' The sound of her voice startled me, as if I had been awakened from a dream. Not only the sounds, but also the words seemed incongruous, intrusive, as though I had slept through acres of time, existing on another plane. The mention of Joszef's name intensified the sense that the last weeks had simply been imagined. Something solid settled and the past few minutes became simply that. I shook my head. *'We can't. We drank it, remember?'*

Ana smiled, cautiously. *'That would be to assume he only had the one bottle. Always prepared was our Joszef. Almost.'* Her correction jagged the image of his slit throat from my subconscious, but Ana had set off across the room before she could see me wince. I waited, anxiously drawing on a newly lit cigarette.

From the third drawer of the filing cabinet, she pulled a bottle of brandy and brandished it hopefully. Despite myself, I returned her smile. She held out a glass of cognac and sat beside me on the edge of her desk. Our glasses clinked and we drank the first brandy down.

'So, the camps.' She tapped out two cigarettes and offered one to me; I stubbed what was left of the one I was smoking and accepted it, along with the flame cupped in her hands. *'They'll be comfortable. There's to be running water, sewerage, power even. Over time, I assume that the inhabitants will be able to build more substantial dwellings.'* She inhaled heavily and released the smoke as a sigh. *'But the inhabitants will have to stay living in the camps. There won't be guards as such, but if they repeatedly seek to move on, that's something we'll have to consider.'*

I said nothing. There was nothing to say. I had already imagined the details they had discussed with von Boehmen and, while it was as bad as I had feared, it was no worse. As soon as the word had been spoken, I had already known that I would never be able to happily visit my neighbourhood again, that Bireli Haluska would never trust another person again, that Kem and I would never sit easily together again. With the force of an electric shock, I realised that I would never see my friend again. The long slow fracture that began with the commencement of my studies had finally, irrevocably ruptured. There was no way back.

'Anton, we don't want to do this. You know that, surely? It's simply that we don't have a choice. The Capital have left us with no other choice.' Her hand rested gently on my shoulder. Her touch startled me, but I accepted its warmth. There was precious little comfort to be found elsewhere. I had made my choice, even if I had not acknowledged the full implications of the decision until then. The bargain with the Capital, the necessity of the course that we had taken, was beyond the control of anyone, even Andreas Hofmans. The price had been set for us by others. We had only to maintain our courage in the face of it.

'Did the Boss argue against it, even though he knew he had no choice?' My hopeful question fluttered up into the darkness. I could not see Ana's face, but I felt her hand tense on my shoulder. It was only the merest flinch, barely a breath, but it was undeniable. She drew on her cigarette and, in the orange glow of it, I could make out the shape of her eyes, watching me.

'Of course he did, Anton. You should know that, without having to ask.'

I looked down, trying to avoid her scrutiny. Even then, even after the sacrifice I had made, that Bireli had made on my behalf, I was still seen as potentially suspect, even by Ana.

'*Of course, of course, I don't need to ask, you're right. The Boss wouldn't sell out the people like that. I know. It's just...*' I wanted to stop, to keep the next thought in my head but it was insistent, would not stay quiet. '*... it's just, well, Georg, before he, uh, left, he noticed something, pointed it out to me. About the bank. The rates are higher, you see. Higher than they were. Before. Before we took control. And the schedule of charges, the schedule setting out what people will pay, those higher rates, it's signed by the Boss himself. And I don't understand...*'

I had stumbled into silence, my tongue tied. I had said too much. I had displayed my doubt, my faithlessness. I knew that there must be a solid reason for the rates being what they were and I should not question it. And yet I had so many questions, so many uncertainties, all set loose by the news that there were to be camps. Too many things made too little sense. I longed for the return of the certainty that I had been able to rely on, the certainty that Andreas Hofmans was the source of our salvation. Of my salvation.

'*Anton...*' Ana sighed the last syllable of my name. A pause followed, then I heard a deep inhalation of tobacco smoke; another pause, then I could see the long stream of smoke pour into the pool of light cast by the desk lamp. Another breath. '*Anton... Georg was already paranoid by then. You should have asked me, I could have set your mind to rest straight away. You shouldn't have let Georg infect you with this nonsense. If ever you have doubts, or don't understand something, always come to me.*' She rested her hand on my shoulder again. I felt its weight but not its warmth. '*Anyway, it's a temporary measure. The money is needed to finance the social programmes, as you know. And most of the fees will fall on the middle classes. I've done the analysis myself, trust me. And when we can, we will reduce the fees, the rates. It's just a stage we need to go through to achieve our aims.*'

I imagined that she would be wearing her most beatific smile, but she was still wrapped in darkness and I did not look at her in any case. I only knew that her reassurance could not tamp down the sourness in my mouth. That her explanation did not explain the price of gas only intensified my unease, but I merely nodded. I had already said too much.

Vertigo

The night passed, but it did not do so pleasantly. Wakeful hours were punctuated by fretful dreams. Every time I woke, the face of Bireli Haluska stared back at me until it faded into the blackness. All too slowly, the black night turned to grey dawn and then the sun cut through the curtains, like a blade reaching across the floorboards. It nagged at my pillow but, despite its insistence, I refused to rise. It was Saturday. I had no reason to be in the world.

Toward ten o'clock, hunger overcame my misery and I stumbled to the washstand to douse my brooding in night-chilled water. I stood for a little while, regarding my blurred reflection, the jumbled hair and puffed eyes. The indistinction of my features was calming and I resented the clarity that came with my glasses when finally I put them on. With a sigh I brushed my hair and smoothed it into some sort of order with a little oil. I retrieved my shirt from the back of the chair and readied myself to re-join the world.

'Oh, I am sorry, Mr Guebler. I have already put away the breakfast things. I could fetch you some coffee, find a little bread?'

I summoned up a smile for Mrs Kettmann to soothe her embarrassment. Too breezily, I thanked her for her kindness and told her not to trouble herself, smothering the hunger I felt. Lying had become so easy. She smiled and nodded in response, relieved not to have to fetch the things so recently put away, and she slipped back into the sitting room. I hung there in the hall for several moments until the thought of a café, of coffee, of bread and ham, pulled me through the door, down the steps and out onto the street.

Mrs Kettmann's building stands on a pleasant side street, fronted by an uninterrupted row of equally polite houses, built during the latter decades of the last century. Very little traffic finds its way along its course and, on that hungry morning, no-one witnessed my appearance on the pavement. I took a confident turn to the left, towards the boulevard, such that I fooled myself into believing that I knew which café I had in mind.

It was only after some ten minutes that I realised that what had appeared to be purposeful walking was in fact aimlessness. I halted by a tram stop and looked about me to gather my bearings, like an adventurer in a new land. Despite the familiarity of the street, I could not summon up the location of a single café, much less how I might find my way to it. The growling in my stomach was insistent and I could only think of coffee and buttered bread. I was walking again. Every so often I would pass a bar or café, the tables spilling across the pavement, and I would slow my pace, consider its clientele, its name, its ambiance. Despite the sounds and smells of eating, of comfort, something about the place would niggle at me and I would reluctantly decide that this was not the right establishment in which to take my breakfast, only to reconsider some fifty metres on, half turn, then feel embarrassed and resume my search.

The cathedral clock struck noon. There would be no breakfast. My stomach clenched in protest and I offered the prospect of lunch to appease it. It gurgled its displeasure. It was only then that I looked around me. Above me, the façade of the art museum leant over with friendly concern. I knew that there was no food to be had inside the museum, but something pulled me towards it nonetheless.

I found my way to the gallery that housed the painting of the riot. There were a few others in the room, but they blurred into the walls, their shifting forms lost in the restless scenes depicted. Only Judith remained concrete, crystal crisp and static, standing a little way from her habitual station. I watched as she worked something loose from under her fingernail, her left-hand pivoting from her immobile right-hand. The sensation of voyeurism was unexpectedly comfortable and I held my breath so that I should not bring the performance to a premature end. I feared that she might look up and catch my gaze. I did not fear my own embarrassment, but hers, that it should erase the naturalness of this scene, of her being. There was no artifice here, no calculation.

I held my shape, unwilling to go further. I had wanted, I realised, to find absolution in Judith. My unconscious mind had brought me here, to her warmth, seeking a way out of my torment. But to bring her my guilt over Bireli Haluska risked extinguishing any affection that she might feel for me. I had already hurt one trusting friend and I did not have the stomach for further callousness, for more shame. To explain to Judith what had happened would mean addressing questions, not only about what I had done to Bireli, but about everything I had done, everything I would continue to do. I toyed with the idea of simply washing myself in her company, but I realised that was impossible. I am ill-suited to light-hearted conversation at the best of times but, in that moment, I knew that my awkwardness would provoke concern and questions, both of which would be unbearable. If my subconscious had led me to her in search of comfort, it had been in error. There was no comfort to be found anywhere, and there was no soul alive that could offer it. I was alone, never more alone, and my abasement swallowed me, like the ground beneath me opening. I retreated to the shadows of the other gallery and let the wall support me until my legs regained their solidity.

I hurried through the museum, barely aware of the people within the galleries and completely oblivious to the paintings on their walls. Past, present and future blurred past me until I stumbled out into the brash light of the day. The city grumbled its thoughts around me, unconcerned by my reappearance. Woozy, I steadied myself with one hand on the cold stone of the doorway's arch. My stomach gave a forlorn whine, eager to let me know that its complaints had still to be addressed. I felt the heat behind my eyes and clamped them shut, so that my despair could not leak out of them. Just two days earlier, the world was opening before me. I had been convinced of my cleverness and of the significance that it gave to me. But everything was now in tatters. What so very recently appeared to be solid, ran through my fingers like water. Everything I had achieved, everything I had believed about myself, was simply shreds of smoke carried on the breeze. My self-pity consumed me.

I was moving again, with even less purpose than before, aimless and lost. After a time, I found myself in the little square, by the café where I had last seen the living Joszef. My subconscious, it seemed, had no interest in bringing me to comfort after all, but rather it sought to torment me. I paused for some minutes, staring at the table where I had sat and drank brandy with him, watched him smoke his guilty cigar. His suspicion of Garcia and his bloodless asceticism sparked connections between my own feelings of remorse towards Bireli Haluska and what I now knew to be my doubts about the role I had assumed within the mayor's office, doubts that had crept up on me as a nagging sense of dislocation, until the word 'camps' had brought them hurtling into my mind.

I was still standing in the square, still staring at the little table, and memories of that last conversation with Joszef bubbled up. I recalled the blood soup his wife was to make for him that evening, and his visceral description twisted in my stomach. The queasiness reminded me that I had still not eaten. I thought about how easy it would be to take my place at that table, order a plate of ham, maybe even a brandy, and to sit and answer the grumbles from within. However, the desire to avoid others, to submerge myself in my aloneness, was now greater than the need to fill my belly. I turned and set off towards the sanctuary of Mrs Kettmann's house.

The greyness of the sky grew darker as I clipped through the back streets. The day had taken an ominous turn and rain would soon crash to the pavement; the bluster of the storm's downdraught already tugged at my coat. I quickened my pace, anxious to avoid further discomfort. I could already feel the embrace of the warmth that awaited me beside Mrs Kettmann's fireplace. The first of the heavy drops slapped against the stone steps as I climbed them, and as the door clicked closed behind me, I could hear the roar of the deluge. I leant against the door for a moment, listening to the rain, my eyes closed, my head bowed as if in prayer. That was how Mrs Kettmann discovered me.

'Mr Guebler? Are you feeling quite well?'

Her voice broke against the white noise of the rainstorm. I opened my eyes without the time to gather myself and, from her reaction, I suppose I must have appeared quite ghoulish. I stared at the hem of her apron to stop the room spinning.

'Yes, quite well. I simply haven't yet had a chance to eat today. Too busy with work.'

At this, the shape of her concern changed from wariness to an almost motherly fussing. She ushered me away from the door and towards the warmth of the sitting room; I felt the firmness of her hand at my back as she steered me through the doorway.

'I swear this job of yours will be the death of you, Mr Guebler, really I do. Now, sit here and I shall fetch you some bread and ham to keep up your strength while I make you something to eat. I have some potatoes and a bit of pork, if that will serve? Anyway, sit.'

She indicated the high-backed chair that was her usual refuge and held my arm while I sank into it. The softness was glorious.

'Oh, I almost forgot. A letter came for you.' She turned to the console table onto which letters and newspapers were placed while waiting to be read. *'Here it is. From the Capital. Maybe a friend?'*

I ignored her curiosity and focused only on the envelope quivering in my hands. I knew no-one in the Capital and the letter felt as ominous as the rain battering the window. I studied the address, conscious that the tight, neat handwriting was familiar, but my hunger had left me dim-witted as well as physically weak; I raked through my memory for enlightenment, but no revelation arrived. Mrs Kettmann reluctantly left the room and I tore into the envelope with just my thumbnail. There was only one sheet of paper within it, filled on both sides with the same dense handwriting. I knew before I found his name at the bottom of the page that the letter had come from Georg.

Correspondence

The lamp light gathered around me in the thickening evening. As soon as was polite, I had thanked Mrs Kettmann for her kindness and left the table to retire. My cursory reading of Georg's letter had been curtailed by her return from the kitchen and I had spent the meal impatient to resume. Even before the door to my room had snapped shut, I had fished the envelope from my jacket pocket and begun to unfold its contents. The page trembled between my fingers as I switched on the lamp.

There was no address at the top of the page, just a telephone number. I traced the digits with my eyes, almost hoping to divine some hidden truth in their sequence, something that could make sense of the day, before I turned my energies towards reading the text itself.

It began as I might have expected a letter from Georg to begin.

My dear Anton,

I trust this letter finds you safely. I realise that in writing to you at all, I may create some difficulties for you…

The brittle familiarity of the greeting and the mannered cordiality of the opening slipped quickly into threat and intrigue, formalities set aside after ten short words. An image formed in my mind of Georg's knowing conspiricism, the self-satisfied smile he wore when he had unpicked a plot that the rest of us were too leaden to even recognise. I smiled with what I can only describe as affection.

...and yet the substance of my request may convince you that it would be better to simply pass it on to Garcia or Ana, in order to absolve yourself of complicity. That would be understandable, if disappointing. I have no reason to assume that you would aid me; there is after all no conspiracy between us. We have barely talked of these matters before.

The nature of the threat now became clear, and I hesitated to read on. Georg had laid out a clear route to my salvation. If I refused to read further and simply handed the letter to Garcia first thing on Monday morning, I would have demonstrated my loyalty and clearly shown that I could, after all, be trusted. And yet, that 'barely' was a barb that could snare me, potentially prompting uncomfortable questions from Garcia. I silently nodded my admiration for Georg's cleverness.

However, if you choose to grant me a little trust and to show boldness, I would be forever in your debt.

At the end of the first paragraph, I paused to rub my eyes, my fingers filling the space under my glasses. Georg's imprecation had an uncharacteristic tone as I sounded the words in my head. He had never given the slightest indication that he could be in anyone's debt. I opened my eyes and straightened my glasses. The lamp light sparkled and span for a moment and I could not focus on the opening of the next line. I looked at my thumb nail, pressed to the bottom of the page, until the pyrotechnics ended their display.

I'm sure that the story of my sudden departure has already been written as one of betrayal and bad faith. I can hear Garcia raging about my infidelity to the cause and see Ana tensing at the strategic blow of the story in the

Tribune. *She would have cursed herself for not foreseeing it, although I'm sure she will have been able to find a way to reconcile herself to the omission.*

I snapped the page over, hungry for more words about Ana, words that could illuminate whatever was being suggested about her. But there was nothing more about her for a little while, just Georg's attempted exculpation.

But my departure was not an act of treachery, nor even of cowardice (although I did have cause for concern for my own safety). Joszef's mistake was in choosing to believe in his own invulnerability and so did not to act in time. I had his example to guide me and, knowing that my own standing was far less secure than his, leaving before I too was visited by Kelemen seemed a rational decision.

His reference to Kelemen sent a chill through me. There was something diabolical about the man, and I still could not understand why the Boss was prepared to tolerate such malevolence. Perhaps it was the fatal weakness in Andreas Hofmans, one which had in the end allowed for the death of his greatest friend. That the Boss's close associate would betray him in this way left me fearing for his own safety, as well as that of Georg and, now, myself.

You see, Anton, I am not the traitor. I know that others, perhaps even you, have doubted the sincerity of my commitment to our cause, but believe me, my departure was motivated primarily by my resolution to pursue the aims that brought me to the office of Andreas Hofmans in the first place. It is Andreas, Ana and Garcia that have betrayed us, not I.

I slapped the bed abruptly, half in exasperation, half in relief. Georg was clearly experiencing some sort of paranoid episode. He was no longer fully in control of his senses, that much was obvious. I imagined the fear that had fuelled him as he had written the letter and felt something like pity for him. I thought of simply handing the letter to Ana, of explaining to her that our former colleague had lost his wits, that he had tried to co-opt me to his paranoid delusions. But curiosity made me read on.

Perhaps history will be kind to the two of us and it will afford us an opportunity to meet again, when I can explain more fully my reasoning. But for now, I have a request. In my haste to leave the city, I only had time to gather some of the documentary evidence that I need. I believe that a folder exists, one that reveals the full extent of the corruption that has infected our work, corruption that exceeds the common or garden corruption of money and privilege, but a corruption that debases the very essence of our purpose. It concerns the plans for the camps that are to house our displaced Roma. It is in the Svankmajer file, which you should find in the cabinets in the mayor's antechamber.

His mention of the camps caused me to shudder. He had named the unnamed thing that had stalked my conscience ever since Garcia had casually uttered the word as he left the office. I knew that these camps would be as benign as they had been presented to me, that even Garcia could not be plotting anything actively harmful to the people of the city, even the Roma, but doubt now rang like a bell and would not be ignored. I resolved to do as Georg asked. I would know the truth. I needed to settle my doubts or else expose the depths of Garcia's malignancy.

I nodded my decision to myself, then paused. How could Georg know about the camps? The idea had not existed until von Boehmen had come with his troops, until Bireli Haluska had delivered his statement and left City Hall. There could be no file, certainly not one of which Georg could be aware. I shook my head to loosen my thoughts, to allow reason to explain this irreconcilable anomaly. When no answer came, the full horror of Garcia's potential treachery shaped in my mind and I felt sick once again.

I need you to retrieve it for me. When you find it – and not before, mind you – call me and I will give you the address to which it should be sent.

The letter fragmented then into cordial blandness, with Georg wishing me the very best fortune with all the sincerity that such language can convey. My eyes skated over them until the postscript, added in a different ink. The full stop beside the S was thick and heavy, as if drilled into the page.

PS. Take care Anton. I wish that I had found it within myself to be a better friend to you these past months. If fate allows, I shall be better in future. G

That G, its elaborate curls contrasted against the primness of the rest of the text, felt like a farewell, teetering on the precipice of abject sadness. Writing those words might well have been the most unguarded moment of Georg's life. A swirl of emotion stirred into the stew of my tiredness and disquiet. The loneliness that had swamped me earlier in the day returned. There was an ache above my right eye. I lowered my eyelids against the glare of the lamp and drifted into a troubled sleep.

Subterfuge

Anxious anticipation accompanied me on the short walk to the office early on Monday morning. The sky was still grey, devoid of feature or interest, and the thick air hung motionless, expectant, muffling the sounds to the street, hushing the bustle of the day. It closed about me, unseasonably clammy. On my arrival at the night door, I barely managed to summon up a nod of greeting for the doorman and I was grateful that he did not feel the need to glance up from his newspaper.

The letter swung with my coat pocket, in time with my steady steps through the corridors of City Hall. Its weight, slight as it was, unbalanced me and I was certain that an observer familiar with my gait would instantly see that I swayed unnaturally, skewed out of kilter by my burden. Were it not before 8am, they might have assumed that I was drunk. But my worries about being discovered at least distracted me from dwelling upon the best course of action. I still did not entirely know what I should actually do. I could not simply walk into the Boss's antechamber and search through his filing cabinets. If for no other reason, the thought of Kelemen seated at his desk, smiling pointedly at my throat, filled me with terror.

I approached the door to the office. The nicotine light spread stickily under the gap at its base; the corridor felt blacker than ever. I breathed in the damp dust that hung in the dead air and imagined myself as if I were already buried. Ahead, I noticed that no light came from the direction of the Boss's office: either he was yet to arrive, or his door was shut. The idea floated through my mind that I could simply continue on towards the antechamber, at least to investigate, but the sound of voices behind the office door dispelled the notion in an instant. My footsteps would alert Ana or Garcia to my unusual detour and I did not feel equipped to answer questions. Inhaling deeply, I opened the door and stepped through it.

The young man sitting at Georg's desk looked across to me briefly, before returning his obedient gaze to where Garcia was still speaking, his right hand chopping the air in explanation. Once the point had been made, he paused.

'Stefan, let me introduce Anton who, along with Ana,' he scowled at the clock, *'completes our merry band. Anton, Stefan joins us to, uh, fill the recent vacancy.'*

Garcia's embarrassment caused his voice to trail off. Perhaps he had made a vow to himself never to mention Georg by name again. I smiled for the first time in days and reached out my hand in greeting. He took it sceptically and, at best, allowed his own hand to be grasped and shaken. I had the sensation of introducing myself to a corpse.

'You're a lawyer?'

I tried to enliven him with a cheery tone, with which I aimed to convey genuine interest, despite its insincerity. My smile fractured in slow motion as his faced formed into incomprehension.

'A lawyer? I don't understand...'

Garcia cleared his throat pointedly, clearly irritated by my inappropriate question. Gruffly he explained that the newcomer was a political adviser, as if such a thing had always existed in the office. Uncertainty swept through me once more and I felt my jaw hang open. It made no sense. There was no vacancy for a political adviser to fill. I was still standing dumbstruck when Ana chose to arrive.

She looked as she always did. The same clothes; the same busy absence in her manner; the same wayward hair. And yet, she seemed different to me: harsher. It was as if the shape and volume of the room had changed, its dimensions skewed by the contents of Georg's letter, by the words resting in my jacket pocket. Everything was as it had been, as it should be, and yet the whole world seemed entirely unfamiliar.

'Morning Roberto, and welcome Stefan. We're so pleased that you able to join us at such short notice. And Anton, my dear, a very good morning to you as well.' She looked at me with a smile, but it fell away almost instantly. *'Everything OK? You look a little out of sorts.'* I stared back at her for a moment, then mumbled something non-committal before crossing to my desk. I sat with my back to the room, trying to mimic my usual shapes and movements until the room settled into a low, industrious hum.

Time passed slowly. Sometime after eleven, once the coffee had been summoned and dispatched, I found myself alone with Ana. Garcia had taken Stefan into the darkness of the corridor, leaving me envious that the newcomer should have an audience with the Boss so soon in his tenure and a little afraid of what might be said. Ana did not look up from her work.

'Cigarette?' I offered my pack to her at the end of an outstretched arm. She looked up with a curious half-smile and nodded. I tossed the pack

across the void between us and she caught it with her left hand, plucking it as easily from the air as if she had taken it from a tabletop. I listened to the fizz of the match, watched her cheeks suck inwards with the first inhalation. I waited for her to say something, but, aside from her thanks, no words were offered.

'*What do you think of him?*' I nodded to Georg's former desk and, when she still said nothing, simply looked at me with something like concern, I continued. '*Nice enough I suppose. But I'm not quite sure what he's doing here. He doesn't replace... fill the vacancy we have.*' Her curious smile became a frown, and her eyebrows narrowed, demanding that I explain myself. '*I mean, he's not a lawyer. I asked. So, I'm not sure what he adds.*'

Her laugh was brief but bitter. '*Really? The Boss made the appointment himself. Personally, I don't think he would bring someone in without good reason. But you might feel differently, of course.*'

I said nothing and simply stared at the page of figures on my desk. This was not a good day even to hint at disloyalty. I could feel her looking at me, could sense the disdain and suspicion, and I wondered if, somehow, she could read the guilty secret in my coat pocket. I didn't speak again until lunch and then declined the invitation to join my colleagues at the café by the bridge. I seldom ate with them, preferring to eat alone, but today I was certain that I would not be able to conceal my awkwardness while we exchanged exploratory pleasantries with Stefan. I claimed an urgent deadline and let them go on without me.

Hunger got the better of me before they returned and I slipped out into the city to find a café that would allow me to fill my stomach unseen by my comrades. By the river I found the doorway to an unfamiliar bar and slipped inside. As I crossed the threshold, it felt as if I had returned home. The warm aromas that greeted me melted my anxiety and when the waiter came to take my order, I asked for a cognac to accompany my soup.

I envied the weightlessness of the café's customers. Life flowed through them carelessly and their conversation babbled brightly. If they had troubles, they had left them elsewhere. Despite my envy, being among their conviviality helped to numb my anxieties and I forgot the world beyond the nicotine-yellow of the net curtains. The brandy arrived to dissolve the concerns that remained.

As I ate my soup, I wondered why I had done this so infrequently since moving into the city. I almost never took time to simply enjoy a drink and some food, except as a means to fuel my subsequent duties. Around me, people were just living their lives. Their duties and vocations were ancillary to the business of being alive. Just a month ago, had I noticed them, I would have dismissed their simplicity as superficiality, as a weakness. It was not the first time that I had considered the possibility that the error was my own: I was still young, but so much of life had already happened without my noticing. I thought of my friend, the only one I had ever had, the one I had abandoned to follow this path. I had betrayed not only Kem and his family, but also myself, in the service of an idea. Sitting in that café, eating soup and drinking brandy, the folly of my life was clear as day.

Imagining Kem's face provoked sadness and guilt, but also anxiety. I thought about Georg's letter. I felt for my coat pocket, searching out the envelope, but there was no fabric hanging from the chair back. Panic raced through me like a startled hare and then the cold realisation settled on me. I had not brought my coat. I had been content to let myself be swaddled in the tepid dampness of the day. My coat hung on the stand behind the office door. Georg's letter was there too, unguarded.

The clock told me that it would soon be two o'clock. There was still a chance that I could be back at my desk before the others returned. I waved to the waiter and, while he told me how much I owed for my lunch and the brandy, I poured too many coins into his hand and scuttled back out into the street, barely able to prevent myself from breaking into a run.

There was no reason to believe that anyone would search my coat, of course. The existence of the letter was unknown to everyone but me, Georg and Mrs Kettman. Whatever suspicions he held about me, Garcia could not see into my soul. The idea that he could was madness, brought on by fear and guilt. I slackened my pace, only to find myself hurrying once more just moments later.

There was a gloss of perspiration at my collar when I reached City Hall and I felt the need to express surprise at the closeness of the day; the doorman grunted in response, pretending not to notice the evidence of my guilt. Through the corridors I counted my steps, listened to my heart thudding in time. At last, I reached the office door and turned the handle.

Ana looked up with a smile. The door clicked shut behind me and I was reassured by the absence of Garcia. I had returned in time.

'Anton, good. I'm glad you managed to take a little break. Did you get something to eat, or would you like me to see if Miss Gelber has any biscuits?'

Her lightness surprised me, and the tension in my shoulders slackened. And yet, I could not resist the urge to check my coat pocket, to reassure myself that the letter was still there, before fishing out a handkerchief and dabbing it at my brow.

'It's warm out there. Very close.' I waited for her to accept this innocent truth before proceeding. *'But yes, I took a stroll to clear my head and found a café by the river. On Eldermeier Street. I had some borsht. And a coffee.'* I stopped, conscious that I had felt the need to lie about the cognac. Instead of continuing, I gave a shrug of my shoulders and returned the handkerchief to its place. My hand brushed against the stiff paper of the envelope.

'Where are the others?' Garcia's coat hung next to mine, and his absence from the office suddenly struck me; Stefan's too.

'Oh, Garcia offered to show Stefan around, introduce him to some of the key people.' She flashed an absent smile. *'I like him. And it's nice to have another economist around.'*

Ana must have seen me flinch before I was able to regain mastery of my body. *'Economist? I thought Garcia said he was a political adviser?'* Even I could hear the tension and urgency in my voice, but I no longer cared. I glared at Ana, demanding an explanation.

'Really? He said that? Funny. No, he's definitely an economist. Garcia must have got the wrong end of the stick.' She smiled again as she dropped her gaze. *'He's nice. I think he's going to fit in well.'*

Shadows

The clock moved past seven o'clock and, one by one, the others left. Ana was the first to disappear into the blackness of the corridor. Stefan made his exit amid blushes, anxious to make the right impression. Garcia watched him leave, then turned to me. He glanced up at the clock, then back to me with a quizzical look. His eyes lingered for a moment, searching for something, before they returned to a dossier on his desk and I could breathe again.

The next ten minutes passed painfully, endlessly. Garcia turned page after page of the dossier. I listened to the flop of paper, the whisper of a draught, the rush of his occasional sighs. Desperate for camouflage, I scribbled into my notebook and traced imaginary lines across the page of a report drafted weeks before, now superseded. At last, he snapped the folder shut.

'Well, I can do no more this evening. I shall leave you in peace to finish that. Whatever it is.' He nodded at the report on my desk with faint amusement. As he stood up, the chair scraped gently against the floorboards and a clench spiralled along my spine, only to dissipate once he had crossed to the coat stand. I had expected him to ask about the report that kept me at my desk into the evening, but he seemed remarkably unconcerned by whatever I was supposed to be doing, and I was unnerved by his lack of curiosity. *'I commend your industry, but don't stay all night.'*

His tone was warm, almost friendly, and the note of concern did not appear to mask any malice; a weak, sad smile flickered across his face as he turned in the doorway. I felt a tremor of guilt that I could even for a moment entertain Georg's suggestion that Garcia had been in some way responsible for the death of Joszef. I spent a few moments scouring my motivations for any hint that my mistrust of Garcia was anything more than a mistrust of foreigners more generally. Perhaps that was it. Perhaps I had taken against him simply because of his otherness. I would know soon enough, I told myself, and turned in my chair to watch the clock pulsing on the wall.

Sometime after eight I heard Miss Gelber click-clack down the corridor heading towards her unknown life. A half hour later, the uneven thud of Kelemen's footsteps followed along behind, heading who knows where. I thought about these lives, of the people with whom I spent so many of my waking hours, and I was struck by how little I knew of them. They were like characters in a film, who only existed while on screen and then simply paused, empty, until their next scene. I wondered briefly if that was how my colleagues saw me, before I had the clammy realisation that that was me: from when I left the office in the evening until I returned in the morning, my life was little more than hibernation. Even the weekends were simply a place within which to rest and feed. Only in a few scant instances, such as those few conversations with Judith Stern at the museum, did my time away from the office feel solid. I promised myself that I would visit Judith again, but that this time I would find the courage to talk to her, not simply skulk in the shadows.

The night-watchman's cheerful whistling snapped me back to the dull light of the office. I recognised the tune, something once familiar that I had left behind in my neighbourhood. The clock showed a quarter to nine and I shook my head in the hope that its face would reassemble itself to show an earlier time. The night-watchman would start to lock the offices soon. I had no time to lose.

This time I remembered my overcoat. I wanted no trace of me left should the night-watchman or anyone else put their head around the door. With a click, I plunged the room into darkness and slipped out of the office. The corridor was thick with impenetrable gloom. Despite its familiarity, I had to feel my way forward, my fingers running over the panels until they found the architrave of the kitchen doorway. The smell of faintly stale coffee, mixed with detergent and cooking oil, turned my nervousness to nausea and I moved on as quickly as the need for discretion would allow.

Another few metres of oak panelling led me to another doorway. I paused, breathless, my palm flat against the door, feeling for the vibration of anything alive that might be beyond it. Nothing stirred. I clenched my fist around the door handle and turned it, degree by degree, until the latch gave a gentle thud and the door swung into freedom.

Inside, the anteroom was as it always was, save for the absence of Kelemen. I imagined him, sitting behind the desk, gazing at me with that chilling smile of his, but the glint of his tooth was simply the reflection of a streetlight on the glass shade of a desk lamp. I reassured myself that the desk was empty, a simple obstacle to negotiate on my way to the filing cabinets arrayed against the wall.

For a moment, I hesitated. I had not anticipated the absence of light, and the streetlamp was too feeble to allow me to make out the labels on the cabinet. My failure to plan for this obvious challenge made me question the wisdom of the whole adventure. But I steeled myself: I needed to know, one way or another. I listened for the night-watchman's whistling, but there was only the thumping of my heart; no sound came from out in the corridor. My terror subsided and I remembered the desk lamp. I shook my head and smiled at the demons I had created for myself. I clicked the lamp into life and sludgy light crawled from the desk to the floor and across to the cabinets.

In the fourth cabinet, my finger stuttered across the spines of manila folders, each named in careful script. I reached *Sabine*, and my finger slowed. Traversing the thirty or so folders seemed to take an eternity, but eventually I found *Susskind* and then *Svankmajer*. I pinched the spine between forefinger and thumb and slid it breathlessly from the cabinet. I had expected it to be fatter. The City had had extensive dealings with the property magnate and I was surprised that this was not reflected in the weight of documentation that was retained. With a shrug, I took the file to the desk and flopped open its cover under the lamp.

There at the top of the folder was the contract that had first been signed with Svankmajer, the document that I had been sent to his office to contest. Beneath that, a report on the progress made in the first three months. There was a receipt for materials, dated sometime after the City had taken over the enterprise, but nothing further. Perplexed, I returned to the cabinet, but there was no second file. I walked back to the desk, shuffled through the pages again, almost believing that I had overlooked the other documents. But there were none. I looked again at the three papers, trying to decide which if any would be of interest to Georg, let alone indicate corruption. The progress report merely told me that things had been moving too slowly, which of course I already knew. It listed a number of sites, some of which I did not recognise. I thought that I had a good grasp of the city's geography, but apparently there were some neighbourhoods that I did not know yet. I looked at the contract, but that had been drafted by Georg himself and so was unlikely to be of interest.

The receipt, too, seemed innocuous. The materials listed were as could be expected in the circumstances: some pallets of brick; some cement, a lot of timber and wire; a tonne of pointed sand; a large quantity of canvas. All were well within the limits of what I knew about construction. Except the wire: I could not comprehend why a building project would require such large quantities of barbed wire. I checked the date once more. The goods had been ordered three months earlier. I carefully folded all three documents and pushed them into my jacket pocket.

I took the now empty file over to the cabinet, slid it back into the space it had vacated. I had removed only a few pages, but even this was sufficient to cause it to sag slightly, its spine bowing into the space its minute diminution had created. I wondered if anyone would notice. I imagined Kelemen opening the cabinet the next morning, his eye drawn to the curve of the Svankmajer file, his thick fingers pulling it hesitantly from its place and flipping open the supple card to reveal its emptiness. I shook my head. No-one would notice the tiny change that I had caused, least of all Kelemen.

The soft thud of the cabinet door blurred into the pad of a footstep in the corridor. The click of a heel sharpened the certainty that I was about to be discovered and I held my breath, tensed my muscles to immobility. My fingernails cut into the palms of my hands. Unseen, a door handle creaked, but it was another door that swung open and closed, somewhere along the corridor. Good sense told me that I should leave, and as quickly, as quietly, as possible. Good sense screamed that I should walk carefully away from the origin of the sound, out into the night without a backwards glance. But I knew the sound of the step. If it had belonged to anyone other than Ana, I may have acted with good sense.

As soon as I turned the corner, I knew that the rectangle of yellow light spreading across the corridor came from beneath the door of our office. I took careful step after careful step until I reached the familiar threshold, made alien by the evening's strangeness. The knowledge that she might appear at any moment, without warning, that she might find me standing there in the doorway, where I should not be, could not drag me from my place and instead I leant closer to the door. I heard voices, hers and a deeper one.

I held my breath and strained to hear what was being said, my gaze falling absently to my feet. The leather held a dull lustre in the low light spilling under the door. The familiar scuffs and creases were obscured, erasing the abrasion of the day to day, making my shoes appear new and unblemished. My toes rose and fell, until the creak of the leather became overwhelming. As if for the first time I was aware that, while shadows threatened, they also provided refuge. They hid the rough edges of things. I thought about the pages within my jacket pocket. Whatever villainy Georg supposed they contained was concealed from me, obscured in shadows, and I could neither see nor understand it.

The sound of conversation burred within the office, a rising and falling of tones without meaning. I leant closer, so that my ear was touching the cool wood of the door. The sounds thrummed, but I could only make out fragments of what Ana was saying.

'No, Franck... haven't had the chance yet... I know, I know... find out about Georg...does Andreas...? Not Roberto, no... No, him too.... Unreliable... Alright, Franck, understood.' Had she not used his name, I doubt I would have recognised the low tones of Kelemen when he replied, but as soon as he began to speak, I could only picture the glint of gold in his mouth. He spoke quietly and in a dull bass, but I heard the words *'fix it'* quite clearly. Silence followed. I pictured the two of

them standing facing each other across the office, and it struck me that I did not for an instant imagine that Ana was afraid. That in itself chilled me more than the finality of Kelemen's pronouncement, and I finally realised that I had indeed sought the wrong ally.

Silence

I kept to the back streets, avoiding the brightly lit boulevards and the lively squares. At every corner, I paused to look over my shoulder. Once or twice, I was sure that I heard the sound of running feet behind me, only to realise that it was my own heartbeat. Streetlight and shadow came in steady waves, each bringing momentary disorientation. I teetered at the edge of a pool of yellow light, finally feeling that sufficient distance had been put between me and the scene of my crime.

The moment of quiet and calm allowed me to think of something other than flight, to notice the other unease that lurked at the back of my mind. The fragments of conversation I had gathered at the office door assembled and reassembled themselves in my mind, their possible meanings shifting and mutating. Georg's bickering with Ana, his mistrust of me, everything meant something darker now. Ana had asked me to prod at Georg's doubts. She had drawn out confidences from my own mind. I rattled through every word that I had ever said to her, seeking out the phrase that would be my undoing.

My solitude was broken by the arrival of another on the street, his hat pulled down and collar turned up. I feared the worst and then I noticed his swaying; at the lamp post, he reached out an arm to steady himself. He looked up, seemingly surprised by my presence, as if I had appeared from thin air. An idiotic smile appeared and his glassy eyes twinkled in the glow.

'Excuse me, sir, do you perhaps have a cigarette? I find myself at a loss.'

He was more than an arm's length from me and yet the schnapps on his breath was overwhelming. It was later than I had thought. I watched his fingers curl more tightly about the post, anticipating the sudden rush of the gale that seemed to buffet him in the still air. He suppressed a convulsion of his chest, his free hand covering his mouth just in case, then he smiled an ingratiating smile.

'Of course.' I made a show of fumbling in my pocket but never took my eyes from him: I did not quite believe that he was not an assassin, despite his inebriation. *'Here you are.'* I held the packet in his direction, then reconsidered. *'Would you like me to light it for you? Since you seem to only have the one free hand?'* I nodded to where his left hand gripped the lamp post. Not waiting for an answer, I took a step back and pulled two cigarettes from the packet. I put both in my mouth together and lit them with a single match. I had seen Joszef do this once, and when the memory hit me, I choked on the smoke.

The drunken man cleared his throat and, looking up, I saw his head flop forward then jerk up again, before falling forwards once more. It took a moment for me to realise that he was nodding, in his own way, at the cigarettes. I took a step towards him and held out his until he took it; if he were an assassin, my moment of distraction would have been ample opportunity to strike.

'Wass up with you, if you... don't mind me asking?' His watery eyes examined me as if it were I that was incapacitated rather than him. He inhaled deeply. *'If you want to talk about it, I know a bar...'* He half-turned, free hand and cigarette trailing into the darkness behind him. He remained that way for a while, as if perplexed by a scene visible only to him. I confess that I gave serious consideration to his offer.

226

The attraction of brandy and of warmth, of conversation with another human being, one of whom I had no reason to be wary, was undeniable. But by the time he had turned back towards me, I had dismissed the notion.

'Thank you, but no. I am already late and should be on my way. But thank you.' I held out my hand without a thought and waited for him to take it. For a time, he studied it suspiciously, but then the memory of correct behaviour broke through the schnapps and he straightened and let go of the lamp post. With exaggerated deliberateness, he shook my hand and nodded a shallow bow. Then he turned and strode off, at least until the next corner where he again stretched out a hand for support.

He disappeared into the deepening night, leaving me alone on my island of dirty lamp light. I do not know how long I remained there, but it was well after midnight when I crept through Mrs Kettmann's door and up the stairs to my room. Again, I had not eaten but, despite my hunger, I fell readily into a tempestuous sleep, filled with shadows and threats. I woke frequently, often damp with sweat, my mind clamped shut with hopelessness.

Before dawn, however, I had convinced myself that I would be able to slip back into the normal flow of things, at least until I had spoken to Georg. I only needed to take some care to avoid further suspicion. No one knew of any of it, after all. The letter from Georg had remained safely in my pocket since its arrival and there was no reason to think that the absence of the Svankmajer documents would ever be noticed. Even if someone should wish in the future to refer to them, and find them gone, there was nothing to link their disappearance to me. In such an eventuality, there might even be an opportunity to cast suspicion upon Garcia. I felt the possibility of security creep into my bones as if for the first time.

Only the conversation between Ana and Kelemen still caused me some little anxiety. I could make no sense of it, neither the content nor it's occurrence. But I clung to the idea that she had named Garcia as unreliable. If all that had gone wrong could be laid at the Spaniard's door, I would be able to reconcile myself with all that had happened. If Garcia could be blamed, then all others could be absolved: Ana, Georg and even myself. And I could finally smother whatever doubts nibbled at my faith in the Boss, and in my work for him. Kelemen's 'fix it' could be innocent. He was the Boss's fixer, after all. My heart grew at the thought that the problem to be fixed was Garcia himself. I clenched my mouth tight shut, my eyes too, and wished to the heavens. The alternative, that Ana was somehow complicit, that Georg had been right about the depths and extent of the betrayal, was unbearable to me. Unlike Georg, I had no-one and nowhere to run to. I had no life beyond the limits of the dark office.

I left Mrs Kettman's house buoyed with wilful resolve. A trace of hopefulness clung to me as I navigated the tangled streets. I would call Georg. He would give me the certainty and clarity that I demanded. He had to: I had done as he had asked, despite the risks to myself. On the old bridge, under the pale morning sky, I paused to delay my arrival at the office for a few moments. I watched the water race away from me, felt the surge of its force filling the air. For an eternity I forgot to breathe, consumed by the cold anger of the river below me. Even here, in the heart of the city, the sounds of the natural world could smother those of man. The clang of the trams, the grumble of engines, all were lost in the relentlessness of water. I felt helpless in the face of its elemental force, and that helplessness crept into my bones. I sighed. I could do nothing until I had spoken to Georg. Until then, I simply had to measure out the day without attracting suspicion.

I reached my desk no later than on any other day. The morning passed in the usual way, and I even managed to complete some minor task that still lingered from the previous day. I constructed a simulacrum of normality that was so banal that even a keen observer would be unable to detect anything worthy of suspicion within it. I was quietly courteous with Ana and authentically awkward with Garcia. I even passed some incidental words with Stefan and poured his coffee once it arrived a little after eleven. Everything had the appearance of complete normality, until just before lunch.

'The Mayor wants to see you.'

Tomasz was in the doorway, razor-blade eyes fixed on Ana. While he lacked the bulk of Kelemen, his presence was just as malevolent. But there was no obvious threat in his invitation and Ana continued writing until the end of the line, where she paused and gave herself a small, satisfied smile. Only then did she look up.

'Thank you, Tomasz. I'll follow you through. Tell the Mayor I'll be along presently.'

She closed the folder on her desk, without hurry or concern, and rose from her seat. Tomasz gave what looked like a bow and began back out of the office.

'We don't often see you in here, my dear Tomasz. Where is your comrade today?'

Garcia's question was conversational, friendly. Like Ana, he was completely at ease with him, unperturbed by the smile that accompanied Tomasz's reply.

'Away. On an errand for the Mayor.' He traced his tongue across his lower lip, then raked his teeth across it. *'Should be back in the morning, once the matter is taken care of.'*

Garcia and Ana exchanged a fleeting glance. At the time, I do not think I even registered that Kelemen's errand required him to be away overnight. I had other things on my mind and barely noticed as Tomasz slunk back into the shadows. When Ana followed a few moments later, she glanced back at me from the doorway, but there was neither smile nor frown.

Her absence from the office tightened my resolve. I made it known to Garcia and Stefan that my hunger was such that I would take an early lunch. Garcia shot a quizzical glance in my direction, but it faded soon enough. I pulled on my coat as breezily as I could and left without further explanation. I knew my destination. Unlike most days, I had already selected a café, not because of its food or ambience, but on account of the discreet telephone kiosk at its rear. Weeks before, when its usefulness to me had been unknown, I had seen customers disappear behind the curtain and return sometime later to pay the cashier. Curious, I had asked my waiter about the mysterious disappearances and reappearances, but I had forgotten his explanation almost instantly. And yet the location of this telephone had tumbled into my mind the instant that I read Georg's letter, even before I knew for certain that I would call him.

The letter and the documents from the Svankmajer file crackled in my pocket as I walked through the town. My pulse throbbed, more than the exertion would merit, and I found myself again looking over my shoulder at each corner. There was no need, I told myself. Garcia could not suspect a thing. No-one could. And yet still I expected to see Tomasz at my heels.

It was midday and yet the heavy sky was dark. The city had lost its definition under the threat of the imminent downpour, but as I scuttled through the streets, the faces of the buildings blurring into unfamiliarity, indistinct and featureless, it did not trouble me. I was anxious only to reach my destination, to complete my task.

I was outside the café. Some customers had taken seats on the terrace, despite the weather, but most were inside, huddled around tables, laughing and talking and eating. The conviviality of the room was almost unbearable and I asked for a table near the back. I ordered the soup without enquiring as to its variety, all the while watching the heavy curtain. I was conscious of the scraping of my left thumb nail against the back of my right, but I did not attempt to control this manifestation of my nerves. I did not care what the other customers thought of me.

A woman appeared from behind the curtain, oblivious to my attention. She crossed to the bar and plucked a few coins from a purse and handed them to the cashier, who took them and recorded some characters in a yellow notebook. I took my opportunity and, in a moment, I found myself on the other side of the curtain, the receiver in my hand, the small distant voice of the operator repeating her question with increasing irritation.

'What number do you require, caller?'

As if awakening, I fumbled for the letter, opened it awkwardly with my left hand and read out the number that Georg had scratched into the paper. The operator told me that she was connecting me and I thanked her numbly. There was a click in the earpiece and I heard Georg's breath at the other end of the line.

'Georg, listen. I can't talk for long. I got your letter and did as you asked. The Svankmajer file. But it makes no sense, there is nothing incriminating there. Practically nothing at all, just three innocuous papers. Well, there is something. An order for materials that seems odd. Not sure what it means.'
A waiter walked past with an empty tray still perched on his upturned fingers. He flashed a smile and gave a curt nod, then lost himself once more in whatever preoccupations filled his dreary hours. I watched him until he disappeared behind a door and was gone. *'Maybe Garcia had already removed the interesting documents? Anyway, what should I do now? With the files, I mean. I have them with me.'*

It struck me that Georg had thus far not said a word and I felt my frustration rise. It was a familiar feeling, one that I had often felt toward him when he was being impossible in the office, before his departure. Before. I paused, disquieted, and left room for him to speak but he just kept breathing.

'Georg, now is not the time for games.' I had wanted to sound righteous, but feared I had only achieved petulance. *'For God's sake, say something, man. I don't have the patience for this. You might think it's funny but you're safe in the Capital. I'm the one that is still in harm's way here and I don't have the time. Just tell me what to do and I'll finish the job.'*

The breathing continued for a moment, more laboured than I would have expected, heavy, like that of a bulkier man. I wanted to lambast him again, but the line cleared and the operator's crystal voice returned, asking her tired question once more. I replaced the receiver in its cradle. It made no sense. Nothing made any sense. Someone cleared their throat behind me. I turned with a start, fearing discovery, but it was just another customer, waiting to use the telephone.

Gravity

I paid the cashier. He did not look up from his ledger, simply stated the amount due and held out his hand. Everything spoke of lethargy and boredom. The man's work seemed to preclude even the possibility of connecting, however briefly, with another person. I imagined him as an automaton, a machine, and realised that nothing about his role in the world would be different if such a thing were possible. I imagined him with a girlfriend, with his family, tried to see him as I thought of myself, and felt a sharp pain at the schism between these two things, the cashier and the man.

My sadness at the cashier's bifurcation only sharpened my anger at Georg. He had put me to so much trouble and then, at the moment of resolution, had chosen to play his games. He had once again demonstrated his unique ability to serve only himself. Georg's conceit was such that he would think nothing of putting a supposed friend in danger simply for his own amusement. I clipped the brim of my hat sharply with my forefinger.

The sudden noise caused one of the nearby customers to look up from her book. The brown eyes of Judith Stern enveloped me momentarily, displacing the swirl of emotion within me. Her gaze felt like the return of gravity and the reeling world steadied, if only for an instant. I remembered, as if from a dream, what it was that was so valuable to me about our acquaintance. Where the rest of my existence moved as a vortex, Judith promised calm, deep seas.

The effect was fleeting, however. I felt embarrassed at the snap that has attracted her attention, and self-conscious of my agitated appearance. As in the gallery, when I had shrunk into the walls to avoid her eyes, I felt certain that my internal anguish was painted across my face, visible to anyone who chose to look, and I felt ashamed of it. But there were no walls to swallow me, and I forced a smile and waved breezily in her direction.

'Fancy seeing you here.'

She smiled and closed the thin paperback, smoothing the cover with her palm before placing it carefully on the table next to her empty plate. I tried to remember how long it had been since we had last spoken together, anxious to find words that I could share without puncturing my fragile equilibrium. I wanted more than anything to spend some time in her orbit, to suspend the tumult of the other life. Despite myself, I asked if I could join her, gambling on her ability to sustain the conversation for both of us.

Once seated, an awkward moment of smiles and stalled sentences soon past. I remembered myself and asked her about her book. The question unleashed her, and she raced backwards and forwards over the plot and characters, never sure where to begin but delighted to have the opportunity to share her private world. Her effervescence almost dissolved the heavy dread that hung from me. Almost. While her thrilled recounting of the redemption of Mario, after his entanglements with the malign magician, rattled in the air, I was able to breathe with ease, and the possibility of optimism that I had experienced that morning returned. Then her eyes dropped to her hands.

'Anton, I need to ask: why did you hide from me? In the gallery. I saw you. I was about to wave but you hid behind a pillar.' Her expression was one of confused sadness, bound together with determined optimism. There was no rancour, just the hope that I could explain away my behaviour with a few words, nothing more; that every imagined injury could be so simply soothed. I wished that I could explain, that I could build a bridge back to the easy friendship that had been blossoming before. But that seemed impossible. The same nausea throbbed in me as it had in the gallery, only now it was more intense. The weight of everything in my life that wasn't Judith crushed me.

I could have told her, let her in. It might have helped. It might have given me some kind of respite. But it seemed too daunting and, instead of telling the truth, I succumbed to what I now know to be my inherent, deeply hidden cowardice. I had spent my life denying it, denying its source too. My father had died during the war, but not in battle, nor even in flight; he had not even had the courage, nor the good sense, to run. He had not been a good thief either, and he had been discovered. He had been led to a wall by his own comrades; they had tied a blindfold around his eyes and then they had shot him when the lieutenant had given the order. He had slumped to the dirty ground and only his pocket watch and his shame had returned to the city after the war was done.

'Oh, that? I was just passing and thought I would pop in on a whim. But when I saw you, I realised that it would be unfair to disturb you. You looked busy, and I just thought that you might get in trouble, talking to a friend during work hours.'

She didn't believe me. Her scepticism was clear in her eyes, but the word 'friend' seemed to be sufficient. Her shoulders loosened and she smiled.

'No harm done. It was funny though. You were so conspicuous. You'd make a dreadful spy.' She laughed at her own joke and didn't notice the steady drum of my heart. *'I'm glad you're not cut out for subterfuge. Anyhow, I told myself over and over that there would be a reason, and so there is.'* Scepticism lingered in her eyes but was swamped by the swelling smile that was filling her cheeks. *'You know, I enjoy our conversations immensely, Anton. Really.'*

Her eyes darted about the table, seeking refuge from her embarrassment. I watched her fingers tussle, listened to her breathing catch. I should have told her then that I too enjoyed our conversations. It was the truth, even if it were a truth only becoming fully apparent to me in the busy air of the café. But I lacked the courage to give her even that small, solidarity part of me. I stayed silent, waited for her to pick up the burden once more, assuming that I would have time to tell her in some unformed moment, in an unimagined future.

'I should go. I'll be late.' I nodded in agreement, hiding my disappointment that she had chosen to end her train of thought there. She was, however, right. I would be missed too, and I risked not simply the rebuke of a supervisor, but an ocean of suspicion. I snapped to my feet to help Judith from her chair. Once we had assembled our outerwear into respectable order, Judith put her hand on my arm, holding me in my place with only the faintest pressure.

'You know, there's a funfair in town. I wonder, would you like to go? Friday evening, perhaps? As friends, of course. I have no-one else I can ask, really. You see, there'll be a huge whirligig there, the biggest in the country, and none of my girlfriends would dare. But, you see, I really want to ride it, and it'd be much more fun to do so with someone beside me.'

I found myself laughing more heartily, more completely, more honestly than I had done for longer than I could remember. Judith looked hurt, as if I were about to ridicule her twice over, first to reject her invitation and second to shame her for her wish to do something as frivolous as ride a whirligig. I settled my laughter as quickly as I could, replacing it with a broad smile.

'Do you know, that sounds marvellous. I haven't ridden a whirligig since I was a child. I used to love the funfair back then, but I just haven't seemed to have the time in recent years. I would love to accompany you, so long as you promise to keep me safe!'

It was her turn to laugh, and I swear that she let out a little squeal of excitement, which attracted the curiosity of the other customers and a withering glance from the cashier. I ushered her out and onto the street, and there we made arrangements to meet on the Friday evening by the entrance to the racecourse, where the fair had set up camp. Before she left, she stretched up and kissed me gently on the cheek. Then she was gone and I watched as she hurried back towards Constitution Square and the museum, surprised by the warmth that the glow of her lips had left upon me. Surprised and a little thrilled, as the tectonic plates of my life shifted once more.

Awakening

The morning came too soon. Light crashed into my dreaming and dragged me into the dull greyness of the world. Chill air brushed against me and the last warmth of Judith's lips upon my cheek was extinguished. The remembrance of the world as it was, rather than as my subconscious wished it to be, was chastening. I longed to return to the warmth of dreams and speculated on the possibility for a few moments.

The sting of the washbasin water extinguished that indulgence and I stared into the day ahead, rooted to familiar streets, tied to known eventualities. There would be the same walk to the office, there would be papers to draft, to edit, to submit. All would be as it had been, and yet all would be other. The events of the past days had altered the foundations of my life, even if its walls looked the same. I allowed the day to take me, and I dressed mechanically, without curiosity, ate my breakfast as if nothing had happened. I left Mrs Kettmann's house without noticing.

However, as I walked through the same streets, under the same grey sky, I found within me an unexpected sensation. I realised, about halfway across the bridge, that I was looking forward to something, something that was not work, something simple, something without complication. The anticipation reminded me most of being a boy, of running down the hill towards the spot by the river where I would find Kem. I felt a pang of guilt and also of regret. I had traded something that had seemed so limited in exchange for the world, and now I found that I had weighed the commodities incorrectly. I had confused the one with the other. Too late of course, with Kem at least, but perhaps my visit to the funfair would open up another chance for me.

I tried to be breezy in my greetings, but only Stefan looked up with a smile; both Ana and Garcia merely grunted a response. It occurred to me that I had still not exchanged more than one complete sentence with Stefan since his arrival. He remained opaque, simply another cog in the machinery of the Boss's plan. Unknown and ultimately disposable. I resolved that I would make it my mission to rectify this over the coming days and weeks, to talk to him, neither to conspire nor compete, but simply to talk to him as another man, complete within himself.

From behind his desk, Garcia stretched himself upright. His head rolled left then right, each twist punctuated by the snap of bone and cartilage. He had an absent look and his movements appeared disconnected. He hung for a moment like a marionette, then recovered himself. *'Stefan, walk with me. I need your counsel.'*

At the scrape of Stefan's chair on the floorboards, Ana looked up briefly, but she was distracted and her smile barely formed before it fell away, along with her eyes. I waited, but there was no further movement. She stared fixedly at her desk, unconcerned by the departure of our colleagues into the darkness of the corridor. As the footsteps receded, the office fell again into uncomfortable silence.

I picked up one of the papers I had left at the end of the previous day. The accounts of the City's bank still made no sense and, if anything, the proposals I had made to stabilise the business had provoked an opposite reaction. Undoubtedly, the City was being very free with the institution's money, but I could not see the underlying rationale and feared that neither the City nor the bank's customers would benefit for long. I stared at the figures in an attempt to grasp again the logic of the Boss's plan.

I turned instead to the latest report on the reallocation of the Roma houses in one of the outlying districts. All were now fully occupied by eligible families, and the former residents had been successfully dispersed. I read the name of the camp to which they had been allocated, trying to guess where it might be located. The name bore no relation to any part of the city I knew but was still somehow familiar. I felt for the papers in my jacket pocket, remembered where I had seen the name before, listed as one of the sites in the progress report in the Svankmajer file. Those unknown neighbourhoods were the camps being constructed. They were the destination for the canvass and wire on the order. An order dated three months ago, long before the visit of von Boehmen.

The realisation that this had been Garcia's plan all along, that he had already ordered the means of Bireli Haluska's incarceration weeks before I had volunteered to cajole him into securing his own imprisonment, came upon me like a flood. I had been complicit in it. I tried to imagine the Haluskas content, settled. My trying, once more, was not enough. The stories of the crackdowns from before the war raced through me instead.

Ana was still focused on whatever occupied her on her desk. She did not notice me, nor my glare. She must have known too. It would be suicidal to challenge her on the matter. My shame and rage made no sense without knowledge of the contents of the Svankmajer file, so to release my anger into the stifling air would be to incriminate myself. I allowed my blood to boil in silence.

'It's not like you Anton.' She was looking at me now, but her chiding was softened by the playfulness of her tone and the gentle creases in

the corners of her eyes. She nodded at the cigarette smouldering in my hand. *'You're normally assiduous in sharing your cigarettes with the office. It's one of the things that mark you out.'*

I had no memory of lighting the cigarette. I stared at it blankly, watched the smoke curl around my fingers, wrapping itself into the spaces between them.

'Are you alright?' Her tone had modulated now, taking on an edge of concern. *'Something troubling you? Anton, say something. You're worrying me now.'* She was caught in indecision, unsure what to do next. It was the first time in our acquaintance that I had felt such uncertainty in her. It felt like power.

'I'm fine. Sorry. That was rude of me.' I tossed my packet of cigarettes across to her, but it skidded off her desk and fell to the floor with a hollow sound. *'I was just a little lost in something. This.'* I held up the document detailing the accounts of the City's bank. *'I'm clearly not smart enough, as I still simply cannot understand these figures. What they mean. Perhaps, when you have time, you could explain it all to me. You have a much better understanding than I of what's going on, of course.'*

I wanted her to explain everything, to smooth away the doubts as she had a dozen times before. I wanted her to make everything whole again. But that time had passed. Nothing she could say could reassure me now. It was plain as day. Garcia could not be acting alone.

Anticipation

After the oppressiveness of the previous day, Friday morning passed briskly. I was able to console myself with the knowledge that the evening would be filled with life beyond the panelled walls of the office. Lights and excitement would replace the deathliness of this dungeon. The expanse of the weekend became a forest instead of a desert. I was able to avoid the thoughts that would torment me if I let them, and this put me in a better mood than I had felt for days.

A little before eleven, there was a sharp, solitary rap on at the office door. It swung open before anyone had a chance to respond and Kelemen stepped into the room, his urgent business beyond the city plainly complete. His demeanour suggested it had been concluded successfully.

'Miss, the Boss needs you.'

Plainly he was addressing Ana, but when I looked up his eyes were on me. Across the room, Garcia kept his own gaze fixed to his desk, while Stefan regarded the bulk of Kelemen's form, unsure of the significance of what was playing out.

'Of course.'

Ana's voice was a little frayed, resigned. She stood slowly and deliberately, never once catching my eye as she passed my desk. And then the two of them were gone, lost in the darkness of the corridor. I wanted to ask Garcia what was going on as soon as the latch had clicked behind them, but it was clear that he had no intention of looking at me, let alone speaking. I turned to Stefan but he too had his head buried in his work. The scratching of his pen and the tick of the clock crawled through the stiff silence.

Garcia only looked up when Ana returned a few minutes later, his eyes searching out hers, their glances conspiring. She looked ashen, as if some terrible news had been delivered to her, and I expected her to announce some new catastrophe to which we would have to respond. But there was no announcement and she slid past my desk, almost within arm's reach and yet a thousand miles distant.

'Would anyone like some coffee?'

Stefan smiled plaintively beside the side table, his fingertip already resting on the handle of the little bell that could summon Miss Gelber. He looked from Ana to Garcia, and finally to me. His raised eyebrow posed bigger questions than those related to my preference for refreshment; I smiled and nodded in answer to both. Next week we would talk, I told myself.

The coffee, when it came, tasted astringent and thin. I tried to tally up how many cups of the stuff I had drunk without noticing its bitterness. It had been two years and eleven months since I first tasted Miss Gelber's coffee. Roughly 150 weeks. Assuming two cups on average each day in the office, that would make 1480 cups of coffee. For a moment I thought to factor in holidays, before I remembered that there had been none; barely a day off at all. The bitter taste on my tongue grew slightly more acrid. The best part of fifteen hundred cups of this coffee and I had never before noticed how unsatisfactory it was. I looked into my cup, watched the gritty dregs swirl, then tipped the remainder into my mouth and swallowed.

The day dragged on without relief but eventually hauled itself to its close. The clock chimed and before the fifth note had sounded I was already on my feet. I felt Ana's curious eyes upon me and turned as carelessly as I might. To my surprise she spoke brightly, as if the day had passed normally.

'You're off promptly today, Anton. Do you have plans?'

There was neither malice nor playfulness, just a wholesome enquiry after a colleague. The safe familiarity of the tone unnerved me.

'Actually, I'm meeting a friend at the fair. She is stupidly eager to ride the whirligig.'

'She?' The tone of her question was open and almost wistful, neither prying nor mocking, and I could only nod in response. *'Well, have fun.'* A small, sharp smile followed, but even after it had fallen away, she watched me as I pulled on my coat. *'Are you walking down to the racecourse, or taking the tram?'* The question was asked in a casual, desultory way, and she didn't even look up from her desk as she asked it. *'Walking. It's a pleasant evening and I have the time. Why do you ask?'*

'Oh, no reason. Just wondered. As you say, it's a lovely evening.' Ana looked up and flashed a smile at me. I smiled back, but was unnerved by the return of some facsimile our previous camaraderie. Stefan offered a cheery 'good evening', but Garcia did not look up as I left the office. His familiar petulance amused me for the first time.

The effort of leaving behind the concerns of the day was so slight, I only realised as I was crossing the bridge that no murmur of the office clung to me. My thoughts were only of what was to come. I strode on with optimism. It seemed so simple. As the streets slid by, their pavements seemed garnished with exuberance: vibrant and alive. The people I passed wanted simply to live, to feel the world around them and entire evenings, open as the oceans, stretched before them. The fading light of the day offered them everything they could want: time to spend in the embrace of family or else in the swirl of friendship and possibility. The city breathed with the rhythm of anticipation. For me, like them, the coming darkness offered conviviality and excitement.

My hand reached into my jacket pocket to retrieve my father's pocket watch. It clicked open at my touch. There was time yet. I patted the pockets of my coat. Reassured by the presence of my notebook and pen, I set off towards Constitution Square.

In Memoriam

On the night that Georg's letter arrived, I started to write my account, to try to keep some record of things. Joszef's first instruction, to keep a diary, took on new meaning, new urgency. So I began to write. I began at the beginning, or as near to it as seemed relevant. At the point where things changed, where my life sprang from my neighbourhood and out into the wider world. I wrote rapidly and soon caught up with the myself. Over the last few days, as my doubts have blossomed, my scribbling has been more frenetic, ever more essential, as if some part of me has known what was coming. The compulsion to record everything has been overwhelming and I have scribbled every thought, every memory, every suspicion and clue into my notebook.

I scribbled the last pages sitting at a table outside a café on Constitution Square, almost in the shadow of the Museum of Art. It felt liberating to express the hope I felt at the time, hope that I might be able to claim a second chance for myself somehow. But that hope now feels painfully misplaced, as painful as the deep ache in my knee. The sharpness has dulled now and I no longer believe that it is bleeding. With my wrists bound behind me, I have no way to be sure, but I can move my leg without the tug of congealing blood against the fabric of my trouser leg, so I can hope. Hope.

Before I left the café, the sun had disappeared completely from the earth and the dusk had thickened. My mind scampered between thoughts, never staying for long, but returning to each again and again, as if I were already within the giddy twist of the whirligig. A face that may have been Judith's crystallised then dissolved before crystallising once more. Two weeks ago, I would have laughed at the idea, barely given it a moment's thought. And yet, as I turned onto the boulevard that led to the fairground, the trace of her lips drew my fingertips to my cheek.

The throng of people had grown and, were it not that everyone was heading in the same direction, the crush would have been unnavigable. A man clattered into my back and kept moving. I was turned shoulder-first into the human current. A woman stood on my foot as she passed and muttered something that sounded more like exasperation than apology. The crowd's earlier embrace had taken on an air of menace; the camaraderie of the street had become an encumbrance, a weight slowing my progress. The thought of being late nagged at me. I scanned the line of buildings, searching for the alley that I somehow knew offered a short cut to the gates of the racecourse, where I had arranged to meet Judith.

The opening in the building line was just ten metres ahead of me, and yet it took me an eternity to reach it. I managed to pull myself from the last of the crowd, felt my coat slipping from my shoulder, squeezed between a mangle of people. I tugged at it, felt the stitching strain. I pulled harder, eyes tight, jaw locked, and I fell backwards into the alley as the fabric finally slipped from between two men at the edge of the herd. In the half-light, I inspected the sleeve and was relieved to see that it was still attached. Two buttons had been lost, somewhere in the river of souls. It had seemed a small price to pay at the time, and now it is barely worth noting.

I'd seen the lights burning at the far end of the alley, but the rest was in darkness. I must have tripped a dozen times, and yet I made better progress than I had under the streetlamps of the boulevard. When I found myself on the avenue, standing on the pavement across from the gateway to the racecourse, I scanned the faces of the crowd until I caught a glimpse of her. Judith was standing in profile, her mint green coat hanging serenely from her shoulders. She had been precisely where she had promised she would be, standing sentry, watching the crowd pouring from the boulevard. Watching for me. I shouted her name and waved my arm, but it had been pointless: the noise of voices and vehicles swallowed the sound. Through gaps in the traffic, I watched her turn left and right, scanning the faces. As she turned, I caught a glimpse of my notebook tucked under her arm: the doorman at the museum had done as I had asked. I waved again and felt sure that she looked directly at me, our eyes creating a bridge across the street, across the swirl of the city and all the life it contained. Elated, I stepped to the kerb and sought out a break in the traffic through which I might slip.

It was then that the car pulled up beside me. I'd cursed its obstruction, oblivious to the intent of the men inside, and I started to move around it. The sound of scuffed feet behind me stopped me in my tracks and I started to turn, fearing an assault, but the bag was over my head before I had chance to see my assailants. The rope bit into my wrists as it pulled tight. The clunking of car doors, the weight of other hands on me, and then the pain in my knee as it struck something metal on my way into the boot.

At first, my mind was consumed only by the pain and the terror, but as the car began on its helter-skelter course I began to speculate on the identity of my assailants. Now it is beyond doubt. When the car stopped a few minutes ago, I heard two men talking. The sound from within the car was muffled but the voice was unmistakable, so much so that I imagined I could see the glint of his gold tooth. I did not recognise the other voice, but it did not require a great deal of imagination to picture his lanky accomplice in the passenger seat. There is no doubt as to who my kidnappers are.

It is less clear to me who commissioned the crime. Undoubtedly, Garcia is involved, but I am no longer sure that he alone is responsible. Ana is also most likely party to it, and logically also to the crime that saw to Joszef. Garcia at least had been unable to perform his grief convincingly, but Ana had me fooled. The thought of it spins my head like a vortex. How had I been so easily duped? Kelemen and Tomasz too. As preposterous as it seems, I cannot escape the logic of it all, no matter how horrifying. All of Andreas Hofmans' most trusted aides have been implicated in the murder of Joszef, and now of me.

Oh god. Georg. Georg is dead. I understand that now. He did not flee far enough, and evil found him. The wordless, breathing man on the phone, it was Kelemen. Kelemen took my confession, unseen and silent, standing over the body of my friend. I told them from my own mouth that I was a traitor, that I had the evidence of their wrong-doing, and now I am to be executed for it. Oh god. I have been loyal, so loyal, to the cost of everything, but that will count for nothing. They will see to it that my death, like that of Joszef's, is presented as something deserved. I will leave no legacy, aside from shame. Except for my diary.

It had seemed the safest thing to do, to leave it for her, with the attendant in the foyer to the art museum. I had realised yesterday that, if they found out, they would be willing to kill me to get back the Svankmajer documents, to make sure that there were no mistakes, that this time the details could not find their way into the newspapers in the Capital. So I had folded the documents into the front cover of my completed journal, and left it at the museum before I went back to Mrs Kettmann's house to change into a new shirt and freshly pressed suit. Mrs Kettmann had kissed my cheek before I set off for the racecourse. Her smile from the doorstep reminded me of my mother.

There is some comfort in knowing that they won't take the documents with my life. They are safe in my notebook, safe with Judith. Ana knows of course that I was to meet a girl this evening, but there are tens of thousands of women in the city. They will never find her. I wrote on the cover that, should anything happen to me, she should speak about the contents to no-one except Andreas Hofmans himself. The Boss will keep her safe, I'm sure of it. I can face what comes next, knowing that Judith will be safe.

She will still be waiting for me, even now. Standing in her mint green coat, staring at the empty boulevard, willing me to appear. She will clutch the notebook, as yet unaware of the importance of its contents, unaware that I will never arrive. I no longer feel the loss of anything, except the loss of what might have been, of what my life could have been had I shared something of myself with Judith. There is only this sense of guilt and of loss, of the unfairness of things. I do not know what, if anything, might have remained between Judith and I, once the whirligig had stopped spinning, but still I feel the loss of possibility like the collapse of a building. And I hope that she will forgive me; that she will remember me kindly. That she will remember me at all.

The rumble of the wheels is now louder than the engine. The streets are cobbled in the steel district, an echo of the wealth that once attached itself to the plant. It can't be long now. I will not cry. I will not give them the satisfaction of my tears. When we reach our destination, when all is said and done, I will retain my dignity, even as I lose everything else. Everything that is, that has been, everything that might have been.

The loss of possibility. That is, after all, what death is. It is dark and I am going to die, and I do not know if it was worth it. I have interrogated the course I took, the choices that brought me to this point. I have hunted for an understanding of what I might have done differently, and I can only think of Judith. All else flows directly and inevitably from my work for Andreas Hofmans and I cannot say that I would change a thing about that. My death was not inevitable. Andreas Hofmans is a force for good in the world, I have to believe that. I cannot believe otherwise, without losing what is left of myself. I cling to my faith in him, because otherwise it has all been for nothing. He has been betrayed, but it was not inevitable. We could have made things differently. I could have made a difference. For all my doubts, for all the numbing terror of this moment, I have greater faith than Georg. Even in the darkness, I still have that.

But, of course, I will cry. When they pull me from the car, pull back the hood and raise the pistol to my head, I shall undoubtedly weep and wail. I will most probably beg for my life in futile desperation as the muzzle of the gun rests against my temple. Or will it be a knife? They slit Joszef's throat, just like the duck that his wife turned to soup. I weigh the sensation of cold steel dragging across my skin, peeling me open, against the disruption of lead passing at speed through what was once my brain. And the tears come already. Of course I will cry. And no-one would blame me.

The car is slowing, and I am not ready. With every spasm of instinctive resistance, my legs are thrashing against the bodywork, and I cannot stop them despite the jolts of pain that each impact sends pointlessly through my knee. Pointless. The sound will not attract the attention of passers-by; there are none in this part of town. Breathe, Anton, breathe. Control yourself. Breathe. You have nothing else. There is not even the rumble of tyres, the squeaking of rusted suspension, just the sound of my breathing, and I want to cling to it for as long as I can.

The doors swing open, then slam shut. I can hear feet scuffing over stone, the flare of a match and the mumbled chatter of two workmen taking a break; a sudden rise and fall of laughter. The noise of a boot swivelling in the gravel conjures perfectly the image of Kelemen grinding his cigarette into the dirt. There are a few steps, then silence. Even my breath has ceased to make a sound.

The handle is turned and the mechanism of the boot door creaks. I feel the hood being pulled from my head, feel the dull light replace the blackness. I blink, blink again and focus. A few stars are visible beyond Kelemen's looming head, but the gold of his tooth glints more brightly than any of them in the sickly ooze of a streetlamp; behind him, Tomasz loiters, thin as a dagger.

'Good evening Anton. The Mayor thanks you for your service.'

END

Acknowledgements

I am indebted to a number of people who have helped me to produce this novel, but I'd like to thank Andy Westwood in particular. Many years ago, on my first day in a new office, he suggested that I keep a diary. Like Anton, I ignored him but that thought eventually percolated into the novel you hold in your hands.

A number of very clever and generous people have helped me to develop the text. Matthew Smith, my erstwhile publisher, gave me helpful but rigorous advice on an earlier draft, which led to what I hope is a much more focused piece of writing. Emma Burnell, Lawrence Mockett, Pam Orchard and Ulla Weinberg all offered detailed feedback on later drafts, which identified a number of remaining weaknesses. Of course, the errors that persist are entirely my own.

This is my first foray into self-publishing and I would not have got this far if it were not for Katherine Heaton, who provided essential emotional and technical support. Finally, I owe Daniel Keeffe huge thanks for designing the cover.

James Townsend can't make decisions. At least not the right ones: about what he wants or who he is. The affair had seemed like a good decision but now that this too has crashed to failure, he has returned into his past in search of something to make sense of how he got here. At home, everyone else is just trying to find some meaning in the debris.

'The writing is absolutely beautiful; mature and with a deep understanding of how to construct characters, the writing is warm and inviting.'
My Little Bookblog review

Fergus Buchanan has led a charmed life: a doting family, a loving sweetheart and the respect of his neighbours. All is as it should be and nothing stands between him and the limitless happiness that is his destiny. But then he is sent from his remote island to retrieve the cursing stone, and his adventures in the wild world beyond cause him to question everything he thought he knew. Succeed or fail, nothing will be the same again.

'The prose lingers over the landscape and the life of the people on it.'
Strange Alliances review

A father and son struggle to overcome the distance between them. Árni left his remote and unforgiving corner of Iceland as soon as he could, seeking opportunities beyond winter and fishing. Married to an English woman, he builds a life as a successful scientist but can never quite escape the pull of the West Fjords and the bleak landscape of his birth, nor shake the guilt he feels towards his distant father. When Eiríkur goes missing, he sets off to find him on the windswept spit of land lost in an angry ocean.

'From the beautiful, rugged descriptions of landscape to the subtle and perceptive observations on relationships, this is a powerful and gripping read. Beautiful and haunting.'
NB Magazine review

Since escaping the East Midlands to find his fortune in the big city, Adrian Harvey has combined a career in and around government with trying to see as much of the world as possible. He lives in north London.

The Whirligig is his fourth novel. His first, *Being Someone*, was selected for the WHSmith Fresh Talent prize in 2015. His other books, *The Cursing Stone* and *Time's Tide* were published in 2016 and 2019 respectively.